# WHITEBLADE

## By

## H A Culley

Kings of Northumbria - Book One
Oswald the Whiteblade,
King of Northumbria, Warrior and Saint

Published by

**Orchard House Publishing**

# TABLE OF CONTENTS

# List of Principal Characters

*(In alphabetical order)*

***Historical characters are shown in bold type***

**Acha** – Widow of Æthelfrith and sister of Edwin, both kings of Northumbria

**Æbbe** – Acha's only daughter; later Abbess of Ebchester and founder of Coldingham Priory

**Æthelfrith** – King of Northumbria who was killed in battle in 616 AD; the father of Eanfrith, Oswald, Oswui and their other siblings

**Ælfric**– King of Deira until 604 AD when Æthelfrith deposed and killed him. Father of Osric

**Aidan** – An Irish monk and missionary; later Bishop of Lindisfarne, who is credited with converting Northumbria to Christianity

Alaric – A Northumbrian in exile; helmsman of the Holy Saviour

Beornwulf – A Northumbrian noble in exile and shipmaster of the Seraphim

**Belin map Neithon** – King of Strathclyde

**Cadwaladr** – Cadwallon's son

**Cadwallon ap Cadfan** – King of Gwynedd

**Congal Claen** – Grandson of Fiachnae and nephew of Eochaid

**Connad** – King of Dal Riada

**Domnall Brecc** – King of Dal Riada after Connad

**Eanfrith** – Oswald's half-brother, King of Bernicia in 633 AD

**Eadfrith** – Edwin's second son; captured by Cadwallon

**Edwin** – Acha's brother, who usurped the throne of Northumbria after the death of Oswald's father, Æthelfrith, the king who first united Northumbria

**Eochaid Iarlaithe mac Lurgain** – Son of Fiachnae of the Ulaidh

**Fiachnae mac Báetáin** - King of the Ulaidh in Ulster

Fianna – The daughter of a farmer on Bute who Oswiu took as his lover

Finnian – A monk originally from Iona who traveled throughout Ireland as a missionary

Fergus – King of Islay

Gytha – The enslaved daughter of a Mercian Thegn, later Oswald's first wife

Jarlath – A captured Irish boy, body slave to Oswald

Keeva – Jarlath's sister, also a slave and Oswald's mistress

**Œthelwald** – Oswald's son, later King of Deira

**Offa** – Oswald's youngest brother

**Osguid** – Oswald's next eldest brother

**Oslac** – The third of Acha's sons, Oswald's brother

**Oslaph** – The fourth of Acha's sons, Oswald's brother

**Osric** – Edwin's cousin, King of Deira during 633 AD

**Oswald** – Second son of Æthelfrith of Bernicia and eldest son of Acha of Deira, later King of Northumbria. A noted warrior and ruler who, with Aidan, spread Christianity throughout Northumbria

**Oswin** – Oswald's cousin who fought at his side in Ulster

**Oswiu** –Oswald's next to youngest brother, who later became King of Bernicia, a devoted Christian who established a number of monasteries

**Penda** – King of Mercia, a pagan

**Rhieinmelth** – Princess of Rheged and heiress to its throne; later Queen of Northumbria

Ròidh – A Pictish prince who became Aidan's acolyte

Rònan – A captured Pictish boy, Oswald's body slave and friend

# Place Names

*(In alphabetical order)*

I find that using the correct place name for the particular period in time may be authentic, but it is annoying to have to continually search for the modern name if you want to know whereabouts the place is in relation to other places in the story. However, using the ancient name adds to the authenticity of the tale. I have therefore compromised by using the modern name for cities, settlements and islands except where the ancient name is relatively well known, at least to those interested in the period. These are listed below:

**Bebbanburg** – Bamburgh, Northumberland
**Bernicia** – The modern counties of Northumberland, Durham, Tyne & Wear and Cleveland in the North East of England. At times Goddodin was a subsidiary part of Bernicia
**Caer Luel** – Carlisle in Cumbria
**Caledonia** – Scotland
**Dal Riada** – Much of Argyll and the Inner Hebrides
**Deira** – North and South Yorkshire and northern Humberside
**Dùn Èideann** – Edinburgh
**Eoforwīc** – York
**Elmet** – West Yorkshire
**Gwynedd** – North Wales including Anglesey
**Mercia** – Roughly the present day Midlands of England
**Northumbria** – Bernicia, Elmet and Deira. At times it also included Rheged and Goddodin
**Pictland** – The confederation of kingdoms including Shetland, the Orkneys, the Outer Hebrides, Skye and the Scottish Highlands north of a line running roughly from Skye to the Firth of Forth
**Rheged** – A kingdom of Ancient Britons speaking Cumbric, a Brythonic language similar to Old Welsh, which roughly encompassed modern Lancashire and Cumbria in England and, at times, part of Galloway in Scotland
**Strathclyde** – South East Scotland

# Glossary

**Ætheling** – Literally 'throne-worthy'. An Anglo-Saxon prince

**Bretwalda** – In Anglo-Saxon England, an overlord or paramount king accepted by other kings as their leader

**Currach** – A boat, sometimes quite large, with a wooden frame over which animal hides are stretched and greased to make them waterproof

**Cyning** – Term of respect used when speaking to a king

**Hereræswa** - Military commander or general. The man who commanded the army of a nation under the king

**Seax** – A bladed weapon somewhere in size between a dagger and a sword, mainly used for close-quarter fighting where a sword would be too long and unwieldy

**Thegn** – In Anglo-Saxon England, a man who held a certain amount of land from the king or from a nobleman, ranking between an ordinary freeman and a hereditary noble. In Scotland, a man, often the chief of a clan, who held land from a Scottish king

**Ulaidh** – A confederation of dynastic-groupings that inhabited a provincial kingdom in Ulster (north-eastern Ireland) and was ruled by the Rí Ulad or King of the Ulaidh. The two main tribes of the Ulaidh were the Dál nAraidi and the Dál Fiatach

**Uí Néill** – An Irish tribe who claimed descent from Niall Noigiallach (Niall of the Nine Hostages), a historical King of Tara who died about 405. The **Uí Néill** tribe was divided into two main branches, each clan claiming descent from one of his sons:

*The Northern Uí Néill branch*:

- Conall Gulban, ancestor of the Cenél Conaill dynasty
- Eógan, ancestor of the Cenél nEógain dynasty

*The Southern Uí Néill branch*:

- Éndae, ancestor of the Cenél nÉndai
- Coirpre, ancestor of the Cenél Coirpri dynasty
- Lóegaire, ancestor of the Cenél Lóegaire dynasty
- Conall Cremthainne, ancestor of the Clann Cholmáin and Síl nÁedo Sláine
- Fiachu, ancestor of the Cenél Fiachach

**White Christ** – A pagan term for Jesus Christ, possibly in reference to the white robes worn for baptism.

# Author's Note

In the early seventh century AD, Britain was divided into over twenty petty kingdoms. I have listed them here for the sake of completeness, though only a few of them feature significantly in the story. A few others get a passing mention. From north to south:

**Land of the Picts** – Probably seven separate kingdoms in all, in the far north and north-east of present day Scotland

**Dal Riada** – Western Scotland including Argyll and the Isles of the Hebrides. Also included part of Ulster in Ireland from where the main tribe – the Scots – originated

**Goddodin** – Lothian and Borders regions of modern Scotland – then subservient to Bernicia and so part of Northumbria

**Bernicia** – The north-east of England. Part of Northumbria

**Strathclyde** – South East Scotland.

**Rheged** – Modern Cumbria and Lancashire in the north-west of England. A client kingdom of Northumbria

**Deira** – North, East and South Yorkshire

**Elmet** – West Yorkshire

**Lindsey** – Lincolnshire and Nottinghamshire

**Gwynedd** – North Wales

**Mercia** – Most of the English Midlands

**East Anglia** – Norfolk, Suffolk and Cambridgeshire

**Powys** – Mid Wales

**Middle Anglia** – Bedfordshire, Northamptonshire and Warwickshire

**Dyfed** – South-west Wales

**Kingdom of the East Saxons** – Essex

**Hwicce** – South-east Wales, Herefordshire and Gloucestershire

**Kingdom of the Middle Saxons** – Home counties to the north of London

**Wessex** – Southern England between Dumnonia and the Kingdom of the South Saxons

**Kent** – South-eastern England south of the River Thames

**Kingdom of the South Saxons** – Sussex and Surrey

**Dumnonia** – Devon and Cornwall in south-west England

Little is known for certain about Oswald's life in exile. We do know he fled to Dal Riada and that he probably spent some time fighting in Ireland, where he acquired the nickname Whiteblade. We also know that he spent part of his exile at the monastery on Iona and that he was converted to Christianity at some stage in his exile.

I have taken some liberties with the accepted historical facts for the sake of the story. This is a time about which there is little written evidence and what exists is sometimes conflicting. The record of kings of the Ulaidh (in Ulster, Ireland) lists different kings at the same time, which probably means that they split into factions, each with their own leaders who called themselves king. The same is true of the kings of Dal Riada.

Aidan was in reality older than Oswald, although I have made them the same age. Connad died and Domnall Brecc came to the throne of Dal Riada later than I have portrayed by a few years. I have simplified the political situation in Ireland because it was far too complex for a novel.

There is little evidence what type of ships or boats the people of ancient Britain used in the seventh century AD. Obviously there must have been some, especially on the west coast, as that was the main means of transport – and the only way of travelling between the many islands of Dal Riada. As many are familiar with the Scottish birlinn – a type of galley – of the Middle Ages, I have used that term.

Apart from a list of their names, nothing is known about four of Oswald's brothers. Only Oswiu, who became King of Bernicia after Oswald's death, is mentioned in various records of the time.

Oswald married the King of Wessex's daughter, Cyneburga, sometime after he became king in 634. He has only one recorded son, Œthelwald, who began ruling Deira in 651. It is thought that he can't have been Cyneburga's son as that would have made him too young to be chosen as king in 651. I have therefore assumed that he was the son of an earlier marriage during Oswald's exile.

# Introduction

At the time of Oswald's birth in 604 AD, the island we now call Britain was divided between the Britons, a Celtic people, in the west and Germanic invaders in the east. Those in the north (Northumbria) and the centre (Mercia) were Angles in the main, whilst those in the south were Saxons, with Jutes controlling part of Kent and much of Hampshire. All three came from the north coast of Germany and what is now known as Schleswig-Holstein. The Celts themselves were divided between those who spoke Gaelic and those who used the Brythonic languages.

Northumbria itself was a recent creation; formerly it was two kingdoms, Deira in the south and Bernicia (including Goddodin) in the north. This is very simplistic, but a detailed explanation of the frequently changing political map of Britain in the seventh century has no place in a novel.

Oswald was the eldest son of Æthelfrith, King of Bernicia and his second wife, Acha, a member of the Deiran royal line who Æthelfrith married after he'd conquered Deira to consolidate his position as ruler of the combined kingdoms. However, Æthelfrith also had a son by his first wife, Bebba, called Eanfrith.

Æthelfrith was killed in battle around 616 by the King of East Anglia. As Oswald was twelve at the time, he was too young to fight for his father's crown and his uncle, Acha's brother Edwin, became king of Northumbria. As he had publicly announced his intention of killing Æthelfrith's sons to eliminate any future opposition to his rule, Acha, Oswald and his brothers were forced to flee from Bernicia. Oswald spent the remainder of his youth in the Scottish kingdom of Dal Riada in the north west of the island of Britain, where he was converted to Christianity. Dal Riada (also written as Dalriata) was a Gaelic kingdom inhabited mainly by a tribe known as the Scots, who later gave their name to the whole country, much as England derives its name from the Angles.

Dal Riada included parts of present-day western Scotland and part of Ulster in Ireland. In the late sixth to early seventh centuries it roughly encompassed present-day Argyll, Lochaber and some of the isles of the Inner Hebrides in Scotland and Counties Antrim and Down in Ulster. Oswald is thought to have gained a reputation as a warrior in Ireland during his period of exile, earning himself the nickname of Whiteblade.

In 633, when Oswald would have been about 29, Edwin was killed by Cadwallon ap Cadfan, the King of Gwynedd, in alliance with Penda of Mercia, at the Battle of Hatfield Chase. Following Edwin's death, Northumbria was divided once more and Oswald's half-brother, Eanfrith, became King of Bernicia, whilst Osric, a cousin of Edwin's and Acha's, claimed the throne of Deira. Eanfrith and Osric didn't last long, as both were killed by Cadwallon when he ravaged Northumbria during the year following Edwin's death.

When Oswald returned after eighteen years of exile to claim the vacant crown of Northumbria, his first priority was to defeat Cadwallon and drive him out of his new kingdom.

# Chapter One – Flight into Exile

## 616 AD

Oswald was fighting a giant with a sword of fire. Each time the giant lunged to grab hold of the small boy, Oswald darted out of his way and brought his flaming sword down to scorch the hairs on the giant's forearms. Suddenly, the monster managed to grab his shoulder and started to shake him roughly. He awoke from his dream to find his ten year old brother Osguid, telling him to get up and get dressed.

'Why? What's happening?'

Before the boy could answer, his mother, Acha, Queen of Northumbria, swept into the room accompanied by three of his other brothers, including the four year-old Oswiu, who was clutching at her skirts.

'Get up now, Oswald,' she said with some asperity.

He quickly did as he was told, puzzled at his mother's tone. She never shouted at him or was cold towards him; not that he was her favourite. She loved all of her seven children equally, or at least appeared to do so.

'Boys, we must flee Bebbanburg tonight. Your brother Eanfrith has already gone to seek refuge with his mother's people, the Picts. Edwin will seek him there, so we will head for Dal Riada. Its king, Connad, was ever your father's ally.'

Eanfrith was their half-brother and at seventeen, was five years older than Oswald. His mother had been Bebba, a Pictish princess, after who King Æthelfrith had named the fortress on the east coast of Northumbria from where he had ruled his kingdom.

As he finished dressing, Oswald turned to the impatient Acha.

'Mother, why must we flee? What has happened? Where's father?'

Acha's shoulders sank and she fought back her tears. At this Oswiu's face crumpled and the small boy started to sob, worried and uncertain about what was happening. Oswald stood staring at the two of them. The three other boys stood there, afraid, but determined not to cry. Oswald's mother had always been his rock – his father was someone he hardly knew – and he felt certain something bad must have happened for her to be this disturbed. Before his mother told them, he knew somehow that his father had lost the battle against Edwin, Acha's brother, who was

14

trying to take the kingdom from him. The cosy world he had known for the past twelve years was coming to an end.

'Æthelfrith has been killed in battle by Raedwald, the King of East Anglia, aiding your wretched uncle Edwin, who has declared himself King of Northumbria in your father's place.'

'But why would he want us dead? Eanfrith, yes; he's father's heir and no relation to him, but we are his nephews,' Oswald asked, puzzled.

'That counts for little when a crown is at stake. Besides, you, your brothers and Eanfrith are all Æthelings.'

*Ætheling*. It meant *throne worthy*. In the Anglo-Saxon world, the eldest son didn't automatically succeed his father. The Witan, the council of nobles, chose the next king from all the Æthelings.

At that moment the nurse entered carrying Oswald's baby sister, Æbbe, wrapped in a blanket and holding the hand of two-year-old Offa, the youngest of the six brothers.

'My Lady, the horses are ready, as is the escort.'

Five minutes later Acha and her children left Bebbanburg and headed north-west towards the inlet from the German Ocean called the Firth of Forth. It would be seven years before Oswald again saw the fortress on top of its basalt outcrop and then only briefly.

~~~

Aidan sat on the hillside, gloomily contemplating the sheep of which he was meant to be in charge. He was the third son of a chieftain of one of the plethora of clans in Ireland, but they seemed to be under fairly constant attack by the larger clans in Ulster – the northernmost province in Ireland – particularly by the Uí Néills, who were fast becoming the predominant clan in the area.

Shepherding was an undemanding but boring job. Provided he didn't let any of the flock get lost, moved them from pasture to pasture as necessary and kept the wolves at bay with the help of his two enormous wolfhounds and the stout stick he'd been given, he didn't get beaten by his father too often.

But Aidan wasn't satisfied with his lot. The boy had been brought up a pagan, worshipping the gods his clan had always worshipped. He didn't really understand the complicated Celtic pantheon which the druids spoke about, but he loved the tales of heroism and mythical creatures as told by the bards. He didn't believe all the stories, of course. He had a questioning mind and life, in his limited experience at the age of twelve, wasn't like that. Nor did he completely believe in the pagan religion as preached by the druids, although he was frightened of them, so he kept his doubts to himself. Although he'd never seen it, they were reputed to make human sacrifices to their gods and to nail the severed heads of their enemies to trees in the sacred groves. As nobody was allowed near these groves, no-one except the druids knew the truth of the stories. It did, however, ensure that the druids maintained control of the people through fear.

Aidan looked down the valley towards the small river near which his settlement was built and was surprised to see a man dressed in a long homespun robe like a druid making his way up towards him. At first he was scared; he tried to keep away from the druids as much as he could; but this man didn't look like one. For a start, druids wore their hair long and this man's hair was cut close to his head and, strangely, it was shaved from forehead to the crown.

'Greetings, my son. May I sit with you a while? I need to rest after the climb up from your settlement.'

'Y-yes,' Aidan stuttered, startled at being spoken to by a stranger. 'Of course. Are you a druid? You look like one, but your hair is different.'

The man frowned. 'No, I am not a heathen druid, may God curse them. I am a monk and I am charged by my abbot to tour this land of ours, preaching the word of our Lord, Jesus Christ, so that the people of Ireland can be converted and saved from the torments of Hell.'

Aidan grinned. 'And did the people of my settlement listen to you?'

'No, they did not! They chased me out of the place with kicks and stones.'

He turned his head so that Aidan could see the cut on the back of his head that was still seeping blood into his hair.

'Why do you do it, then, if people just attack you?'

'Because my work is important; nay, vital. Not all clans are as unwelcoming as yours. Many are prepared to listen, at least, to what I have to say. Some have even been converted to Christianity.'

Seeing the puzzled expression on the boy's face, he explained that *Christianity* was the name of the religion of those who believed in one God and Christ, his son. He went on to explain how Christ had died to save the world and Aidan sat entranced, listening to him. But then something happened that drew the attention of both boy and monk back to the valley. The sound of fighting carried up to them on the wind.

'It's the bloody Uí Néills,' Aidan exclaimed in horror. 'They're attacking my settlement! I must go and help!'

He had taken no more than a step or two when the monk pulled him back. Seeing their master being held by the stranger, the two wolfhounds started to growl a warning and got to their feet, their hackles rising. The monk pulled the boy to him, ignoring the dogs.

'There's nothing you can do, son. Your family won't thank you for getting yourself killed needlessly.'

'You hate them because they wouldn't listen to you!' Aidan yelled. 'They're my people. I can't just watch them die!'

'I hate nobody. Just calm down, boy. I have a feeling that God has a special purpose in store for you. I had a vision last night in which Jesus came to me and told me to seek you out. That can only be because he wanted me to save you from getting killed today.'

The twelve-year-old looked at him in wonder. Somehow he knew that the monk was telling the truth.

'You came to save me?'

The monk nodded. Without saying another word, the man turned and started to walk further up the valley away from the settlement, which was now burning fiercely. Aidan stood there undecided for a minute and then turned to follow him. The two big dogs watched him go, then started to pad after him. The sheep would have to fend for themselves.

~~~

Oswald was getting saddle-sore. It wasn't helped by the fact that his four-year-old brother, Oswiu, was also sitting on the mare immediately in front of him. Of his siblings, only Osguid was old enough to ride his own pony, but at least he had it to himself. Oslac, Oslaph and Offa all rode in front of nobles who had elected to go into exile with Acha rather that stay and pledge allegiance to her brother. Æbbe was fast asleep in a sling on her mother's back. Her nurse had never ridden in her life, so she too shared a horse, this time with one of the warriors who were escorting the queen and her sons. To judge by the grin on his face, he wasn't finding having a young woman riding in front of him as uncomfortable as Oswald was.

It started raining on the second day after leaving Bebbanburg and everyone was soaked to the skin. Morale sunk lower and lower, but as they headed through the Pentland Hills, the clouds parted and a watery sun appeared. Gradually the warmth started to dry their sodden cloaks and they began to gently steam. When the expanse of water to the north of Dùn Èideann came into view, there was a collective sigh of relief.

Oswald could dimly make out the point where a river flowed into the the wide firth. This was where the northernmost province of Northumbria, Goddodin, met three other kingdoms: Strathclyde, to the south-east, Dal Riada, to the north-east and the land of the Picts, to the north-west. Acha had felt that they would be safe once they reached Dal Riada, or so she hoped.

It was as they neared Strathcarron that they ran into trouble. Stirling was a Pictish fort which guarded the junction of their territory with Dal Riada and Strathclyde. The settlement sat on an escarpment high above the surrounding countryside and below it lay the first crossing point over the River Forth. Once north of the river, they would be in Dal Riada, but first they had to get there and the bridge was guarded.

'They'll let us past, won't they?' Oswald asked naively, when they'd halted a safe distance from the narrow wooden bridge. 'After all, Eanfrith is half Pict and he's our half-brother.'

'You've a lot to learn, Oswald. It's because he's your half-brother that I don't trust him. With you and your brothers dead, he would be the only son of Æthelfrith left with a legitimate claim to the throne of Bernicia.'

'Oh! I see. So what do we do? Kill him first?'

His mother laughed. 'Now that's an idea, but it would seriously upset the Picts. No, I think we'll leave that to others. We need to lie low and hope that we're forgotten about until the time is right.'

Oswald nodded. 'Meanwhile, we need to cross that damned bridge. How do we get past those Picts without killing them? I assume you want to avoid that?'

Acha smiled. He eldest son was learning.

'We send someone down to negotiate,' she replied, looking round for the right person.

One of the nobles, a thegn called Hussa, went riding down with an escort of three mounted warriors, just as a group of men appeared from Stirling. A few were mounted, but most were on foot. Acha looked anxiously from the group at the bridge to the other, larger, body of men that was still a couple of miles away. Suddenly, those who were mounted broke away from the rest of the men on foot and headed for the bridge at a gallop. It would take them less than ten minutes to get there. The last thing she wanted was a fight between her men and the Picts, but she could see little option. Not only was it a risk, as she only had a few more men than the sentries guarding the crossing, but word would also get back to Edwin about where she and her sons were heading. Her mind was

18

made up for her when Osguid pointed behind him and yelled, 'Riders approaching!'

At first Acha thought that they were Edwin's men, but their bodies were painted with woad in intricate blue patterns and their hair was plastered to their heads with lime. They were obviously a party of Picts returning north from Strathclyde and she wondered what they had been doing there. There was an uneasy truce between the two kingdoms at the moment, but they were hardly allies.

'Get my children in the centre; we're going to force our way over the bridge.'

The few nobles who had accompanied her and the dozen warriors of her personal household formed up round Oswald, Osguid and the men with a boy or the nurse riding in front of them. Acha handed Æbbe to the nurse and, drawing her sword, took up position in front of the surrounding cluster of horsemen. At her signal, they bounded forward and headed for the bridge.

At first Hussa was so intent on talking to the sentries that he wasn't aware of what was happening but, when he saw the Picts looking behind him in alarm, he turned to see what had distracted them. Being slightly quicker witted than the Picts, Hussa wheeled his horse out of the way just as one of the men painted with woad thrust his spear at him. He pulled his sword clear of its scabbard and turned his horse in a tight circle so that he could bring it down on the unlucky Pict's head. The sharp blade cut through the mass of lime-plastered hair and shattered the skull beneath. The blow sent a shudder up the thegn's arm, but the man dropped like a stone, spewing forth blood and a grey substance which resembled the porridge he'd had for breakfast from the top of his head.

The three men of Hussa's escort urged their horses forward to drive back the rest of the Picts who were trying to kill him. Once they had gained a momentary respite, all four of them withdrew just as Acha and her party reached the bridge. The charging Northumbrians had moved into a column, as the wooden bridge was too narrow to allow more than three people riding abreast to pass over it. The Picts scattered out of the way of the galloping horses, so Acha, half her men and the children reached the crossing without difficulty. They rode across, but the second half of the column was attacked in the flank by the sentries, who had now recovered their courage.

Two of the rear guard were killed before Hussa and his three horsemen could wade in and start to cut down the Picts. After three more of their men had died, the rest of the Picts fled, allowing the remaining Northumbrians to ride across the bridge. However, by this time the mounted party from Stirling were approaching fast. Hussa assessed the situation quickly and decided he had to delay the mounted Picts or risk their fresher mounts overtaking Acha and her children.

'Those who have a bow dismount and string it quickly,' he yelled, hoping that at least some of the men with him had brought a hunting bow.

Five men did as they were bid, whilst the rest watched the approaching Picts with mounting apprehension. They numbered 10 against perhaps 25 Picts. Less than a minute later the first arrow arced up into the sky, followed quickly by several more. By the time the first volley had struck home, the archers were putting a third arrow to their bowstring. One man and two horses were hit initially; that didn't slow the oncoming horsemen, but the second volley brought down two horses and several more crashed into them, breaking legs and causing chaos.

Without waiting to see the effect of the remaining arrows, Hussa called for his men to follow him and he raced after Acha. The Picts at the head of the mass of mounted men were milling about in confusion, but those at the rear sped past them without giving them a second glance. Hussa glimpsed behind him and saw that a dozen Picts were closing on him and his men, so he halted once more and the archers leapt from their horses to nock another arrow to their bows. Two more volleys managed to kill or wound another three men and the same number of horses. When Hussa made as if to charge the remaining handful, they fled. The Northumbrian thegn grunted in satisfaction and turned once more to follow Acha into Dal Riadan territory. He was fairly certain that the Picts had had enough; even if they hadn't, they would hesitate to provoke Connad by an incursion into his kingdom.

Eventually he caught Acha up.

'Did you learn anything from the Picts at the bridge, Hussa?' she asked after congratulating him on his bravery and quick thinking.

'Only that they had instructions to capture or kill you and your children.'

'I see. It seems that Edwin is not our only enemy, then. Eanfrith obviously has the ear of the local Pictish king. I only hope that we find some friends in Dal Riada.'

'I thought that King Connad was Æthelfrith's ally? Your husband's nephew, Oswin, is already under his protection and serves him as a warrior in Ulster, or so I've heard.'

'That's true and the king and I are distantly related, but I've learned that kin can be either useful or a nuisance. After all, we are fleeing from my own brother. Connad is just as likely to seek favour with Edwin or the Picts by handing us over as he is to offer us sanctuary.'

'Why then flee to him?'

'Because we have no-where else to go.'

~~~

Aidan was enjoying himself. He and the monk, whose name was Finnian, had got on well from the start. At first they argued about who was right: the druids, or men like him who followed the teachings of the White Christ. At least, Aidan argued and got quite agitated, whereas Finnian remained calm, pointed out the fallacies of Irish mythology and began to talk to him about Christ's life and his teachings.

Despite his ingrained faith in the old gods like the Dagda, Lugh and the Morrigan, Aidan hadn't accepted what he'd been taught at face value and he gradually came to accept that belief in them had evolved from the tales of ancient heroes from Ireland's past, some of who seem to have had supernatural powers. His traditional religion was not written down, but spread by the druids by word of mouth and, more importantly, by the bards who had preserved Ireland's cultural heritage over the centuries.

Finnian explained that each time a saga was recited, it changed slightly, the truth being embroidered to make the tale more exciting. Bards depended on their story-telling skills in order to earn their living and had to keep their, usually drunken, audiences entertained. Aidan had only just been allowed to attend the gatherings of men in his father's hall, but he and his friends had often snuck in unnoticed at the back of the hall to listen to the bards. He reluctantly agreed that those tales he had heard more than once differed each time they were told.

At first Aidan had been less than impressed when he discovered that Christ was a preacher and not a warrior. He associated Christ with the bards and couldn't see what was so special about him. However, as time went on and he heard about the miracles Christ was responsible for and began to understand his philosophy, he grew more interested.

Every time Finnian came to a settlement he would try and convert the people to Christianity. Sometimes they would give him a courteous hearing, provide him and Aidan with food and place to sleep and then send them on their way unharmed. Others, especially those settlements where the druids were powerful, gave them a beating before driving them

21

out. In a few cases Finnian found that the settlement was already Christian and had a small church and a priest. In every case these communities had been converted a century or more before by Saint Pádraig or one of his acolytes. It was such a settlement that saved Aidan's life.

They had arrived at a settlement in the south of the province. The inhabitants were from a clan called the Uí Néill, who were gradually forcing out the original populace, the Ulaidh. The latter were Christians, in the main, whereas the Uí Néill were pagans. As soon as the inhabitants discovered that Finnian was a Christian monk, they attacked him with spears and Aidan bravely interposed his small body between the attackers and the monk. His two dogs had been slain by others two weeks previously and he had reacted instinctively to protect the monk, much as his dogs had done for him when they had been killed.

'Leave him alone; he is a man of God, not a warrior,' he yelled, but it did no good and one of the inhabitants thrust his spear over the boy's shoulder, aiming at Finnian's neck. Aidan put up his hands and grabbed the spear, pulling it down and to the side so that the point hit the ground and such was the momentum of the attacker that the point stuck fast in the earth and the man wielding it was forced to let go as he stumbled and fell face down in the dirt. Aidan and Finnian were lucky that the spearman was disliked by his fellows as being pompous and arrogant. The other men laughed at their sprawling comrade, which only made the man more furious than he was already. He climbed to his feet, but Aidan was quicker. He pulled the spear from the earth and thrust the blunt end into the man's distended paunch. The air whooshed out of his lungs and he bent over, winded and in pain. The other men hooted with laughter and Aidan threw down the spear before taking Finnian by the sleeve and curtly telling him it was time to go.

The monk was stunned by Aidan's courage and meekly allowed himself to be led from the place. However, the man who had been humiliated wasn't content to allow them to go unmolested, as the others were. He retrieved his spear and hurled it at the retreating pair. He had aimed at Aidan and it was Aidan he hit. The boy felt a sudden thump in his shoulder and after a few seconds he fell to the ground screaming when the pain hit him; then searing agony coursed through his small frame and he was unable to move.

Finnian ignored him at first, turned on his heel and walked slowly and deliberately back towards the rotund man who had thrown the spear. The fellow quailed before his angry gaze and fell to his knees, mumbling like an idiot, while the others watched in amazement. They made no move to help the man or to attack the monk, as he raised the crucifix he wore hanging from the rope around his waist to his lips, kissed it and held it over the quivering man. He told him that the wrath of God and Christ his beloved son would be visited on him for the rest of his days. Then he turned on his heel and went to help Aidan.

The inhabitants pulled the mumbling wretch to his feet and led him away, casting superstitious glances over their shoulders at the monk. The crowd of women and children who had come to watch, expecting to see the monk and his boy beaten to death, broke up in silence, wondering at the power of the monk. Had Finnian stayed, he could probably have converted the settlement, so in awe of him were they, but his priority was to save the boy.

Luckily the thrown spear had lacked power and the point had ricocheted off the left scapula. Finnian searched in his pouch and gave the boy some herbs to chew on. A short while later Aidan lost consciousness and the monk was able to pull the spear point out. Immediately the wound started to bleed copiously and Finnian wondered how he was going to staunch it. He sensed rather than heard a movement behind him, but instinctively he knew it wasn't a threatening one.

A girl knelt beside him and handed him a clean cloth and a bowl of water. Finnian cleaned the wound and pressed the cloth over it whilst he took a bone needle and a length of catgut from the girl. He expertly stitched the two flaps of skin together, washed the blood away and then bound a fresh bandage in place. He nodded his thanks to the girl who, without a word, gathered up the bowl, soiled rags and the needle and went back into the settlement. Finnian picked up the unconscious Aidan with one arm around his shoulders and the other under his knees and carried him away without looking back.

The monk was near the point of exhaustion when he came to another settlement. This one was on the coast and it was inhabited by Ulaidh fishermen, some of who were trained warriors. These wanted to launch a reprisal raid on the place where Aidan had been attacked, but Finnian and the local priest managed to persuade the headman that this would only stir up the whole area which, up to that point, was enjoying a short period of relative peace.

The priest led the way into his hut and they laid Aidan down on the rough-hewn table so that Finnian could examine the wound. He took off the bandage and cut through the stitches so that he could see inside. He gently explored the wound and found that a bit of bone had been chipped away, but the spear hadn't broken the scapula.  Using a pair of bone tweezers, he pulled the fragment out, washed the wound again and stitched it up once more.  This time he poured a quantity of the priest's whiskey into the gash before dressing it.

Finnian left Aidan with the Ulaidh whilst he continued with his mission to convert the Irish.  It would be years before he saw him again.

~~~

Oswald was getting more and more angry.  Connad, King of Dal Riada, sat on his throne on a raised platform at one end of his great hall at Dùn Add, a hillfort on top of a mound that dominated the surrounding flat lands.  The nearby inlet of Craignish provided a natural safe harbour for his small fleet of birlinns.

'My Lady, I would remind you that your husband, the cursed Æthelfrith, defeated my grandfather at the Battle of Degsastan a decade and a half ago.  We were enemies then; why should I regard you differently now?'

'Because Æthelfrith allowed your grandfather to continue to rule Dal Riada as an independent kingdom, merely insisting on a treaty of friendship between our peoples.  He could just as easily have incorporated your lands within Northumbria.'

'How generous of him,' Connad sneered.

'How dare you speak so to my mother, the daughter and wife of kings far greater than you, like that?'

Connad's face suffused with anger.

'You had better teach your whelp to mind his tongue, woman, or I will cut it out and make him my thrall.'

'Be quiet, Oswald,' Acha snapped.  'You are not helping.'

'King Connad.'  She turned back to the young man covered in a wolfskin, sitting on the throne.  'It seems to me that you have three choices.  You can either bid us leave in peace, or you can try and make us your thralls – in which case you will have a fight on your hands and you will lose more warriors, something you can ill afford after your recently setbacks in Ulster.  The Ulaidh are losing ground to the Uí Néill and you are losing more warriors supporting your Christian allies than you can afford.  After all, you are spread thinly on the ground from the Isle of Mull in the north to Kintyre in the south and you are beset by other enemies – the Picts and the Strathclyde Britons, to name but two.  You need my men to bolster your numbers; and they are all trained warriors, not armed farmers,' she added contemptuously, referring to the young men standing around the hall armed with no more than a rudimentary spear.

'You mentioned a third option, my Lady?' Connad asked softly.

'We can join you and make common cause with you against your enemies.'

'And what would you want in return?'

'A safe home for me and my children.'

'Hmm. I agree, but with two conditions.'

'Which are?'

'You, your men and your brood become Christians and your sons join my war band as soon as they attain fourteen summers.'

'That seems fair, but fourteen is over young to go to war.'

'No, you misunderstand. That is when they will be old enough to start their training as warriors. At sixteen they will be old enough and strong enough to fight.'

'I see. And in the meantime?'

'You may keep the four youngest with you for now and the baby, of course. The other two will leave for Iona on the morrow to become novice monks.'

After a pause, Acha nodded her head in agreement.

Oswald and Osguid had been excited by the talk of becoming warriors, but now they were to be shipped off alone to this place called Iona to become monks, a term they were unfamiliar with and they became anxious about what the future held for them.

# Chapter Two – The Isle of Iona
## 618 AD

Oswald and Osguid ran down to the shore to meet the birlinn, which had just beached. The Master of Novices would beat them for leaving the abbey when they should have been practicing their reading of the scriptures, but the arrival of their brother Oslac, now ten, was an event not to be missed. However, the birlinn didn't contain their younger brother, but fierce looking warriors who spoke a tongue not dissimilar to the Gaelic they had learned since their arrival, but with a strange accent.

The man who appeared to be their leader was dressed in a chain mail byrnie which came half way down his arms between elbow and wrist and just covered his knees. His metal helmet consisted of a rounded cap made from four pieces of iron riveted together and had a mask type of face guard around the eyes and nose. His neck was protected by a chain mail aventail. He had a sword and a shorter seax in leather-covered wooden scabbards hanging from the studded leather belt around his waist and he carried a throwing axe in his hand. Osguid thought that the overall effect was of a fearsome fighter and he felt scared. Not so Oswald. He coveted the helmet, armour and weapons and envied the man who could afford such things.

Several of the crew also wore byrnie and helmet, but many of these had obvious repairs and the majority of the helmets were no more than segmented domed iron caps. Some wore leather jerkins to give their torsos some protection, but the majority wore simple tunics and brightly coloured trousers, gathered below the knee by ribbons wound around their legs.

A boy of perhaps thirteen or fourteen, presumably the leader's son, leaped from the prow of the birlinn and came to stand by his side. He wore a jerkin made from some sort of animal fur, probably rabbit and a seax hung from his belt. He was bareheaded and his dark hair, encrusted with sea salt, hung in lank bunches down to his shoulders. Evidently it hadn't been washed for a while.

The abbot of Iona, Fergno Britt mac Faílbi, stepped forward and welcomed the warrior, who pulled the helmet from his head. The two boys could see that he was an older version of his son, but with a long moustache and two scars which disfigured his face. When he smiled at the abbot he appeared to leer at him and looked even more frightening.

Oswald asked a monk standing nearby who he was and was told that it was Fiachnae mac Báetáin, King of the Ulaidh in Ulster and one of Connad's sub-kings. He had apparently stopped at Iona to pray at the shrine of Saint Columba before continuing to Dùn Add to discuss the forthcoming campaign against the Uí Néill with the Dal Riadan king. Oswald and Osguid looked in awe at the other scars on his arms, as well as at the many arm rings he wore to indicate both his wealth and his success in battle. Oswald knew that many of them must have been taken from enemies he had killed in personal combat.

'If you insist on running away like thralls trying to escape, you will be treated like slaves,' the novice master told the brothers when they returned at last to the scriptorium, where their fellow novices were bent over their desks laboriously copying pages from an illuminated Bible.

'We're very sorry, Brother, but we thought it was the ship bringing our brother Oslac to Iona and thought it only polite to go and greet him,' Oswald replied, trying to appear contrite and failing miserably.

'Did you really? Well, as you have no doubt discovered, it is the King of Ulster and his son, Eochaid, who have honoured us with a visit.'

Oswald didn't like to correct him and point out that Ulster was currently divided between several kings, only one of which was the redoubtable Fiachnae mac Báetáin.

'Abbot Fergno has asked me to find a suitable novice to look after Eochaid whilst he is here with his father, which means doing whatever he so desires and so, Oswald, you have just selected yourself for the task.'

'You make it sound as if I am to be his thrall, Brother.'

'If that's what you want to call it, well then, yes, you are to be his thrall whilst he is here. It is your penance for disobeying me. Perhaps it might teach you a little humility.'

'I am not here to learn humility; I am here to learn about the Christian faith, which is something you have singularly failed to teach me about so far, Brother. May I remind you that I am the son of a King of Northumbria and nobody's thrall?'

The Master of Novices grew puce with rage.

27

'How dare you speak to me like that? You are here to learn to be a monk, that's all I know and I care not who your dead father was. I will ask the abbot to have you flogged for your impudence to me.'

Oswald felt his own temper rising to match that of the furious monk, but he had enough sense not to exacerbate the situation. He regained control and forced himself to calm down. He bowed his head.

'I apologise, Brother. I should not have spoken to you like that. However, I refuse to act as a thrall to some whelp spawned by a minor Irish chieftain. That is not why I and my brothers are here. King Connad was quite specific in his agreement with my mother, the Lady Acha. We were sent here to learn about Christianity prior to returning to be trained as warriors.'

'I know nothing of this,' the Master of Novices replied, not in the least mollified by Oswald's attempt to smooth things over. 'The rest of you get back to work; you too, Osguid. Oswald, you and I are going to take a little walk to see the abbot.'

After the monk had finished explaining Oswald's transgressions to Fergno, the abbot looked a little uncomfortable.

'It's probably my fault for not explaining the situation with regard to the children of the Lady Acha, Brother. Oswald is correct. In fact, the ship carrying his brother, Oslac, is due to arrive here in the next day or two. The ship is a merchantman on its way to Ireland to trade. Oswald is to return to Dùn Add as soon as a ship going there arrives on Iona and I can secure passage on it for him. I agree that Oswald was quite wrong to speak to you, his superior, in the way that he did, but you say he did apologise? Good. Then let this be an end to the matter.'

The monk looked even angrier, if that were possible, but he held his tongue.

'Now as to Eochaid, he too is travelling to Dùn Add to train as a warrior and I had thought, as he is only slightly younger than Oswald, that it might be a good idea if they became acquainted with one another. There is no question of Oswald becoming his servant, let alone his thrall. I really can't think where you got that idea. I merely thought that Oswald might show Eochaid around the abbey and the island and explain our life here to him.'

'I do think that you could have explained that to me, Father Abbot. It would have saved me from an embarrassing situation.'

'Yes, well, I've said I apologise for that oversight. I don't intend to repeat myself, Brother.'

'No, of course not. Thank you, Father Abbot. Will that be all?'

'Yes, thank you, Brother. Oswald, I expect you'll find Eochaid in the guest hut. You had better go and introduce yourself.'

Oswald bowed slightly and followed the far from pacified Master of Novices out of the abbot's cell. As soon as they were out of earshot, he turned and grabbed the front of Oswald's habit.

'You've made a fool of me in front of the abbot. You may be about to leave here, but I'm going to make your life hell before you do.'

'I don't think so.' Oswald smiled sweetly at him. 'If you do, I'll return one night and quietly deprive you of the equipment hanging between your legs, which you have no use for in any case. You'll never get a decent night's sleep, wondering if that sound you heard outside the novices' hall is me, coming for you, or just one of the dogs taking a piss.'

Oswald again smiled sweetly at the red-faced monk.

'Now take your grubby hands off me so that I can go and find this Eochaid.'

As the monk stomped away angrily, Oswald didn't feel particularly proud of himself. He knew that he was guilty of the sin of pride and that he had been unnecessarily insolent. The threat he'd made was just to get his own back on the man for the threat he'd made, but that still didn't make it acceptable. However, he told himself, if a warrior, even a Christian one, didn't have his pride and his honour, he was nothing – and would soon be a dead nothing, too. He forgot about the tiresome monk and set off to find Eochaid.

He wasn't at all sure that he would want to get to know this boy, but he could see the abbot's intention was a sensible one. If they did get on, then it would be valuable to have someone who was a friend during the tough days of warrior training that lay ahead of them. The trouble was that, from the brief sight of him he'd had down at the beach, Eochaid had seemed to be rather full of self-importance. He sighed and knocked on the rough-hewn door of the guest hut.

~~~

It had taken Aidan several months to recover and regain full use of his arm. Finnian hadn't returned and so, to repay the inhabitants for their kindness in taking care of him, he joined them when they went out fishing and worked for nothing except for food and a corner of a hut in which to sleep. As often as he could, he would go and spend time with the settlement priest to learn more about Finnian's religion. Unfortunately, the man only knew the rudiments and could answer only a few of the many questions the boy had.

'I was a monk on Iona before I was ordained as a priest to come here and look after these people. Perhaps you should go there if you want to learn more,' he told Aidan one day.

On a clear day Aidan could see Kintyre, one of the sub-kingdoms of Dal Riada, from the hill above the settlement, but the priest told him that Iona was off the tip of a larger island called Mull, some distance to the north of Kintyre. Nevertheless, Aidan often climbed the hill and gazed at that part of Dal Riada he could see across the relatively narrow stretch of water, then looked to the north where Iona lay over the horizon. For reasons he didn't understand, he longed to make his way to the monastery on the small isle. Perhaps Finnian would be there? He missed the itinerant monk and his teachings. He had known so much more than the local priest.

After Aidan had been with the Ulaidh for over a year there had been a storm. That wasn't unusual in the winter, but this was in the middle of summer and it was really severe with winds that howled around the squat huts in which the fishermen and their families lived. For miles around it tore ships free of their moorings so that they were either lost at sea or broken up on the rocks. One man who had ventured outside to check that his chickens were safe had been blown off his feet and had to crawl back to the safety of his hut.

In the morning, as the Ulaidh inspected the damage done by the storm to the settlement and the fishing currachs, they saw a birlinn in difficulties limping towards the beach. It had lost its mast and was being propelled by no more than eight oars, instead of the usual forty for a ship that size. As it got closer, they could see that those who were not rowing were frantically bailing out seawater, using everything they had, including helmets.

When they had managed to run the ship onto the sandy beach, the exhausted crew collapsed where they stood, except for one man who managed to haul himself over the side and stagger ashore. The inhabitants, uncertain whether the arrival was friend or foe, had armed themselves and watched as the lone figure wearily approached. As he drew closer, the headman recognised him as one of Connad's chieftains from Lorne, an area of Dal Riada on the mainland opposite the Isles of Mull and Iona and rushed to his aid.

The great storm had tossed the birlinn hither and thither after the mast had been reduced to a stump. The hull had flexed so much in the heavy seas that some of the caulking had been washed out of the strakes that formed the hull and the ship had started to take in water at an alarming rate. By the time they had sighted land they were knee deep in brine. Only frantic bailing had stopped them from sinking before they reached the shore.

Two days later, the surviving twenty-seven men had recovered sufficiently to begin the task of repairing their ship. Aidan had asked and received permission to help them, so he walked down to where the crew were examining the hull of the birlinn. He spotted a boy who looked to be a little bit older than he was and he approached him timidly.

'Hallo, I'm Aidan. Is there much damage?' He was half afraid that the boy might give him a pitying look and ignore him, but he didn't. He turned to him with a broad smile on his face.

'Hallo, I'm Niall, the son of the helmsman over there, Ruairi. This is the first time I've been old enough to accompany the men and I thought it was going to be my last.'

Aidan responded to the other's friendly grin with one of his own. Feeling encouraged, he asked a question that might display his ignorance, but he took the risk.

'What's wrong, apart from the broken mast, obviously? Why did you take on so much water?'

'How much do you know about ships?'

'I know how to sail our fishing currachs, but they're made by stretching waterproofed skins over a light wooden frame. I've only been here fifteen months and I lived inland before, so I don't know much about ship construction, or its problems.'

'I see. Why? Only fifteen months, I mean. If you don't mind me asking.'

Aidan gave him a brief account of his life, playing down the reason he'd been wounded.

'Huh, I'm supposed to be a warrior and have suffered nothing more serious than a nick to my thumb when sharpening my seax, whilst you have already got yourself an impressive scar to prove your valour.'

It took Aidan a moment or two before he realised that he was being teased. He blushed and returned to his original question.

'Tell me about ship construction.'

'Well, you lay down a keel, then add the frame before encasing it with planks butted up to each other as tightly as possible. The strakes, or planks, as you might call them, overlap slightly along the long edge. The trick is to make a ship which is light but strongly built. To do that you have to accept a certain amount of flexing of the frame. Obviously this means that the strakes move slightly as well. To overcome this, we pack the gaps between the strakes with shredded fibres of cotton or hemp soaked in pine tar and driven into the seam between the strakes with a caulking mallet and a broad chisel-like tool called a caulking iron. In the storm, the ship flexed so much that some of the caulking came loose, allowing water to seep in.'

'You seem to know a lot about it, Niall.'

'My father is our best ship-builder as well as being our helmsman,' the older boy said modestly. 'He's teaching me.'

At that moment Ruairi yelled and beckoned Niall to his side. Aidan followed him without consciously thinking about it.

'We'll need more pine tar, Niall. The fishermen only have enough for waterproofing their skins. We'll have to try and find a source elsewhere.'

'We get ours from a larger settlement a few miles to the north of here along the coast,' Aidan blurted out without thinking. 'Mind you, it's not cheap and I know the elders have talked about making our own.'

'Oh and who might you be?'

'Father, this is Aidan. He arrived here a year or so ago with Brother Finnian, having been badly wounded in a fight with the wretched Uí Néill.'

Aidan wanted to protest that it wasn't quite like that, but before he could open his mouth, Niall carried on.

'We could take one of the larger fishing currachs to this settlement to buy more pine tar and perhaps more hemp too. It's better than cotton, which is all we have left.' He turned to Aidan. 'Do you have a currach?'

'Not of my own; I usually crew for one of the fishermen and his son. Should I go and ask him if he'll take us?'

The next day they returned with a pile of hemp and as many pots of pine tar as the currach could carry and work started on the hull. The currach turned around and Aidan and the crew headed back to fetch more. Meanwhile, a new mast had been fashioned from a tall pine tree, as had a new spar to carry the mainsail. A replacement sail was being made by the women in the settlement by sewing together several of the smaller sails used for the fishing currachs. The men were also busy making oars to replace the ones lost in the storm.

Once they had sufficient supplies, Aidan helped enthusiastically with the caulking process, but found out that the pitch tar didn't wash off in sea water. Niall laughed at his efforts to get rid of the tar and showed him how to use sand to get the stuff off his hands and arms – a painful process, as it took off layers of skin along with the sticky tar.

32

The whole process took a week before the birlinn was ready to set sail. The crew had been making for home with a cargo of furs purchased further south. Luckily the wolf and brown bear pelts had been sewn into oiled leather bags for the voyage and so had survived their immersion in sea water. The crew presented the settlement with a bundle of the furs to thank them for their hospitality and that night everyone got uproariously drunk, including Aidan.

When he awoke the next morning he was surprised to feel as if he was being tossed around in a barrel. The floor on which he lay seemed to slope at an alarming angle in two directions at once and the motion made bile rise in his gullet. He knew that he was about to vomit – and quite violently.

Suddenly, powerful arms lifted him up and held his head over the side of the ship as he heaved up everything he'd consumed the previous night. He slumped back onto the wooden deck of the ship and looked up to see Ruairi grinning down at him.

'Believe it or not, you're in better shape than my son,' he told him. 'He's still sleeping like a baby and he spewed all over his tunic in his sleep, dirty little bugger. I've a good mind to throw him in the sea to wake him and clean him up.'

'But he told me he can't swim!'

'Nor can he; pity that.' And the brawny helmsman bellowed with laughter.

Aidan grinned, despite his pounding head, then a thought occurred to him.

'Er, what am I doing here?'

'The headman said you wanted to go to Iona, so we're going to drop you off when we get there.'

'Oh.'

Aidan would have liked to say goodbye to the people who had tended him and treated him as if he was one of their own, but it couldn't be helped. Perhaps one day he'd return so that he could say how grateful he was. But he never did, though he always thought of it as the perfect example of Christian charity.

Aidan went and found a leather bucket and one of the crew showed him how to fill it with sea water without it tugging him over the side. Niall was curled up asleep in the prow of the ship. The front of the woollen tunic he was wearing was, as his father had said, covered in vomit. Aidan threw the contents of the bucket over him, washing off him most of the stinking residue of the meat and ale he had consumed the previous night.

The boy awoke spluttering and reaching for his seax. When he saw Aidan through his bleary eyes, he groaned and curled up again to go back to sleep.

'Shall I get another bucket, or is one enough?'

'If I didn't like you so much you'd provide the first band on the hilt of my seax.'

A seax had a short blade used for close fighting where the longer blade of a sword was too cumbersome. Typically, it was the blade a young warrior was given first, before he was old enough to wield a heavier weapon. Putting a coloured band around the hilt was the traditional way of marking how many men you had killed in battle. It was an unsubtle way of boasting about your prowess.

An hour later, the two friends had recovered enough to stand at the prow watching the blue-green coastline of Kintyre slide past as they proceeded north under sail. The mainsail wasn't something to be proud of. Most birlinns sported sails dyed in bright colours, with a device to declare their clan or kingdom. The patchwork of spare buff, off white and dirty grey fishing boat sails depressed the men aboard and they decided to call in at Tarbert, halfway up the Kintyre peninsula and get the sail dyed a uniform yellow. The sail would lack the black wolf's head of Dal Riada, but at least they wouldn't be such a laughingstock when others spotted them.

Tarbert had a natural harbour which, thankfully, was devoid of any birlinns at the moment. They easily found a berth alongside the wooden jetty amongst the few fishing boats still in harbour. Not all were currachs; a few were built of timber, like the much larger birlinn. The men carried the sail up to the dyeing works whilst Niall and Aidan climbed the low hill above the settlement. From there they could see the Hebridean Ocean on which they had been sailing and behind them, the waters of Loch Fyne.

'That's the Kingdom of Strathclyde over the other side of the sea loch,' Niall told him. 'We're at peace at the moment, but that's a rare occurrence.'

'How far up the coast does Dal Riada stretch?'

'Well, it's really a group of petty kingdoms who've come together and elected a High King to rule them. It's for their protection as they couldn't survive long on their own. At the moment it consists of Lorne in the north, Kintyre, where we are at the moment, the Isle of Islay, which is probably the biggest of the kingdoms as it includes Mull, with Iona at its south western tip, Jura and several more smaller islands further out from the mainland. To the south of us, near where we've just come from, there's Ulster. However, we no longer rule all of it, as the pagan Uí Néill are struggling with the Ulaidh for control of it.'

'And the Ulaidh are part of Dal Riada?'

'Well, they're our allies, at any rate. My father says that they used to be part of Dal Riada and subject to the High King, but now it's more like a federation. I suspect that it depends on the personalities of the kings of the Ulaidh and of Dal Riada. Their king is too strong a character to bend the knee to a devious weakling like King Connad of Dal Riada.'

'But I thought that the Ulaidh were part of the Scots people and that it was the Scots who settled Dal Riada. Why is the High King of Dal Riada not the King of the Ulaidh?'

'Because Ulster, in fact all of Ireland, is wracked by fighting, intrigue and power struggles. The Caledonian western seaboard was much less populated and a much better place to live in peace – well, at least comparatively speaking. The Scots population in Caledonian Dal Riada is now much, much greater than it is in Ulster.'

After a pause whilst Aidan digested this information, Niall asked the question that had been at the forefront of his mind ever since they had sailed.

'Are you set on staying on Iona and becoming a monk?'

'It's been my dream for awhile. I was fascinated by what Brother Finnian told me about Jesus Christ and I need to know more about him and his teachings. Why?'

Niall shifted uncomfortably on the tussock of grass on which he was sitting.

'I like you. I've other friends back home, of course, but we're always competing with each other. You're the first friend I've had with who I can be myself. I'm sad at the thought of us parting.'

Niall's answer surprised Aidan. The helmsman's son was older, bigger and stronger and to some extent, he was a role model for the younger boy. It had never occurred to him that Niall thought of him as anything but a mildly amusing buffoon. He was tempted to ask if he could stay with Niall's people and train as a warrior when he was a little older, but then he remembered what Finnian had told him about God having a special mission for him, so he kept quiet.

The next day they left Tarbert and hoisted the mainsail again. It was still a patchwork, but at least the patches were all roughly the same colour. They made good progress with the wind coming from the south west, so they didn't have to row until the wind died, just as they approached a dangerous whirlpool called Corryvrechan between the Isles of Jura and Scarba.

'It's said that it drags unwary ships down into its depths and they emerge in Hell,' Niall told him. Aidan didn't know whether to believe him or not. He had discussed the concept of Hell with the priest back in the settlement, but the man didn't know much more than that those who led evil lives were condemned to live there for all time. He shuddered and kept a wary eye on the distant maelstrom as they rowed hard well to the east near the mainland. Once clear of its danger, they rowed between two more small islands. This stretch of water was quite narrow and there were several rocks that either just broke the surface or lay a few feet below, waiting to rip the bottom out of any ship that didn't know the passage well.

Niall was sent to watch for the rocks from the prow and Aidan went with him. The birlinn edged forward slowly as the two boys leaned out as far as they dared to point out where the rocks were. Suddenly Niall called out that there was a rock a few feet off the port bow and Ruairi pushed the steering oar a little to the left. However, Aidan could see a jagged point over which the sea broke every few seconds about twelve feet dead ahead.

'Rock dead ahead,' he yelled in alarm.

'How far?'

'Less than ten feet now.'

'Back oars,' Ruairi ordered and handing the steering oar to another, he ran forward. The ship slowed and then slowly started to move in reverse as the rowers put their backs into it.

'Cease rowing. Well spotted, Aidan, that would have ripped us apart.'

Now the tide was carrying the practically motionless birlinn back towards some rocks it had just navigated around.

'Forward slowly left bank of oars only.'

As the ship started to move and the head came round, Ruairi ordered all the rowers to pull together, but slowly. They inched forward, but there were no more rocks and soon everyone relaxed as they pulled hard for Loch Buie on the south coast of Mull. They beached the ship for the night and started the campfire to cook the evening meal just as the sun started to set in the west, bathing the sea and the long peninsula called the Ross of Mull in orange light. The sky had turned turquoise with streaks of dark grey cloud here and there.

Aidan didn't think he had ever seen such a beautiful sight. Niall and his father joined him and they watched the sky change to a riotous mix of orange, red, indigo and various shades of grey as the sun went down. By now the land was almost black but the sea reflected the colours of the sky, only mottled and moving with the waves.

'Make the most of it, it'll be raining before dawn,' Ruairi said gloomily. 'You did well today, Aidan. I shall be sorry to leave you at Iona and I know that my son feels the same. You have the makings of a fine sailor.'

'I'm sorry, Ruairi. Brother Finnian said that God has a special task for me and I think that it will start on Iona. Don't ask me how I know; it's just a feeling I have deep down. I hope that I shall see you both again in the future, though. Thank you for showing me such kindness and friendship.'

The next morning Aidan said nothing as they rowed into the driving rain along the south coast of the Ross of Mull and across the narrow sound between the main island and its tiny satellite. They raised their sail to catch the strengthening wind as they neared Iona and as luck would have it, a birlinn appeared around the end of the peninsula just at that moment. They were challenged, but they were left alone as soon as the shipmaster was recognised. However, one of the crew did call across asking where they had acquired such an unusual sail, followed by the sound of uproarious laughter, much to the annoyance of Ruari's crew.

As they approached the shore, they saw that there was another craft already beached on the small stretch of sand to the south of the abbey. However, as they made ready to beach alongside it, it was pushed back into the sea by the monks and it turned to round the north of the small island. Aidan was scanning the island eagerly, especially the group of monks in their brown habits, in the hope that Brother Finnian might be there.

All that the departing birlinn seemed to have done was to deliver a small boy of about ten, who was being greeted enthusiastically by another boy in a habit who appeared to be couple of years older. He thought it was likely that they would be novices, just as he hoped to become.

The ship ran up the beach slightly before coming to a halt and Aidan leaped over the side. Niall had already said goodbye to him and now he threw down the bundle containing Aidan's few possessions. Ruairi followed him over the side and walked with him up to the one monk who had remained behind when the others had returned to the abbey, taking the two boys with them.

'Father Abbot.' The burly helmsman greeted the thin, rather aesthetic monk with a brief bow. 'This is Aidan, who desires to become a novice here. He has a letter from the priest of his settlement and he was the companion of Brother Finnian for a time.'

'Greetings in God's name, Ruairi; and welcome to Iona, Aidan. If you were Finnian's companion I'm sure we can find a place for you here. Will you and your men stay for a meal, Ruairi?'

He already knew the answer to that, as the steersman and his crew had stayed aboard, but it was common courtesy to issue the invitation.

'Thank you, Father Abbott, but we are long overdue and must return home with all speed.'

It was then that Aidan realised that their families would be worried about them after the great storm and it was because of him that they had delayed their return. He couldn't image his late father's people going out of their way like that to help a stranger.

'Farewell, Aidan. I hope that our paths will cross again someday.'

Aidan would have liked to watch them depart, but as the abbot set off at a brisk pace towards the abbey buildings, Aidan grabbed his bundle and hurried after him.

~~~

At first Oswald thought that his initial impression of Eochaid as an arrogant boy had been correct. When he was admitted to the guest house, he greeted the King of the Ulaidh courteously and explained that the abbot had thought that Eochaid might like to be shown around the monastery and the island.

Before his father had a chance to reply, the boy, who was sitting on a chest sharpening his seax, looked up and glared at the young novice.

'Why would I need some snivelling boy to act as my guide? I'm quite capable of finding my own way around this tiny little islet.'

Oswald was stung by this response to an offer he hadn't wanted to make in the first place and replied without thinking.

'I'm no snivelling boy, you spoiled little brat. My father was Æthelfrith of Northumbria and if you want to keep that head on your shoulders you'll show me some respect!'

As soon as he'd spoken, he thought that his hot temper and his intemperate tongue had got him into trouble again; however, the boy's father roared with laughter and smacked his son on the side of his head.

'Well said. I think Eochaid may have met his match in you. Now put your toy sword down, boy and go with this young monk and try to learn something useful.'

38

With bad grace the boy rubbed his head and shoved his seax back in its scabbard. He got up and stalked out of the hut, barging Oswald with his shoulder as he passed him. Oswald spun around and kicked the other boy in the back of the knee so that his leg collapsed and he went sprawling through the door. He stooped down and grabbing Eochaid's long greasy hair, pulled his head up so that he could look him in the eye.

'I told you to show me some respect, Eochaid, or I'll do more than make you eat dirt.'

To his surprise the Irish boy's face crumpled and Oswald realised that he was trying not to cry. He immediately let go of his hair and pulled him to his feet.

'Come on, we'll start in the church.'

He led the way, to give the boy a chance to recover his composure. He was astute enough to realise that Eochaid's arrogant bravado was all show; underneath, he was an insecure little boy trying to live up to his father's expectations.

The Irish princeling sulkily followed Oswald into the church and stood in the aisle of the small, austere stone building as his companion went and prostrated himself in front of the altar. Oswald ignored the other boy's surliness and began to explain about the life of a monk. He went on to talk about his own conversion to Christianity on Iona, having been a pagan for the first twelve years of his life. Suddenly, something he'd said caught Eochaid's attention.

'How did you escape from Northumbria after your father was slain?'

Oswald recounted the skirmish with the Picts and Eochaid's eyes lit up with excitement.

'I envy you. My father expects me to become a warrior, but he won't let me do anything remotely dangerous. The nearest I've come to anything at all risky is coming on this voyage with him. Even then, I have to stay safely in the bowels of the ship so I don't fall over the side.'

He spat to express his disgust and Oswald laughed. He had begun to sympathise with Eochaid and understand why he behaved like a petulant child.

'I take it that you've never climbed up a rock face, then?'

'You are in jest. Of course not.' Suddenly his eyes lit up with excitement. 'You mean there are places here that we can climb?'

Oswald nodded.

'They aren't very high or steep, but they can be challenging if you crave a little excitement. Come on,'

A few minutes later they reached the top of a cliff above a small sandy cove at the southern end of the small island. Eochaid peered over the edge at the beach fifty feet below, where the waves rolled in gently and lapped the shore, but Oswald grabbed his sleeve and took him to the other side of the rocky outcrop. Here there was no beach but just jagged rocks against which the sea crashed. Suddenly he didn't seem quite so keen.

Oswald peeled off his habit and, yelling for Eochaid to follow him and copy what he did, he started to scramble down the rock face. When his head disappeared, the Irish boy gritted his teeth and undid his belt, dropping his seax on the grass before gingerly lowering his legs over the edge. He was waving his feet about trying to find a foothold when he felt his left foot grabbed and placed on a protruding bit of rock. Oswald continued to help him find foot and hand holds until he was confident enough to proceed on his own. A few minutes later, the two boys stood on a ledge just above the rocks being pounded by the waves. As they were splashed by droplets of spray, Eochaid put back his head and whooped his delight at what he had just done. He had never in his short life felt so alive.

The climb back up was a lot easier and the two lay side by side grinning at one another.

'Do you wrestle?'

Eochaid shook his head. 'But I've watched our warriors and I think I know the fundamentals.'

Oswald spent the next hour teaching the other boy the basic holds and the techniques for throwing and pinning one's opponent. By then they were sweating profusely, so Oswald took Eochaid down the much gentler scramble on the other side of the outcrop to the cove with its white sandy beach and they washed themselves in the sea. Neither boy could swim and Oswald panicked when a larger than normal wave swept his companion off his feet and he disappeared below the surface. He groped around under the water and found an arm. A moment later he pulled a laughing Eochaid to his feet.

'Perhaps your father was right to protect you from harm,' he grumbled. 'Have you no fear?'

'Not with you, Oswald. You have given me the confidence in myself that I lacked. How wrong I was about you when I first saw you.'

The two made their way back to the monastery chattering away. Oswald realised with a start that he had made a friend of the Irish princeling. He was glad that they would be sailing together when he left for Dùn Add. However, he did wonder what had persuaded King Fiachnae to let Eochaid train as a warrior and said so.

'Oh, I think my father fears for me because my two elder brothers were killed in battle and he's afraid of losing his last son; that said, he realises that I have to learn to fight well, or, living where we do, I'll be as good as dead anyway. I suspect it's a case of, "if he can't see me he can't worry about me." That's why I'm to train at Dùn Add.'

That night a great storm hit Iona and the birlinn fought against the ropes that held it secure halfway onto the beach. The ropes held, but the strakes at the stern were severely stressed by the action of the agitated waves. Like Aidan, miles to the south, Eochaid was pressed into service re-caulking the damaged stern and he was delighted when Oswald and his brother came and stripped off their habits to help him. Unlike Aidan, the two had lived by the sea at Bebbanburgh all their lives and had done this before, until they had been forced to flee.

Once the birlinn had been repaired, Oswald packed his few belongings and changed his habit for the tunic he had arrived in. It was now ridiculously small for him and after Eochaid had finished laughing at him, he lent him one of his. Osguid was sad to see him go, but his elder brother reminded him that Oslac would soon join him and the boy cheered up a little.

Oswald and Eochaid left Iona just three days before Aidan arrived.

# Chapter Three – Coll and Tiree

## 620 AD

For the next two years, Oswald and Eochaid learned how to fight with sword and shield, how to use a seax in close quarter fighting, how to use a spear and a bow and how to hunt. The latter gained them useful skills as trackers, mastering the stealthy approach and how to face a charging enemy when they hunted boar. Finally, they were being taught how to fight in a shield wall. Soon they would be ready to be classed as warriors.

Oswald had been looking forward to Osguid returning to start his training at Dùn Add, but he was to be disappointed. His brother had elected to stay on Iona and become a monk and now Oslaph had turned ten and gone to join his brothers as a novice. Connad had given Acha and her family a hut to live in when they first arrived, but Oswald lived in a separate hut with Eochaid and the other trainees. Naturally he visited his mother, but not very often. Acha would like to have seen more of her eldest son, but she consoled herself that she still had Oswiu and Offa at home to keep her company, as well as her daughter, Æbbe, who was now nearly five.

'Have you heard?' an excited Eochaid asked Oswald as he burst into the hut that they shared with six other youths training to become warriors.

'Heard what?' his friend replied, continuing to sharpen his sword with a whetstone.

'Some Picts have landed on Coll and slaughtered or enslaved the people there. Apparently it's not just a raid this time; the rumour is that they've brought their families and intend to settle.'

'Really? Where did you hear this?' Oswald's eyes lit up at the prospect of some action at last. Dal Riada had been too peaceful for his liking over the past few years.

'Two men and a boy managed to escape in a fishing boat and they've just arrived here. Connad has told Lorchan to gather the crews of five birlinns to go and recapture the island.'

The Isle of Coll was one of two small islands that lay to the north west of the much larger Isle of Mull. If Coll had been invaded, then the other, Tiree, was probably under threat as well. The eight boys in the hut had all turned sixteen and hoped to be included in the force being sent to retake the islands. If Lorchan, one of the most experienced shipmasters, was taking three big and two smaller birlinns, then he would need at least two hundred and fifty warriors to man them. That would mean every man from Dùn Add except the elderly would be needed. Connad would presumably have gone himself, but he was recovering from a bout of fever that had left him weak and bedridden.

Later that day they were told that they would be crewing one of the smaller birlinns and found out that another one would be joining them from Mull. They would rendezvous off Iona and then sail up Mull's western coast and across the seven miles of open water to Coll. As it was probable that the Picts had also invaded Tiree, Lorchan was sending Oswald's birlinn there on its own to find out exactly what the situation was. They were not to fight, but merely to assess the enemy's strength and disposition.

Oswald's shipmaster, Cael, re-iterated Lorchan's instructions about not trying to tackle the Picts on their own, but Oswald made up his mind to ignore him if he got the chance. He had trained for two years for this moment and he wasn't to be denied his first fight.

The wind was against them as they rounded the end of the Ross of Mull and entered the sound between Mull and Iona. Rowing demanded all his concentration and effort, but Oswald glanced at the monastery as they passed and wondered how his three brothers were. He had found the life of a novice monk restrictive, but during his two years there he had become a devout Christian and he could understand Osguid's attraction to a life of prayer and meditation.

They anchored for the night in Loch Scridain, a deep inlet on Mull's west coast and set off at dawn for the two outer islands. As they left the loch, Cael steered north-west directly towards Tiree, whilst the rest continued along the coast. The crew were still rowing, but now they had the wind on their beam to help them. The direct crossing was twenty five miles or more, so it would be the middle of the afternoon before they reached the island.

However, it took them a little longer than that, as Cael steered for the south coast of Tiree as soon as the island came in sight. He hoped that it would appear to anyone on the isle as if they were heading around Tiree for the Isle of Barra further out.

Once they were out of sight of Scarinish, the only settlement on Tiree, he turned the birlinn and headed into Balephuil Bay. Once they had beached the ship Cael left Oswald and his seven friends to guard it and divided the remaining men into three groups to explore the island.

Needless to say, Oswald, Eochaid and the others had been bitterly disappointed to have been given such an unexciting task. Oswald immediately took charge and started to plan how they should defend the birlinn, should they be attacked. Although Oswald had been accepted by most of the others as their leader for the past two years, one of the youths had never accepted this and constantly disputed anything he proposed.

Ultan was a nephew of King Connad – his sister's eldest son – and he thought that this gave him the right to lead. The others told him repeatedly that this had to be earned, but it made no difference; he repeatedly challenged Oswald and this time was no different.

'All we have to do is stay here with the ship. There's no one for miles around. I'm going to sleep.'

The others ignored him and Oswald took one other youth with him to keep watch inland from a clump of marram grass on top of a small dune above the beach, whilst Eochaid stayed with the rest on the ship. Because the wooden benches and deck of the birlinn were uncomfortable to sleep on, Ultan stretched out on the sand and soon started to snore gently. Eochaid scooped up a bucket of sea water and crept up on Ultan before tipping the cold water over him. The others hooted with laughter, but Ultan was not someone to take a jest in good part.

He leaped up with a roar of rage and drew his sword. Eochaid had his sword and his seax belted to his waist but he made no effort to draw either blade. Instead, when Ultan rushed at him and tried to spit him on his sword, the Irish boy merely stepped to one side and tripped Ultan up as the momentum of his charge took him past. Of course, this made the others laugh even harder.

Suddenly Oswald appeared and cuffed both Ultan and Eochaid around the head.

'Shut up, you idiots. You're meant to be keeping a lookout. There's a sail over there,' he said, pointing to the southern tip of the island. 'Quick, into the ship and cover yourselves with whatever you can find to make it look as if it's been left unguarded.'

Ultan, still angry, was about to question him, but the glare that Oswald directed at him convinced him to do as he was told and all eight hid under the spare mainsail beneath the small area of deck in the stern on which the helmsman stood.

'Good. If you had questioned me again, Ultan, I'd have had no compunction about killing you to save the lives of the rest of us. Now we wait here until they put a crew aboard and they've put to sea; then we emerge and kill them.'

'But they'll outnumber us,' Ultan objected.

'You stay hidden and become a slave, then,' Eochaid told him brutally.

'They'll be busy rowing and won't be expecting us. Now, quiet.'

The eight boys held their breath and gripped swords and seaxes tightly. Shields would have only encumbered them. They heard the Picts clamber aboard and felt the birlinn shudder as it was pushed off the beach. The splash of oars and the slight rocking motion told them that the enemy were backing the ship and then the change in motion meant that it was turning out to sea. There was a shouted exchange between the two shipmasters and then they felt the ship pick up speed.

'Now,' yelled Oswald and sprang from his hiding place. He had stabbed the three rowers nearest the stern before the Picts realised what was happening. Without waiting to see what the others were doing, he jumped up onto the helmsman's platform and cut the astonished man's throat. The ship slewed round without his hand on the steering oar and Oswald stumbled before regaining his footing. This gave the man standing beside the dead helmsman – presumably the shipmaster – a chance to draw his sword.

Oswald could hear the shrieks of the rowers as more of them were killed where they sat, but then the clash of metal against metal indicated that at least some of the Picts were now fighting back. However, Oswald had other things to worry about. The man facing him had several scars on his legs, arms and face and they, along with the rings around his upper arm, indicated that he was an experienced warrior as well as the ship's master.

Suddenly the man feinted at Oswald's head, then changed direction to stab down at his thighs. Oswald was slightly disappointed. He had been expecting such a move and he twisted sideways to avoid the thrust and, at the same time, stabbed the man in the right biceps with his sword and slashed at his body with his seax.

It was unwise to wear chain mail whilst at sea, unless you wanted to sink like a stone if you fell overboard, but the man was wearing a thick leather jerkin which absorbed most of the blow. Nevertheless, blood began to seep out of the cut in the leather and he had to change his sword over to his left hand, as his right arm was now almost useless.

The Pict looked at his young adversary with new respect and growled something at him which Oswald didn't understand, but he guessed that it wasn't complimentary. This time the man decided to make a sustained attack and it was all that Oswald could do to parry the other's cuts and thrusts. However, the man was far from the first flush of youth and he began to tire.

Now it was Oswald's turn to attack and the man was forced back against the sternpost. Oswald stepped forward to press home his attack, but then slipped on the blood coating the deck. In trying to recover he stumbled forward and head butted the Pict shipmaster in the belly. The man took a couple of steps backwards trying to regain his balance. He failed and fell over the side.

Oswald thanked God for his good fortune and turned to see how the others were faring. Suddenly Ultan appeared in front of him. The boy stabbed out with his seax, hoping to gut Oswald, but he misjudged it and opened up a long, shallow wound in the other's side instead.

Oswald felt nothing for a moment and then an agonising pain shot through his body and he fell to his knees. His head drooped so he didn't see Eochaid come up behind Ultan and thrust his sword into the boy's torso. Putting his foot into the small of the traitor's back, he straightened his leg and Ultan followed the Pict shipmaster over the side. As it happened, Ultan couldn't swim, but it would have made no difference. His spinal cord had been severed and he had lost control of his limbs. He floated face down for a while and then sank beneath the waves.

Eochaid and his friends had managed to kill all the other eighteen Picts on board. It would have been more of a feat had more than three of them managed to reach their weapons, but even so, the boys had good reason to feel proud of themselves. However, their euphoria was short lived once they realised that Oswald was wounded. To make matters worse, the crew of the other birlinn had realised that their prize was no longer following them and had turned around to investigate.

Unlike the unprepared men they had just slain, this ship had a crew of twenty, all fully armed and ready for a fight. Six inexperienced boys – Oswald was too wounded to be of any use – couldn't hope to defeat them.

~~~

Aidan knelt beside Osguid as they took their vows to become monks. Both had completed two years as novices and at sixteen and fourteen respectively, were considered old enough to progress to become full members of the Iona community. The previous night had been spent in prayer and at dawn they had been shorn of the hair from their foreheads to the crown of theirs heads. This form of tonsure was exclusive to the Celtic Church and gave both monks and priests a distinctive look.

After the ceremony was over, both monks visited the abbot separately in the beehive hut in which he lived. Osguid was told that he would join the other monks who farmed the land and looked after the livestock on the island; Aidan would become the assistant to the new infirmarian. This monk was responsible for looking after the sick and the injured and had himself been the assistant infirmarian until two weeks ago when the previous incumbent had died in his sleep at the age of fifty-five.

Aidan had been healthy during his time as a novice and so he hadn't had occasion to visit the infirmary, but of course he knew Brother Brendan and from what little contact he had had with him, he'd liked him. For his part, Brendan knew that Aidan was a kind boy with a pleasant disposition and was a hard worker. Of all the monks available to assist him, Brendan had asked for Aidan. He was not to be disappointed.

Aidan had enjoyed his time as a novice, although he shared Oswald's dislike of the Master of Novices, who he thought was too strict and lacking in any attractive qualities. He had managed to keep his nose clean, though and had never been beaten. Not so Osguid and his brother Oslac, who always seemed to be up to mischief. Aidan was therefore surprised when Osguid had asked to remain as a monk instead of leaving to train as a warrior like his elder brother. When Aidan asked him why, Osguid confessed that he had spent his life to date in Oswald's shadow and although he loved his brother, he didn't want to spend the rest of his life being known as Oswald's brother. He liked the life on Iona and he was devout in his way, so he had decided to stay. However, he had been fascinated by Aidan's stories about Brother Finnian and confessed that he would like to become a missionary in due course.

Aidan thought long and hard about what Osguid had said and wondered if that wasn't what he himself wanted to do. However, there was a great deal to learn if he was to become a good healer and he concentrated on that for now.

'This is how you make a poultice,' Brendan was explaining, when Osguid came bursting into the infirmary.

'Brendan, come quickly,' he panted, forgetting in his agitation to address the infirmarian as Brother. 'You too, Aidan. Oswald has just been brought here from Tiree. He's been badly wounded.'

~~~

Eochaid had taken one look at the approaching Pict birlinn and realised that he had but moments to act.

'Quick, get the mainsail up.'

The others obeyed without question. Now that Oswald was out of action, they looked to the Irish prince as their leader. They undid the sail ties and hauled on the halliard to raise the yardarm from which the sail hung. It took scarcely more than a couple of minutes before the sail began to fill with the wind coming from the west, but in that time the other ship had narrowed the gap between them to about half a mile.

Eochaid directed them to let out one rope and pull in another until the sail was set to take them to the south of the Picts' birlinn. Predictably, the other ship turned to intercept them. However, they were now picking up speed and the Picts' shipmaster had failed to allow for this when setting his new course. His men were putting their backs into extracting every ounce of speed out of their vessel, but they were rowing against the wind and the shipmaster had steered a circular course in his attempts to come alongside Eochaid's ship. They had therefore rowed further than necessary.

The young Dal Riadans cheered when it became obvious that they would be able to slip past to the south of their foes. But Eochaid surprised them by suddenly changing course towards the enemy.

'Trim the mainsail,' he ordered brusquely and when they hesitated, unsure what he was doing, he added, 'quickly now!'

They did as they were bid and then they realised what he was attempting to do. It was risky, but it would put an end to any pursuit. He was headed directly towards the side of the Pictish craft. At first their shipmaster thought Eochaid intended to ram them, so he turned towards him whilst his men prepared to board. At the last moment Eochaid pushed the steering oar over and the two ships passed within two feet of one another.

Two Picts had grappling hooks ready and they swung them to couple the two ships together, but then the prow of the Dal Riadan birlinn hit the first oar, which was still in the water. The oar snapped with a crack and the inboard end of it smashed into the rower's chest, caving in his ribcage. The sharp ends of the broken bones pierced his lungs, ensuring his death in due course. The same thing happened all the way along that side of the birlinn, except for the last oar. The rower there realised what was happening and just managed to haul it inboard in time.

The Dal Riadan birlinn sailed on undamaged, apart from a few scars on its hull, leaving behind a ship full of dying men with only eleven oars instead of the usual twenty. By the time the Picts had sorted themselves out, Eochaid and his small crew had rounded the point and disappeared from view.

The problem now was that they didn't know where Cael and the rest of their crew were and if they stopped to try and find them, they might run into more Picts ashore, or more likely, give the other birlinn the chance to sail after them and catch them up. Eochaid came to the conclusion that the sensible thing to do was to make for the Isle of Coll and hope that he could find Lorchan and the other ships.

In the event Eochaid found them quite quickly as they had landed on the beach in Brechacca Bay at the southern end of Coll. However, to get there the boys had to run directly into the wind, so they lowered the sail and got out two pairs of oars to try and row. They were making barely any progress against the wind, but they were spotted and another birlinn soon came out to investigate.

'What's happened? Where're Cael and the others?'

'We were left to guard the ship, but it was captured by a Pictish birlinn. We managed to re-capture it and they've lost most of their crew, but they're just behind us,' Eochaid yelled back. 'Oswald is badly wounded,' he added.

Lorchan was dying to know how a handful of boys had managed to kill most of a Pictish crew, but that could wait. At that moment the other ship appeared and Lorchan immediately set a course towards it.

The Picts tried to raise their sail and escape, but they had scarcely managed to get turned back facing the way they had come before Lorchan overtook them and came alongside. The fight was brief and bloody and within ten minutes the only Pict left alive was a boy of about twelve who kept spitting at Lorchan and trying to bite his captors.

'Tie him up and knock him out if he keeps that up. He may be able to tell us if there are any more of the pagan devils around.'

'And so I killed the treacherous dog and fed him to the fishes,' Eochaid told Lorchan after explaining how well Oswald's plan had worked.

'I never liked Ultan anyway, but I'm not looking forward to telling the king. How did you evade their birlinn?'

When Eochaid had finished his tale, Lorchan was tempted to congratulate him and the others for their cunning and their bravery, but he was wary of his king's reaction to the killing of his nephew. He confined himself to nodding sagely.

'Well, we've killed every Pict we found on Coll, but it will need to be re-populated. We rescued most of the women and children who the Picts had taken as slaves, but they've killed all the men and older boys. It's too late now to go and find Cael and as far as we know, the birlinn you encountered was the only one sent to Tiree, so he should be safe. Still, he won't be going anywhere.'

'What about Oswald? He's been sewn up and bandaged, but he's lost a lot of blood and my stitching is not very good.'

Lorchan grunted. 'It was his plan that saved your birlinn and your lives. I'll send someone back to Dùn Add with tidings of what's happened and they can drop Oswald off with the monks on Iona on the way. You'd better stay on Iona with Oswald for now; that way Connad will have time to get used to the death of his nephew without you there for him to take revenge on.'

# Chapter Four – Rònan

## 620 - 621 AD

Oswald tossed and turned, yelling out in delirium as Aidan tried to restrain him from hurting himself or others. His wound had become infected before he arrived at Iona and although Brother Brendan had cleaned it and re-stitched it, it had started to fester. Brendan and Aidan had cut away the infected flesh and the wound had started to heal, but not before the infection had spread through his body via his bloodstream. Brendan had explained that either the fever would kill him, or it would break and he would slowly recover.

Osguid, Oslac and Oslaph had tried to visit their brother, but Aidan didn't want them to see Oswald like this and had sent them away, promising to send for them as soon as there was any change. Osguid had taken them to the church to pray with him, but after a while the two novices were sent back to the scriptorium and Osguid had to go back to work. Eochaid had stayed in the infirmary, however and had helped Aidan bathe Oswald's body with cold water to keep the fever down.

It wasn't until the early hours of the fifth morning that the fever broke and then Oswald began to recover slowly. It had left him very weak, though and the tightness and loss of muscle in his right side would take some time to mend before he could move normally again.

His brothers came to see him as soon as he was lucid once more, but soon got bored just talking to him and left him alone again. One or another would drop in for a few minutes, but now that they knew he was on the road to recovery, their visits became less frequent and he was left with only Brendan and Aidan to talk to. Eochaid had become bored on Iona once he knew that his friend was getting better and had joined a ship that was returning to Islay. There were a few warriors on Iona, but they didn't see it as part of their duty to give Eochaid the weapon training he needed. There would be other young men on Islay with who he could train. He felt guilty about leaving his friend, but Oswald insisted he go.

'By the time you return I shall be fit enough to start weapon training again and I shall need you here so I can beat you,' Oswald told him. The other smiled back at him.

'If you are truly fit enough to beat me on my return, no-one will be more delighted than me.'

The two thumped each other gently on the shoulder and Eochaid ran down to the beach to convince Oswald that he was glad to be going, when in fact he had rarely felt so sad.

When Oswald was able to get up for a few hours a day he went for short walks, but soon got tired. When he came back one day Aidan was mixing some herbal remedies and Oswald asked him if he could help.

Aidan explained what he was doing and Oswald sat down beside him on the bench and began to help him, copying what he did exactly. Brendan smiled as he saw that the two were becoming good friends and wondered whether Oswald would now stay on Iona as a monk. However, he soon realised that it was the last thing Oswald was likely to do. He became increasingly irritated at his forced inaction and often had to be cautioned about doing too much too quickly. His response was to glare at Brendan or Aidan and roundly curse them. It was a good job that they both realised that he was just giving vent to his frustration. Deep down, he knew how much he owed the two of them.

~~~

Lorchan had sailed into the loch below Dùn Add, dreading the reception he would receive from the king. However, Connad had congratulated him on his success in driving the Picts out of Coll and Tiree and discussed repopulating the islands with him. He didn't mention Ultan at first, which worried Lorchan a little.

He had brought the Pict boy he had captured back with him and had him taken before the king. The boy's behaviour hadn't improved and he spat at his guards and cursed Connad.

'My, he's feisty, isn't he? He'd make a good warrior if he could be tamed. I'm not sure he's going to be much good as a slave, though. What will you do with him? Kill him?'

'No and I don't need another slave, but I thought that Oswald deserved a reward after saving Cael's birlinn, so I'll give the boy to him when, or perhaps I should say if, he recovers.'

'Yes, that was a bad business. Why should my nephew try to kill Oswald? I can't believe that of him.'

'I gather that the others chose Oswald as their leader, but Ultan couldn't accept it; he demanded that position for himself because of his kinship to you.'

'Still, Eochaid didn't have to kill him. My sister and her husband are furious and demand that I execute Eochaid. However, that would alienate his father and he is my vassal in Ulster. You've put me in a difficult position, Lorchan.'

The other man was about to point out that the king was hardly being fair; it wasn't his fault that Ultan was a treacherous dog. He didn't blame Eochaid for killing the king's nephew; on the contrary, it was what he deserved. Striking one of your own side during a battle was unforgivable. However, he held his tongue.

'It would be better if Eochaid didn't return here, Lorchan, if you understand me.'

'Perfectly, Lord.'

He therefore sent word to Iona to warn Eochaid to return to the relative safety of Ulster, but by the time the message got to Iona, Eochaid had already left for Islay. The abbot went to find Oswald and told him about the warning, so he paid one of the island's fishermen to take the message on to Eochaid.

He realised that this meant that his friend wouldn't be returning and that only increased his foul mood. If he couldn't start training again - and that meant having a skilful opponent with whom to practice - he wouldn't be much use as a warrior, even when he was physically fit again.

He became increasingly distant from his brothers, who were frightened by his outbursts of temper and the only one who was prepared to put up with him was Aidan. His soothing voice seemed to calm Oswald down and he came to rely on his friend as his only companion.

Things might have continued down this unsatisfactory path if a ship hadn't arrived to take Oswald back to Dùn Add. He left Aidan with reluctance, but he knew that he would become unbearable if he stayed. His farewell to his brothers was a little uncomfortable and he apologised for being like a bear with a sore head. However, he was now happy again. Returning to Dùn Add meant that he could start to train once more. As they put out to sea he suddenly felt free and even the nagging residual pain in his side seemed to be less important.

'Welcome back, Oswald. We have missed you these four months. I hope that you have recovered from your unfortunate injury.'

'It wasn't unfortunate, Lord; it was deliberately inflicted by the treacherous Ultan.'

His mother had cautioned him about mentioning the king's nephew, but her plea had fallen on deaf ears.

'Be very careful, Oswald. You and your family are here as my guests. If you make unfounded accusations against my own family, you and yours will no longer be welcome here.'

Oswald had the good sense to know when he was flogging a dead horse, but he felt better for having made his complaint.

'As you know, Lord, we are more than grateful for your hospitality. However, I hope that whatever trifling service I may have been able to render to you during the re-capture of Coll and Tiree may, in some small way, repay you for your kindness.'

Connad knew that Oswald had neatly turned the tables on him and he laughed.

'You've a clever tongue in your head, boy. Make sure it doesn't trip you up one day. Mentioning Tiree reminds me that Lorchan has a gift for you, to thank you for what you did that day.' He beckoned Lorchan forward and he came gripping a boy of twelve or thirteen by the shoulder. The lad was dressed as a slave with a wooden collar fastened about his neck.

'We captured this little vixen on Coll and I thought you might like a body slave, Oswald. I'd like to say that he's house trained, but he'll still spit at you or bite you given half a chance. Beating him doesn't seem to do any good, but perhaps you can do something with him. If you tire of trying, then perhaps you could set him free and hunt him down with your friends. It would be good sport, if nothing else.'

The boy's eyes had widened at this suggestion and he looked at Oswald with fear in his eyes. At least he understands some of what we are saying, Oswald thought, even if he pretends not to. He knew that the Picts spoke Brythonic, the language of the majority of Britain prior to the arrival of the Romans, but he had obviously been taught, or had picked up, some Gaelic.

He beckoned the boy over to him and he came after a moment's hesitation. When he got close enough, he spat at Oswald and the globule of mucus and spittle landed on the young man's tunic. Oswald spat back, but this time the contents of his mouth landed squarely in the youngster's right eye. He reared back in astonishment and blinked several times to clear the muck from it, then he grinned at Oswald and knew he had met his match.

'Take the collar off him, Lorchan. If he runs, he knows he'll be the quarry for my friends to chase and kill. I know you understand me, boy, so don't pretend otherwise. What's your name?'

'Rònan ab Teàrlaidh. My father was King of Lewis, an island to the north of Skye.'

The boy fingered the chaffed skin around his neck where the rough wood had rubbed it raw. Not unnaturally, he'd hated the collar and he was delighted to be rid of it. He looked at Oswald and nodded his thanks.

'I see. Will he pay to get you back?' Oswald asked.

'I shouldn't think so; you pigs killed him on Coll. My uncle will be king now and he'll want me dead so I'm not able to challenge him when I'm older.'

'Well, Rònan ab Teàrlaidh, it looks as if we're stuck with one another. One word of warning though. If you bite me, I'll set the dogs on you and you'll find out what it's really like to be bitten.'

'Don't worry. You I like; not these swine, though.'

The boy grinned at him and Oswald couldn't resist giving him a half smile in return. Connad and Lorchan had listened to this exchange, first with anger at the boy's temerity, then with admiration at the easy way Oswald had won him over. The king looked at Oswald with new eyes. The boy was dangerous. He was clever, cunning and people liked him. Moreover, they would follow him. Oswald was a threat and one way or another, Connad determined to get rid of him.

~~~

Oswald had intended to return to his mother's hut to complete his convalescence, but he didn't entirely trust Rònan yet and he wasn't sure it was sensible to expose his two youngest brothers and his sister to him. Nor did he want the two of them to live in a hut with other warriors. They would tease Rònan and order him about. He would undoubtedly react badly and with weapons lying about, that just wouldn't be sensible.

So Oswald decided to build a small hut for just the two of them. The weather was fine and, being spring, it wasn't too cold at night, so they slept outside until the hut was built. Rònan and Oswald went out to cut saplings for the end walls and Oswald found that the exercise, whilst painful, helped to develop the muscles in his right side. He selected five straight trees to form the frame to hold the roof in place and watched whilst Rònan chopped them down. He borrowed a horse to drag the trees back to the building site, once he and the boy had trimmed the branches from the trunks.

Next they enlisted the help of Oswald's friends to erect the frame. The following day they put the uprights for the walls in place at each end and wattle was woven in between the uprights to form the two walls. They mixed water and earth to make mud and plastered the wattle to make the walls. Once this had set hard, it would keep out the wind and the rain.

When they had finished they were filthy and Rònan suddenly picked up a handful of the leftover mud and threw it at Oswald, who responded. Soon they were both covered from head to foot in the stuff and laughing their heads off. They ran down to the river to wash it off and Oswald discovered to his amazement that he'd run all that way without his side troubling him once.

That night it rained for an hour and they both got soaked. Oswald became determined to finish the hut before the end of the next day. They went and cut a lot more saplings, which they tied in place in a grid pattern to make the frame for the roof. This would come down to the ground on the long sides of the hut, as that was the simplest construction. Finally, they worked to tie bundles of straw on top of the roof frame to form a waterproof thatch.

That night they were exhausted, but they had their own place. Working together had cemented the bond between the two of them and Oswald found that, although Rònan was his servant, he no longer thought of him as just his slave. For his part, Rònan found that he no longer wanted to return to Lewis and kill his uncle so he could become king; he was content to stay with Oswald and serve him.

Just as he was drifting off to sleep, Oswald decided that he would try and convert Rònan to Christianity.

~~~

Working on the hut had built up the muscles in Oswald's right side and toned up the rest of his body, which had got decidedly flabby since he'd been taking things easy. Now he wanted to get back into fighting form as quickly as possible. He started by going for a run first thing each morning. At first Rònan stayed behind and prepared their breakfast, but after a week he asked if he could come, too. His legs were shorter that Oswald's, but he managed to keep up and as they both got fitter, Oswald found he was having to put a lot of effort into not letting Rònan beat him.

A week later, Oswald went and joined his old friends and started practice fighting with sword and shield, sword and seax, spear and shield and with a battle-axe. At first he was a poor opponent, but as he got fitter, he started to win more bouts. When Rònan had finished his chores in the hut, he got into the habit of coming to watch.

After a couple of weeks, the boy asked if he could join in. Oswald was dubious, but he had established a close rapport with Rònan and to reject his request would show that he didn't trust him with a weapon, so he compromised.

'We had to start our training with a wooden sword, so this afternoon we'll go and find a suitable piece of timber and I'll show you how to fashion a practice sword out of it. I'll go and find mine in my mother's hut and then I'll start to teach you.'

The boy's eyes lit up and he could barely contain his excitement until the training session ended. The others thought that Oswald was mad, but he had become convinced that Rònan now identified himself more with him than he did with his former people.

After a lunch of hard bread and goat's cheese, Oswald and Rònan went over to Acha's hut. The former was guiltily aware that it had been over two weeks since he had last seen his mother and siblings and the feeling intensified when Oswiu, Offa and Æbbe ran up to greet him enthusiastically. His sister even threw her arms around his legs and hugged them. Rònan smiled to see such affection, then looked sad. He had a sister on Lewis who he had been just as fond of, but he knew he would never see her again.

Distracted, he didn't hear Oswiu's question. He had asked if Rònan liked being his brother's slave. Their mother had a slave to look after them and the hut, but she was elderly, sulky and the children didn't like her. Oswiu sensed that the relationship between his brother and his slave was rather different.

'Rònan may be my servant, but he is also my friend,' Oswald told him.

When Rònan heard himself being described as a friend he felt elated and grinned broadly at Oswiu.

'He's going to teach me to be a warrior like him,' he told the younger boy proudly.

'Do you think that's wise, Oswald?' Acha asked, coming out of the hut to greet her eldest son.

'There's no-one I would trust more to guard my back, outside of my closest friends.'

Rònan didn't think he'd ever been happier. At that moment there was nothing that he wouldn't have done for Oswald.

After promising to return to eat his evening meal with his family, Oswald collected his old practice sword and he and Rònan went in search of a suitable length of wood. By the time the sun was setting, they had fashioned the rough outline of the sword, but finishing it would have to wait until the next day.

Rònan had expected to have to fend for himself that evening, but to his delight, Oswald took him along to eat with his family. Oswiu came and sat next to him and told him how he envied him.

'I can't wait until I'm old enough to learn to be a warrior, but I've another two years before I am even old enough to go to Iona and then I've got to spend two boring years there before I can start to learn how to fight. It seems ages away.'

Rònan was about the average size for a twelve year old boy, but Oswiu was much bigger than the norm for nine year olds. In fact, he wasn't that much smaller than Rònan, which gave Oswald an idea. He already knew that Oswiu, although a devout boy, was destined to be a fighter, not a monk and he saw no harm in him starting early. He turned to his mother and whispered in her ear. At first she shook her head, but after a few minutes Oswald had evidently persuaded her and he turned to the two boys.

'I'm too big to be Rònan's practice partner,' he began. 'How would you like it if I taught the two of you how to fight and you can practice together?'

It was, of course, a rhetorical question.

~~~

Aidan had missed Oswald's friendship after he departed Iona, but a month later he cheered up when Eochaid returned, bringing with him Brother Finnian. The young monk was delighted to see his old teacher again and they spent many hours telling each other what had happened to the two of them since they had last been together.

Eochaid, on the other hand, was not so happy. He was disappointed to find that Oswald had already left for Dùn Add and for a while he thought of following him there. Aidan pointed out the folly of that idea, as Ultan's father was bound to demand his death as soon as he arrived. He had only been safe on Islay because Connad didn't know he was there.

'I honestly think that your best course of action is to return to your father in Ulster,' Aidan told him. 'Brother Finnian is returning there in two weeks' time; why don't you go with him?'

Eochaid nodded. 'Yes, at least I'm a warrior now and he can't keep me shut away from danger; but I need to see Oswald first.'

'That's madness!'

'Not if I travel there in disguise. I only want to see him and then I'll return to Ulster.'

'How are you going to do that?'

'I've a little gold and silver now. I'll pay a fisherman to take me and go as his assistant.'

'Yes, that might work, if you're very careful. I know which of the fishermen on the island are trustworthy – not that I think that the others would betray you – but the man I have in mind is as honest as the day is long.'

Four days later Eochaid landed at dusk near Dùn Add and whilst the fisherman went on to the fishing settlement at the head of the sea loch to spend the night, Eochaid made his way up towards the hill fort and the sprawling mass of huts below it. He had no idea where Oswald might be living, but Osguid had explained where his mother's hut lay.

The inhabitants took refuge in the hill fort in the event of a raid, so there was no need for a palisade around the settlement itself. It was therefore relatively easy for Eochaid to slip into the place and find a path through the narrow passageways that ran between the huts. He made his way towards Acha's hut in the light of the moon, but before he got there, he bumped into a boy carrying some firewood. The boy uttered a Pictish curse as a few of the logs slipped out of his arms and Eoachaid knew that he must be a slave. He breathed a sigh of relief.

'Do you know Oswald?' he asked the boy, who was muttering under his breath as he tried to pick up the dropped wood whilst keeping the rest in his arms.

Eochaid stooped to pick up the wood for him and looked into the boy's eyes. They had a wary look, as if the boy was frightened.

'Who wants to know?'

'Don't be impudent.'

Eochaid was about to call him *slave* but then he noticed that the boy didn't have a wooden collar around his neck. Yet he had definitely sworn in the Brythonic tongue.

'Fair enough. I won't be impudent, but I won't tell you where Oswald is until you assure you that you mean him no harm.'

Eochaid sighed, not knowing whether he could trust this strange boy.
'I'm Eochaid –' he began.

'Why didn't you say? He's always talking about you. Come on, this way.'

'I've got a surprise for you,' Rònan told Oswald as he dropped the pile of wood next to the hearth.

'Eochaid? Is that really you? What are you doing here? You know that it's not safe!'

Rònan was pleased to hear Oswald so happy and he smiled to himself as he began to prepare the evening meal, but the smile disappeared when Eochaid asked Oswald to come with him to Ulster. He was really enjoying life at Dùn Add. Oswald was teaching him and Oswiu to fight and he had made friends with the younger boy. If Oswald left, would he take Rònan with him? If not, what would happen to him? Even if he went with him he would miss learning to fight with Oswiu and he knew that the younger boy would be devastated.

He was so engrossed with his own thoughts that he missed Oswald's reply. He knew he shouldn't interrupt, but he had to know.

'Will you take me with you, Oswald? What about Oswiu?'

'Do you allow your slave to talk to you like that, Oswald?' Eochaid asked, puzzled at the relationship between the two.

'I do more than allow it, I encourage it. Rònan may be my servant, but he is also my friend. I'm even teaching him and my brother Oswiu to fight with sword and shield.'

'To what end?'

'So that he can fight alongside me. He's too young at the moment, but he'll make a great warrior one day.'

Eochaid looked at Rònan with new eyes.

'I see. I've evidently misjudged you, Rònan. I apologise. Can we start again?'

He smiled at the boy, who nodded back, albeit somewhat sulkily. He had decided he didn't like Eochaid, mainly because he was trying to take Oswald away.

Oswald sensed the tension in the air and realised that the two were jealous of each other's relationship with him. Unusually, he didn't know what to do to resolve the situation. He wanted to go to Ulster, partly because of his friendship with Eochaid, but also because it offered the possibility of more fighting. On the other hand, he knew how disappointed Oswiu would be if he took Rònan away. There was no question in his mind that the boy would be going with him, if he went. That certainty was about to change.

He slept fitfully that night, dozing, then waking to ponder his options. He was just about to fall asleep again when he was conscious of movement in the hut. He swivelled his head slowly and saw Rònan creep outside. Thinking he was going to take a piss, he turned over to go to sleep again, but there was something about the furtiveness of the boy's movements that convinced Oswald that he hadn't gone outside just to relieve himself.

He got up quietly so as not to wake the gently snoring Eochaid and left the hut. He looked left and right and caught a glimpse of a vague shadow making its way towards the hill fort. He quietly followed Rònan until the boy stopped suddenly and stepped into the shadows. Some sixth sense must have told him that he was being followed. Oswald waited patiently and a few minutes later he glimpsed a movement in the shadows as Rònan continued to make his way towards the hill fort and the hall of Connad.

When Rònan got to the gates, he found that they were shut for the night, but he could see a sentry on the walkway beside them. He opened his mouth to shout up to him, but before he could do so, a hand clamped his mouth shut and an arm gripped the boy tightly.

'Not a sound, Rònan, or I will kill you.'

The boy recognised Oswald's voice and he slumped dejectedly in his arms. The latter led him away from the gate and then pushed him up against the wall of a hut.

'What were you about to do, Rònan? Were you about to betray me?'

'Not you, never! But I couldn't let Eochaid take you away from me.'

'What do you mean?'

'I know you want to go with him and you'll leave me here as the slave of someone else. They wouldn't treat me like you do and besides, I couldn't bear to be parted from you.'

Oswald had to smile to himself. The boy obviously had a bad case of hero-worship.

'I was going to take you with me, as it happens.'

'Oh! I thought you would want to leave me here.'

'Well, you were wrong, but now I can no longer trust you. To betray one of my friends is to betray me.'

The boy started to sob. 'I'm so sorry. I was jealous and I wasn't thinking straight. What will you do with me?'

'I don't know. Go back to the hut and try to get some sleep. I need time to think.'

Oswald wandered down to the shore and gazed down the loch. He had become very fond of Rònan but he was appalled by what he had tried to do. His faith in the young Pict had been badly shaken. Perhaps he'd been a fool to allow the boy to get close to him. His instinct was to get rid of him, but he knew how much Rònan would hate being someone else's slave. As a general rule slaves were treated very badly, being beaten for no reason and having little or no self-respect. It would break Rònan and he suspected he would prefer death.

The more he thought about it, the more he realised that the boy had acted out of affection for him. Perhaps part of the reason was also his developing friendship with Oswiu. He realised that his brother would be upset if Oswald left taking Rònan with him.

Apart from the fact that his relationship with Rònan had taken a bad knock, there was the antipathy between him and Eochaid to consider. The boy didn't know Eochaid like Oswald did and he had just seen him as a threat to be disposed of. When he thought of getting rid of his body slave, he realised that the prospect dismayed him, but he wasn't sure that he could truly forgive and forget either. That would take time and that was one thing he didn't have if he was going to leave.

He eventually came to the conclusion that he would go with Eochaid, but he needed to think further about Rònan. Having made his mind up to go with Eochaid, if not about his slave, he went back to the hut to try a get a little sleep before dawn. He heard Rònan snivelling in the corner, which surprised him. The boy he knew would be too proud to cry. It convinced him that Rònan truly repented what he had tried to do.

The next morning Oswald made his way up to the king's hall and stood in line with the other petitioners. Eventually it was his turn to speak.

'Lord King, I am pleased to say that I am fully recovered from my wound and now I seek further battle experience. I ask your permission to go and serve Fiachnae mac Báetáin in Ulster, to help him in his battle against the Uí Néill.'

Connad looked surprised.

'You must be a mind reader, Oswald. I have just received a plea from Fiachnae for me to send some warriors to help him recover the Island of Rathlin, which lies between the Mull of Kintyre and Ulster. Let me think about it and come and see me again tomorrow.'

'Yes, Cyning.'

He left the hall trying to hide his excitement. Of course he would take Eochaid with him; his father could hardly object to him fighting if he was a member of Oswald's war band. He was already planning on asking the five of his friends who had trained with him to come along. Then his euphoria faded. He still needed to decide what to do about Rònan.

# Chapter Five – Rathlin Island

## 621 AD

When Oswald returned to see Connad, he got a pleasant surprise.

'It seems that you are in luck, Oswald. I have had a string of young warriors wanting to join you in your venture to help regain Rathlin Island for King Fiachnae. One of them is the helmsman Alaric. I have therefore decided to loan you one of my birlinns, the Holy Saviour. Bring it back in one piece.'

'My lord, I don't know what to say. I am most grateful.'

'Don't thank me; it's my young warriors you should be thanking. And Alaric, certainly.'

'I definitely will.' He paused. 'But if Alaric is to be the helmsman, who will be the shipmaster?'

'Why, you, of course.'

Oswald left the hall stunned. At first he wandered around in a daze, wondering if he'd be up to the responsibility. He had never captained a birlinn before, or any craft, come to that and although he had Alaric – an Angle who had fled with him and his family from Bebbanburg – to help him, he wasn't sure he'd be up to the task. Then he remembered that Eochaid had brought the birlinn back from Tiree to Coll safely and that he would also be with him.

That reminded him that Eochaid was still in his hut. He would have to smuggle him on board somehow and he would also have to decide what to do about Rònan. He mulled the problem over and prayed to God for inspiration. Suddenly he had a thought and feeling much happier, he made his way back to the hut.

When he got there he found that a large group of young men and a few boys had gathered around the hut and were talking to Rònan, who stood in the doorway protectively. Oswald smiled when he realised that the boy was trying to stop anyone from entering and finding Eochaid inside. Perhaps his idea would actually work.

As soon as they saw Oswald approaching, the men crowded around him, all offering their oaths to follow him if he wanted them. They were bored at Dùn Add, where nothing ever seemed to happen and craved excitement and danger. The Holy Saviour had twenty oars a side, which meant that he needed forty rowers and she could comfortably hold another twenty warriors. With shipmaster, helmsman and a few ship's boys, she could take a crew of seventy all told. He did a rough calculation and thought that there were perhaps forty young men and a few older warriors who had no family. At first he discounted the few warriors in training, who were between thirteen and fifteen, but then decided he could take the older boys if he couldn't find any others.

By the end of the day he had signed up sixty men and youths and two of the thirteen year olds as ship's boys. With Eochaid, himself, his original five friends, all of who wanted to come along and Alaric, he had his seventy. Then he noticed Rònan standing with his head bowed, wondering about his fate.

Eochaid was due to go down to the beach to meet his fisherman after dark and Oswald asked him to take Rònan with him.

'Sail back to Iona and I'll collect you from there, Eochaid. If I decide I can forgive you, Rònan, I'll take you with me too; if I can't, then you'll stay and serve the Christian brothers. At least they will treat you a lot better than the men here.'

In truth he wanted to see if Eochaid would forgive the boy and whether Rònan could put his jealousy of Eochaid behind him. If both happened, then he would do his best to trust the boy again.

His next problem was unexpected. Oswiu crept into his hut that evening and said he had come to look after his brother now that Rònan had left. Oswald had no idea how Oswiu knew that his servant had gone, but when he asked him, Oswiu just said that he'd had a dream. It took several days to get the birlinn ready for sea and during that time Oswiu looked after him as Rònan had done. The two brothers got to know each other much better in those few days than they had over the past nine years. Oswald even put his brother through his paces with practice sword and shield and was impressed how quickly he had picked up the basic moves. He decided that he would buy Oswiu a seax as a present before he left.

The young boy was delighted with the gift and had to practice moves with it there and then.

'Oswiu, put it away now. You need to get on with preparing our meal.'

'Oh, I won't need to. Mother wants us to eat with her and the others on our last night here.'

The use of *our* rather than *your* puzzled Oswald, because Oswiu would be going back to Acha's hut to live with Offa and their sister once he'd sailed. He was going to ask him about it, but then Alaric arrived with a question about the ship and he forgot.

Oswald had enjoyed the boy's company, which had surprised him because most seventeen year olds don't have a lot in common with boys of nine. Of all his brothers, he realised that he now felt closest to Oswiu.

The next morning he nearly decided to wait another day. It was raining hard and the wind was blowing a gale. However, only the first part of the journey to Iona was difficult and Alaric assured him that he had sailed through the Gulf of Corryvreckan at slack water before and it wouldn't be the maelstrom it was when the tide was running.

The water still boiled and waves ran in all directions as they crossed between the islands of Jura and Scarba, but there was no whirlpool. After that, it was an exhilarating sail with little excitement until one of the warriors found a stowaway. The crew's personal gear had been put under the rowing benches or under the platforms at stern and prow. Oswiu had been hiding under a load of cloaks under the stern platform. Oswald took one look at the crestfallen boy and his heart lifted. He would never have taken Oswiu with him; he was far too young and Acha would never have forgiven him. Nevertheless, now that he was here, he was pleased to see his brother.

'Shall I throw him to the fishes, Oswald?' Alaric suggested.

'Good idea.'

Oswiu grinned, thinking that his brother was in jest, but then he screamed in panic when the man who had found him lifted him over the side so that he dangled above the waves, which seemed to lick hungrily at his feet as they crashed against the side of the birlinn.

'Or we could just leave him on Iona. He's nearly old enough to become a novice anyway.'

'You can't. I'll just run away.' Oswiu had recovered his composure once he had been hoisted back onboard and set on his feet again.

'How? It's a small island.'

His brother looked so dejected that Oswald was tempted to relent, especially as he admired his pluck in hiding away on board. Besides, he was secretly glad he had done so.

'Have you thought how worried Mother will be when she discovers that you're missing?'

'I told Offa to tell her once we'd sailed; besides, she knows you'll look after me.'

Oswald sighed. 'I know I'm going to regret this, but you can join the ship's boys.'

Oswiu's face broke into a broad grin.

'Thank you, Oswald. You won't regret this.'

'On the contrary, I'm sure I will. Now, your first task is to climb the mast and let me know when you see land.'

It was something one of the other boys would have had to do soon, but the Ross of Mull and Iona were still some miles away over the horizon and wouldn't appear for some time yet, even on a clear day – and this day was anything but clear. However, an hour or two sitting in the rain on the spar that carried the mainsail, clinging to the mast as it waved wildly to and fro with the ship's pitching and rolling, would soon dampen Oswiu's enthusiasm for a life afloat.

The motion made Oswiu vomit several times, but he maintained his vigil without complaint and, after spotting land and describing it to Alaric, he descended to the deck with an excited grin on his face.

'Well done, brother. You'll do,' Oswald told him and the boy positively basked in his praise.

Two hours later they gently beached the Holy Saviour below the monastery. The rain had stopped and the wind had eased, but that did little to lift Oswald's spirits. Now he would find out if Eochaid and Rònan had managed to overcome their differences. Fighting an enemy was far preferable to trying to keep one's friends happy, he decided.

~~~

In the event it wasn't a problem. Once they'd cleared the air, Eochaid and Rònan had got on well together. Rònan resumed his duties as Oswald's body servant and Oswiu was content to be the junior of the three ship's boys, looking after the crew and doing the simple tasks on board. Just so long as he was with Oswald, he was happy.

The two were able to spend time with their other brothers whilst they were there and Oswald came to the conclusion that, like Osguid, the other two were likely to become monks or priests rather than warriors.

He also visited the infirmary to see Brendan and Aidan and thank them for the care they'd taken of him.

'You seem to have made a full recovery,' Aidan smiled.

'Yes, it took a long time before I lost the stiffness in my side, but now you'd not know I'd been wounded – apart from the six inch scar, that is.'

Just as he was about to take his leave, Oswald turned back to Aidan and asked something he'd been longing to know the answer to.

'From what you told me about your time with Brother Finnian, I'd half expected to find that you'd gone with him when he left.'

'I think I want to be a missionary in due course, but I like it here and I'm fulfilling a useful purpose in helping Brother Brendan to heal people.' Aidan paused and then asked something he'd refrained from mentioning before.

'You said when you were recovering that your greatest desire was to regain the throne of your father, but now you're getting embroiled in a war on the other side of the country. Have you reconciled yourself to staying in Dal Riada?'

Oswald didn't reply immediately.

'The short answer is no. I will take back Northumbria one day, but it is a job for a mature warrior, not a youth. I need experience in warfare and to build up a reputation before I can hope to succeed. One day I will do it, though and then my mission will be to convert the kingdom to Christianity; but that might be an even bigger battle than getting the crown. I will need help with both.'

~~~

The five brothers had joined the monks and the crew in the small church for a service of prayer before departure the next morning and the abbot blessed the Holy Saviour before she was pushed off the beach to resume her journey to Lough Larne, on the north-east coast of Ireland. They had to row against a headwind for most of the day and consequently made slow progress. By late afternoon they had only reached the south-western tip of the Isle of Islay, so Oswald decided to turn and run before the wind up into Loch Indaal, which pointed like a finger into the heart of the island.

At the end of the loch there was a bay with a sandy beach where Fergus, King of Islay and the Isles – a vassal of Connad's – had his base. They were treated most hospitably and that night they feasted in the king's hall. Predictably, departure the next morning was rather later than Oswald would have liked and he was less than pleased to find out that some of his crew had managed to get Oswiu well and truly drunk; so much so that he was still distinctly merry the next morning. His merriment soon disappeared, however, once the birlinn hit the large waves rolling in from the west and after he had spewed over the leeward side several times, he vowed never to drink ale again.

Leaving Islay behind, they ran before the westerly wind to the southeast, passing Rathlin Island on the horizon to the west of them and turned south until they saw the coast of Ireland fine on the steer board bow. The wind dropped as they entered the lee of the mainland and they had to row the last few miles to King Fiachnae's main town of Larne and the entrance to the sheltered sea lough beyond. The shore was rocky, but a wooden jetty had been built out into the lough and a wharf ran the length of the shore in front of the settlement. Six birlinns of varying sizes and a couple of trading ships were tied up alongside. The traders were similar to the warships, but broader in the beam to carry cargo and they had fewer oars, as they mainly relied on the wind for propulsion. Their crews were also much fewer in number.

Alaric brought them alongside the last space on the jetty and Oswald went off with Eochaid to see King Fiachnae. He took two warriors along as an escort, as well as Rònan in case he needed to send a message back to Alaric. Somehow Oswiu tacked himself onto the rear of the party too.

Fiachnae hadn't seen his son for several years and their reunion was emotional, with much back slapping and comments about how much he had grown. Oswald stood by, patiently waiting to be greeted, whilst Rònan and Oswiu gazed wide-eyed about the king's hall. What had most caught their attention were several rotting heads hanging by their hair from the rafters.

'Dead Uí Néill,' one of the warriors escorting Oswald explained and the two boys shuddered delightedly. It was the first of their enemies that they had seen, but it wasn't to be the last, by a long way.

At last Fiachnae turned to Oswald and welcomed him, thankfully without all the hugs and backslapping. The version of Gaelic spoken in Ireland was a little different than that of Dal Riada, but it was similar enough for Oswald to follow most of what was being said. When Oswald looked a bit blank, Eochaid, who spoke both dialects and also English, the common language of the Angles, Jutes and Saxons, translated.

During the conversation, Oswald was reminded that Eochaid was not Fiachnae's first born son. There had been two elder brothers, both of who had been killed in battle when Eochaid was still a child. No doubt this explained his father's protective attitude when they had first met. However, one of them had a son called Congal. He was twelve, but if he grew to adulthood before the elderly Fiachnae died, he would have a better claim to the throne of the Ulaidh than Eochaid.

Oswald first met Congal at the feast given in honour of Eochaid's return and the arrival of the contingent from Dal Riada. Eochaid was seated on the left of the king and Oswald in the place of honour on his right. Congal sat on Oswald's other side. The rest of the men on the high table were the various chieftains of the Ulaidh who had brought ships and men for the re-conquest of Rathlin Island. No women were present and Oswald realised with a start that he had seen none in the king's hall. All the slaves serving the revellers were men and boys.

This time he had ordered Oswiu to remain with those guarding the Holy Saviour and told Rònan to make sure that he didn't sneak off to the hall. He was fairly confident that his brother had learned his lesson, but the boy had a nose for mischief and Oswald didn't want him making a fool of himself in front of the Ulaidh. They had already made fun of the youth of most of his crew and he had had difficulty in keeping his temper in check. He didn't want to give them a chance to ridicule his brother.

After he had made polite conversation with Fiachnae for a while, Oswald turned to Congal, who was sitting morosely eating his food. The chieftain on the boy's other side was exchanging bawdy stories with the man to his right.

'Tell me about your father, Congal,' he said with a smile.

Eochaid had said nothing to him about his two brothers in all the time he'd known him and he was curious as to the reason.

'What's to tell? He died when I was too young to remember him.'

Oswald ignored the boy's sullen rudeness and tried again.

'You must have heard about him from others, though – your mother, perhaps?'

'She burst into tears the one time I asked about him; she's dead now in any case.'

'So you've been brought up by your grandfather?'

'Hardly! He ignores me. It's my right to succeed him as the son of his second son, but he hates me and wants Eochaid to follow him. It's not fair.'

The boy returned to picking peevishly at his food.

'So who looks after you?'

'I look after myself! Oh, I have slaves, but there's no-one who cares about me.'

Oswald was forced to the conclusion that the boy was self-centred and resentful. He could understand why, but he began to worry for Eochaid. His friend was brave and a good fighter when he had to be, but he was also kind-hearted and generous. Congal was mean-spirited and

70

Oswald was fairly certain that he wouldn't hesitate to kill his uncle if he stood in the way of his ambition to rule the Ulaidh. He would have to warn Eochaid.

Later, when he told his friend of his conversation with his nephew, Eochaid merely smiled.

'Congal's welcome to try and rule the Ulaidh. When they aren't fighting the other clans, they're fighting amongst themselves. It's the curse of the Irish; we love a good fight. Besides, I have no desire to be king.'

'But your father has nominated you as his heir.'

'Then let's hope that he lives long enough for Congal to grow up.'

~~~

Acha had been furious when Offa told her that Oswiu had stowed away on the Holy Saviour. She had watched Oswald and his brother grow close over the short time that they had shared the former's hut and had been pleased. Now she saw that it had been a mistake. The younger boy obviously idolised his eldest brother and that had led him to seek the perilous life of a seafarer and warrior years before he was old enough. It was bad enough that Oswald put his own life in danger every time he put to sea without dragging his brother along.

She tried to comfort herself with the thought that Oswald would leave the boy on Iona and let her know that he was safe, but she heard nothing and imagined the worst. Offa was too busy playing with the other boys at Dùn Add to notice how distracted his mother had grown, but her daughter immediately knew something was wrong. Acha was touched by the way the little girl tried to comfort her and, if only for a moment, she wished that she had given birth to fewer sons and more daughters. At least Æbbe wouldn't cause her the anxiety that Oswald and Oswiu were doing.

Acha had been relieved at first when Osguid had decided to remain on Iona as a monk, but later she realised that this meant she was unlikely to see him again unless he came to Dùn Add. Some Celtic monastaries allowed women to visit – some even housed both monks and nuns – but not Iona. When both Oslac and Oslaph sent messages to say that they would also be remaining there as monks she felt hollow inside.

The nobles and warriors who had accompanied Acha into exile had either been given land elsewhere in Dal Riada, or had entered Connad's service. One or two sometimes came to visit her, but this grew less as time went on. They had married and had families of their own now, even if they had left wives and children behind in Northumbria. The chance of being re-united with them was remote and in any case many of their first wives had found other husbands.

Acha hadn't made any real friends at Dùn Add. Connad had ignored her after giving her a hut, slaves and a small grant so that she could buy food, clothes and other essentials. The other women were conscious that she had been a queen and, although they respected her, they made no attempt to get to know her. Whilst she had her children around her, that hadn't mattered so much; now that most of them had left, she was beginning to feel her isolation.

She found consolation in prayer and Æbbe often accompanied her when she went to up to the little stone-built church near the king's hall. At first Acha prayed for the safety of her two sons in Ireland. She knew now that Oswald had taken Oswiu with him when he left Iona and she found it hard to forgive him for putting the little boy in danger.

Oswald had wanted to write to his mother whilst he was on Iona, but he couldn't find the words to explain why he'd decided to let his brother remain on board. He knew that Acha would be worried and that she would blame him; he just didn't realise how angry she would become as her resentment festered.

~~~

The morning after the feast in King Fiachnae's hall, the fleet put to sea in a fine drizzle that managed to penetrate everywhere. Rònan had greased Oswald's chain mail, helmet and weapons in an effort to keep the rust at bay, but he wasn't sanguine about its effectiveness.

Fiachnae had wanted Eochaid to lead the expedition, thinking that this would bind his chieftains to his son's side. For his part, his son was certain that his father was mistaken and in any case, he was sworn to follow Oswald as a member of his crew. His father had accepted this with bad grace and had eventually decided to command the fleet himself.

The local bishop had come down to bless the fleet and the four hundred men it would be taking into battle. Oswald was now a devout Christian, but standing in the drizzle for over an hour whilst the bishop droned on sorely tested his faith. Then, as if on cue, the rain stopped and a few patches of blue sky appeared through the clouds. Unfortunately the wind also dropped and they would have a long, hard pull up the coast to the island.

'If only that damned cleric had shut up half an hour earlier we'd have been halfway there whilst there was still some wind,' Alaric commented to Oswald, who made a non-committal grunt in reply.

There was nothing for Oswald to do at the moment. They were following the king's birlinn and it would be hours yet before they had to arm themselves. So he went and turfed the youngest rower, a brawny lad of fifteen, out of his seat and enjoyed the exercise that rowing gave him. The other rowers grinned to themselves. There were few shipmasters who would endure the hardship of rowing when they didn't have to. Oswald was already popular and this made him even more so, but that wasn't why he'd done it.

Oswiu, who was helping the other boys prepare portions of smoked meat and cheese to hand out at midday, glowed with pride at the high regard in which Oswald was held. Rònan looked up from putting a better edge on his master's sword and thought he was mad. Rowing was hard work and Oswald wasn't used to it. Rònan thought he would give up after a while, but he didn't. The boy became concerned. If Oswald became tired he wouldn't be any good when it came to fighting. Eventually he became exasperated and went over and whispered in his ear.

Oswald hadn't thought about it and saw the sense in what Rònan was saying. Not for the first time, he was impressed by the boy's instinctive common sense. He got up and the young rower took his place again. Shortly after that, Oswald ordered those who had been doing nothing to take the place of the rowers on the left hand side. He would rest them for an hour and then he'd change them with those on the right.

When Rathlin Island came in sight Oswald was puzzled. It appeared to be L shaped and little bigger than Iona. He doubted whether it could support more than forty or fifty inhabitants, so why had the King of the Ulaidh assembled an army over four hundred strong to take it back?

They sailed into the large bay to the south-east of the island and Oswald could see that most of the shoreline was peppered with rocky outcrops. Alaric had already told him there was no suitable landing place for birlinns on the northern or eastern sides; the only place to beach them appeared to be a small stretch of sand where the peninsula in the north met that in the east. One small birlinn was already there, along with a few fishing currachs.

'What's Fiachnae playing at?' he asked the helmsman. 'He doesn't need a fleet of seven birlinns to capture this place. There isn't even room for us all to land.'

73

Spotting Eochaid sitting sharpening his sword with his back to the mast, he called him over.

'What's your father up to? He doesn't need all these warriors to retake this place.'

'I know as much as you do. The only guess I can make is that he intends to punish the Uí Néill for their temerity to invade. As you know, there has been an uneasy truce between us for a little while now, but that seems to be coming to an end. Part of the problem is that the Uí Néill don't have just one leader. Up here in Ulster they are divided into two main clans, but there are other smaller septs – that is, large families – as well. The dominant clan had been Clan Connel, but their chieftain died recently and now Clan nEógain, led by Suibne mac Fiachnai, has come to prominence. It was the nEógain who ousted our people from Rathlin. I suspect that my father plans to go on to attack their main settlement as a punishment. If he can do them enough damage, then the new chieftain of Clan Connel might be able to assert himself as head of the Northern Uí Néill.'

'And I thought politics in Northumbria were complex! Where is this main settlement of the nEógain?'

'I believe it's a place called Cullmore, at the head of a large sea inlet called Lough Foyle, or at least it used to be.'

Their conversation was interrupted by a hail from Fiachnae.

'Eochaid, I want you and Oswald to have the honour of massacring the invaders. We'll stand by in the bay ready to help you, if needed.'

'Have I told you recently that I think your father is a cunning bastard?' Oswald grinned at Eochaid, who looked furiously across the sea at his father. 'Come on, let's do this. Everyone don your armour and have your weapons ready. Rowers, take her in slowly. Oswiu, climb up the mast again and tell me what you can see inshore.'

He had every intention of leaving his brother up there out of harm's way, or so he thought.

'I can see men massing back from the beach, Oswald,' Oswiu called down in his high treble voice.

'Can you estimate numbers? How well are they armed?'

'There might be thirty or more but some of them are no more than young boys. Only a few are wearing chain mail and a helmet; a few have leather jerkins; the rest are unprotected. They have a variety of spears, hand axes, a few hunting bows and very few swords. Those that have shields only have those small targes.'

74

'Thank you Oswiu.  Stay there and call down if you see any more appearing from anywhere.'

'I can see some women and children now.  They have come out of the huts behind the men and are running off to the south.'

'Father,' Eochaid shouted across the bay.  'The women and children are heading for the south of the island.  Is there a beach on the other side where they could have a boat or two?'

'Yes, there are two small sandy coves.  I'll send one of our birlinns to cut off their escape.'

A few moments later Oswiu saw the rearmost vessel hoist its sail and head off to round the southern tip of the island.  Even if the women and children had made it to the coves, there could only be a few small boats there, which the birlinn would have no trouble in catching.

Oswiu turned his attention back to the beach, which was now no more than a few yards away.  He was ready for the impact as the keel ran into the sand and stuck there, but nevertheless, he wasn't expecting the way the mast leant forward as the ship's forward momentum suddenly ceased,  and then whipped back well beyond the vertical before coming upright again.  He managed to cling on as it bent forward, but when it whipped back he lost his grip and went flying backwards like a stone from a catapult.

He was momentarily aware of flying through the air before he plummeted into the sea just behind the stern post.  Luckily the beach shelved quite steeply, so there was enough depth of water to cushion his fall, though it still winded him badly and stung his back and legs.  Unfortunately, however, he had never learned to swim.  He started to move his legs and arms wildly and his head broke the surface briefly before he disappeared again.  When he came back up, something hit him on the head.

As he sank once more he saw that it was the end of a rope and he struggled frantically to reach it.  His lungs felt as if they were going to burst and everything was turning black when his left hand touched the rope and he grabbed it.  He reached it with his other hand just as someone started to pull the rope inboard and his head broke the surface once more.  He coughed up a mouthful of seawater and then started to draw in great lungfuls of air.  Finally he reached the side of the ship and saw Rònan grinning down with the other two ship's boys on either side of him.

'Come on, Oswiu, stop mucking about.  You're missing all the fun.'

They pulled him along beside the hull of the ship until the water was shallow enough for him to stand, then left him to wade ashore whilst they rushed to the prow to watch the battle, such as it was.

Oswald had been the first man to leap onto the beach. He had vaguely heard a startled cry as the ship grounded on the sand, but by then he was already in motion. He stumbled briefly when he landed, recovered and then ran forward. The solid ground felt strange after the moving deck and it took him several paces before he was running normally. By then he was only thirty yards from the enemy line. It wasn't a shield wall as such, more a disorganised line of men shouting abuse and waving their weapons. Oswald almost felt sorry for them. One or two arrows thudded into his shield before he reached their line, but they did him no damage.

He punched the first man he reached in the face with the boss of his shield and thrust his sword into the throat of another. The man behind them was wielding a heavy woodsman's axe. He raised it over his head, intending to bring it crashing down on Oswald's helmet, but Oswald was too quick for him and stabbed him in the belly before his axe could make contact. It fell from the man's hands and clattered on Oswald's shield as it dropped to the sand. The man screamed in agony and fell to his knees, clutching his stomach.

Then Eochaid was on his right and Alaric on his left and together they smashed their way through the enemy before starting to roll up the left hand side of their line. More and more of Oswald's warriors arrived and it wasn't long before the surviving men of the nEógain threw down their weapons and surrendered.

The Ulaidh women and children had been enslaved and roped together in one of the huts. Oswald released them from their wooden collars and asked about the men. Apparently the nEógain invaders had taken them out into the bay and thrown them over the side, telling them to swim back to the mainland. Of course, very few could do so and they used those who could as target practice for their archers.

Oswald was enraged by this tale and was about to order the execution of all those who had been wounded or who had surrendered, but two things stopped him. Several of those who had fought against him were no more than boys and Eochaid pointed out that his father wouldn't thank him for usurping his prerogative to decide their fate. He nearly replied that, if Fiachnae had wanted to dispense justice, he shouldn't have used Oswald's men to do his dirty work, but he held his tongue. There was no point in having an argument with Eochaid.

It was only then that he noticed a bedraggled Oswiu sitting in the sand beside the prow of the birlinn and he ran over to him. The boy was sobbing and Oswald picked him up and held him in his arms.

'What happened?'

Before he could reply, Rònan jumped down from the prow and told him.

'You should have seen him. He flew through the air like a bird, but one with no wings. He made a hell of a splash when he hit the water, too.'

Oswald was annoyed at Rònan's seemingly callous attitude and was about to go up and berate the grinning boy when Oswiu gripped his sleeve.

'Don't be cross with him. He saved my life. He was quick witted enough to throw me a rope and pull me to safety. If anyone was to blame, it was you for sending me up that damn mast!'

Oswald looked contrite, then grinned.

'I'd have liked to see you flying through the air though!'

Oswiu looked at him in astonishment, then he too grinned.

'If I hadn't nearly drowned, I'd have liked to try it again. It was a fantastic sensation.'

~~~

The following day the small fleet sailed down Lough Foyle, keeping to the eastern shore so that they would be hidden from Cullmore for as long as possible. Fiachnae had put some of his warriors in the small birlinn he had captured at Rathlin Island, so there were now eight ships in the fleet. Unfortunately, they met two Uí Néill birlinns coming the other way. Those were quickly overcome and the surviving members of their crews thrown overboard, thus increasing the Ulaidh fleet to ten, but Cullmore had now been warned.

Fiachnae beached his ships two miles short of the place and, leaving fifty men and the ships' boys to guard the fleet, he led three hundred and fifty men along the coast towards the settlement. Oswald was surprised to see that less than twenty per cent of the Ulaidh warriors wore armour or carried sword and shield. Most looked like the rabble they had faced at Rathlin Island. All his men wore a chain mail byrnie or a leather jerkin and all had a helmet of some sort. Furthermore, all had a sword and shield. Most supplemented this with a throwing axe, seax or spear and about a third carried a bow and a quiver of arrows.

Oswald could see why his men had been chosen to carry out the assault of Rathlin Island. His men had suffered no more than a few minor flesh wounds. Had the Irish carried out the attack, they would undoubtedly have suffered many more casualties.

Fiachnae sent out scouts when he thought that they must be no more than half a mile from the settlement. They soon came back to report that the defences consisted of a ditch some six feet deep and a palisade on top of an earth ramp perhaps seven or eight feet tall.

This time Oswald and his men were tasked to fight their way through the place and capture the chieftain's hall, which would undoubtedly be in the centre. In essence, they would lead the assault once the gates were open, whilst the Irish followed on, no doubt raping and pillaging as they went.

Fiachnae's way of opening the gate was simple. He sent a hundred men forward who climbed the far side of the earthen rampart, whilst his archers kept the enemies' heads down. Then a hundred more men rushed down the bank into the ditch and climbed the other side. The first hundred, less the few who had been killed by now, put their backs against the palisade and cupped their hands. The second wave, almost as one, put their feet into their comrades' cupped hands and were lifted up so that they could grasp the top of the palisade. They heaved themselves over it and dropped down on the walkway, where they attacked the defenders, driving them back. Once inside, their task was to secure the gates and throw them open so that the rest could storm into the settlement.

The Ulaidh lost quite a few men to arrows fired at them as they approached and to rocks dropped on them whilst they were trying to scale the wall, but they succeeded. Seventy or eighty were left after they had captured the walkway near the gates and once inside the settlement, they made for the gates, ignoring the distractions of booty and screaming women – at least most of them did.

Ten minutes later the gates were thrown open and Oswald, Eochaid and Alaric led the crew of the Holy Saviour into the settlement. There was little resistance. As soon as the men of the settlement saw them coming they ran to hide and those that didn't were quickly dealt with. Oswald saw two of his younger men dart down a narrow alley after a girl of about twelve. He sent Eochaid and another man after them and, as he suspected, it was a trap.

Three men came out of the shadows armed with daggers and a spear as soon as the two youths had passed where they were hiding and three more appeared in front of them. They were trapped but they prepared to take as many of the Uí Néill with them as they could. They stood back to back with their shields in front of them and waited for the six men to attack. It never came. Eochaid ran one of the half-naked warriors through before the Uí Néill men knew he was behind them, whilst his companion killed the one with the spear. The third man was trapped between Eochaid and the two youths, who, up to a couple of seconds ago, had been their quarry. He dropped his axe and pleaded for mercy, but one of the youths stabbed him in the neck and he fell to the ground.

Seeing that their trap had failed, the other three ran off and Eochaid led the way back to re-join the rest of the crew.

'Oswald will deal with you two later,' he told them as they ran.

'What will he do?'

'Probably cut your pricks off to stop you being so stupid again,' he replied with a grin.

There was a brief fight outside the chieftain's hall, but it was quickly over. The sacking of the settlement continued for the rest of the day and on into the night, but at nightfall Oswald and his men went back to the Holy Saviour. They had amassed a good deal of plunder, much of it from the chieftain's hall as they were the first ones there and had captured a number of women and children as slaves.

One of the women, a girl of perhaps fifteen, had caught Oswald's eye. She was a real beauty and unlike most of the Irish, she had long blonde hair like many of the Angles and Saxons. He took her from the rest of the slaves and told Rònan and Oswiu to guard her. Then he and Eochaid went to find Fiachnae.

Oswald presented the king with a small chest full of coins as his due as the leader of the raid and in return Fiachnae told Oswald that he could have the small birlinn that he had captured at Rathlin Island. This suited him well, as the Holy Saviour on its own would have been too crowded on the return journey with the slaves that they had taken. Oswald made Eochaid shipmaster, which pleased both father and son and Eochaid asked Fiachnae if he had a man who would make a good helmsman.

Eochaid christened his new ship the Gift of God and the next morning the two birlinns set off to return to Dùn Add. If Oswald had been aware of the reception he and Oswiu would receive when they got there, he might have stayed in Ulster.

# Chapter Six – Loch Fyne

## 621 AD

Oswald had never seen his mother so angry. Instead of greeting her two returning sons, she rushed at them and started to hit and scratch them, screaming all the while. Oswald had difficulty in restraining her, but eventually she stopped struggling and broke down in tears. Oswiu was a quivering wreck, cowering on the ground by this time and even Oswald was badly shaken. Offa and his sister sat in a corner of the hut, hugging each other and crying.

'What on earth possessed you to take Oswiu with you? He could have been killed! I was beside myself with worry. The least you could have done was left him at Iona and written to me to let me know he was safe.'

'Yes, you're right. But he refused to stay there and you knew he was with me. Surely you trusted me to keep him safe?'

As he said the words he had an uncomfortable moment when he remembered that his brother had nearly drowned at Rathlin Island.

'Refused? He's a boy of nine, for heaven's sake! You should have made him stay.'

'Yes, you're probably right, but we are back now safe and sound and he has gained a wealth of experience that will stand him in good stead when he becomes a warrior.'

'Becomes a warrior? Isn't it enough that you are always risking your life, Oswald? He's going to join his brothers on Iona and become a monk after he's completed his novitiate. I may not see him again after he leaves here, but at least I'll know he's safe.'

At this Oswiu pulled himself together and stood up.

'No.'

'What did you say?'

'I said no. I'm not going to Iona and I'm not going to be a monk. I'm staying with Oswald.'

'I'm your mother and you'll do as I say.' she yelled at him.

Oswiu didn't say another word but turned on his heel and started to walk towards the hut that Oswald and Rònan had built.

Acha stared after him, her mouth set in a determined line and Oswald knew that this was beginning to become a battle of wills. His heart sank; the last thing he wanted was for his family to be torn apart.

'Leave him be for now, mother. I'll talk to him when he's calmed down, but he'll never become a monk and you need to accept that. I must go and see Connad to give him his share of the plunder and thank him for the loan of his birlinn. You need to look after Offa and Æbbe; you've scared them half to death.'

As he left, he dabbed at the scratches that Acha had inflicted on his face and arms. He knew that he was in the wrong for not writing to her from Iona, but that didn't excuse the way she had treated him and Oswiu. He feared that a rift had developed which would be difficult to heal.

Connad was delighted with the gold and silver that Oswald lay at his feet and congratulated him on his success.

'Not only have you brought me back plunder, but you have bound Fiachnae closer to me. I'm well pleased.'

He paused before continuing, looking past Oswald at Eochaid.

'I'm surprised – pleased, but nevertheless surprised – to see you've brought Fiachnae's son back with you again. I would have thought that Eochaid's father would have wanted his heir to remain by his side.'

'But I'm not his heir, Cyning. My elder brother had a son and my nephew will succeed my father.'

'I see, but isn't this nephew still a child?'

'He's twelve, Cyning and hopefully my father will live for many years yet.'

'Yes, of course. Let's pray so. It will need to be a long time, though. I'm not sure that the Ulaidh would want an inexperienced youth to rule them, with the Uí Néill waiting like hungry wolves to gobble up more of their land.'

He transferred his gaze back to Oswald.

'What are your plans, now that you're back?'

'I hadn't really thought that far ahead, Lord.'

'I have need of someone skilful as a warrior and as lucky as you. Neithon, King of Strathclyde, has recently died and his son, Belin, is flexing his muscles. As you know, his lands adjoin those of Lorne, which is part of Dal Riada. He recently tried to launch a raid on Lorne through the Pass of Brander. It is narrow, steep sided and easily defended, so he got a bloody nose, but he is likely to try again. My advisers think that his likely route is

81

through the mountains that lie between Loch Awe in the north and Loch Fyne in the south. It's wild country and few people live there. If you are willing, I would like you to take a few birlinns up Loch Fyne and also scout the land to the north to see if Belin is up to anything.'

'You honour me, Cyning, by the trust you have in me. Which birlinns would I take?'

'Just make sure my faith is well placed. I'll give you the Holy Saviour and you can take Eochaid's Gift of God, assuming he is willing to go with you.'

When Eochaid nodded, he turned back to Oswald.

'I'm also sending Beornwulf with you.'

He was one of the Angle nobles who had fled with him and his family from Bebbanburg and who had been serving the King of Lorne as a shipmaster for the last five years.

'His ship is called the Seraphim and has a crew of sixty,' he continued. 'They are all hardened warriors, but they understand that you are their leader. I don't want to start a war with Belin, at least not yet, so be careful. If you are forced to fight, don't leave any witnesses.'

'I understand.'

When he left, he found Beornwulf waiting for him by his hut.

'You've turned into a man, Oswald,' he grunted by way of a greeting.

'It's good to see you again too, Beornwulf. Did you think I'd stay twelve forever?'

'I'm sorry to hear of the rift between you and the queen.'

It was so long since he'd heard his mother referred to by her former title that at first Oswald didn't realise that he meant Acha. He sighed.

'Yes, it's a bad business and not something I sought. She would like to keep Oswiu a baby, I think, but he's got more spirit than many a fully grown warrior.'

'Would you me like to speak to her on your behalf?'

Beornwulf had been a member of his father's council, so his mother had known him well in the past. He couldn't see that it could do any harm. He would dearly like to be reconciled to his mother, before they left, if possible, although, as Oswiu would be coming with him, he didn't give much for Beornwulf's chance of success.

In the end Beornwulf came to see Oswald as night was falling and said that his mother would like to see him. He went over to his mother's hut, worried that another meeting might make things even worse if she hadn't changed her mind. However, her opening topic of conversation caught him by surprise.

'Oswald, come in. I hope that you'll join me in eating this delicious venison stew that my slave women have prepared.'

Acha had two slaves, an old woman and her granddaughter. Both were Cymri from a mountainous land well to the south and as ugly as sin.

'I understand that you now have a slave yourself and I don't mean Rònan.'

'You are well informed, mother.'

He risked a weak smile and was gratified when she returned it. It would seem that she too sought reconciliation.

Oswald had kept the blonde girl he'd captured at Cullmore. He'd found out that she was called Gytha and was the daughter of a Mercian thegn who had been captured by pirates and sold to the Uí Néill. She was being kept as a gift for Suibne mac Fiachnai, the chieftain of Clan nEógain and so was still a virgin, a rare condition amongst pretty young slaves. As the daughter of a minor noble he might have freed her, but she was a pagan, so he decided to wait and see if she would convert to Christianity first.

He was sexually attracted to her, but for now he kept his desires in check. It was beneath his dignity to force a slave to sleep with him.

At first Rònan had been affronted when Oswald had announced that Gytha would take over his duties in looking after their hut, cooking and washing their clothes. However, he'd been mollified when he was told that he'd still be responsible for looking after Oswald's armour, weapons and two horses that he'd recently bought so that they could range further afield when they went hunting.

'It'll also give you more time to train with me and Oswiu,' he added.

That had brought a broad smile to the boy's face. He was now thirteen and although Oswald hadn't said anything, he intended to free him and officially induct him as a trainee warrior when they returned. There was only one proviso. The boy would have to be baptised as a Christian. None of Oswald's war band was a pagan.

Gytha seemed happy to be Oswald's slave and as Rònan and Oswiu both told him, she kept looking at him whenever she thought herself unobserved. She had certainly improved the tidiness and cleanliness of the hut and insisted on cooking outside whenever it wasn't raining, to try and minimise the acrid smell of smoke from the central hearth.

Oswald supposed that it was too much to hope that his mother hadn't become aware of the change to his domestic arrangements.

'Have you bedded her yet?'

He was slightly taken aback by his mother's bluntness.

83

'No, she's a virgin and the daughter of a Mercian thegn. She deserves better than to be treated like a whore.'

'You wouldn't be in love with her, would you?'

'Possibly,' he grinned. 'Would you be horrified if I was?'

'No, I had hoped that you would marry a princess as your father's heir, but as an exile, that's too much to hope for. And I would like grandchildren.'

'Hold on! I don't know whether I want to marry the girl yet and she would have to be willing to convert to Christianity first.'

'That's important to you?'

'Yes, I want my children to be brought up by two Christian parents and taught about God and his Son. I don't want a tug of war between the one true God and the Anglo-Saxon deities.'

'I think you are very wise.'

By this time they had finished the venison stew and Acha decided that it was time she raised the question of Oswiu.

'Oswiu is very like you. I can see that now, but both of you have caused me a great deal of distress and I cannot allow Oswiu to speak to me in the way that he did.'

'I have apologised and I sincerely repent not writing to you from Iona. It was wrong of me. I hope that in time you can forgive me. However, I don't regret taking Oswiu with me and to pretend to you that I did would dishonour both of us.'

Acha sighed. 'I understand that. Do you propose to take him with you when you go on this Loch Fyne expedition?'

'Yes. He would never forgive me if I left him behind.'

Acha seemed agitated. 'I wish you wouldn't, but if you do, make sure he is well protected. And you need to be on your guard, too.'

'Why, what do you know?'

'Know? Nothing. Suspect? Quite a lot. Connad pretends to favour you, but secretly he seeks your death. You are too popular amongst his young warriors and he thinks you seek his throne.'

'That's nonsense! There's only one throne I want and it's that of Northumbria.'

'I know that, but it is the sign of a weak king to be paranoid about those who would make a better ruler than he is.'

'But how am I in danger in Loch Fyne?'

His mother looked uncomfortable.

'Your father never entirely trusted Beornwulf. However, he was never a friend of Edwin's and so he had no option but to flee with us. Do you not

84

think it strange that Connad has asked the King of Lorne to loan him Beornwulf? He thinks you will trust him because he's a Northumbrian. Don't.'

'He has sixty men, but Eochaid and I have nearly twice as many as that. What can he do?'

'I wish I knew. Lead you into an ambush by Belin and the men of Strathclyde perhaps?'

'Thank you for the warning, mother. I'll be on my guard.'

'Now you know why I don't want Oswiu to go with you. You have no choice, having accepted the expedition, but you don't have to take him with you.'

Oswald glared at her.

'So that's what this is all about,' he accused her. 'It's all a ploy to stop Oswiu going with me!'

He got up in anger and made to storm out of the hut, when she put a gentle, restraining hand on his arm.

'Do you think so little of me that I would try and trick you?'

'No. No, of course not. I'm sorry. I know you mean well. I'll watch out for Beornwulf and I'll make sure that Oswiu is kept safe. However, it is me that Connad wants to get rid of, not my little brother.'

'No, but it would enrage you and make you reckless if anything happened to your favourite brother.'

Oswald nodded in understanding.

'Is he my favourite? Yes, I suppose I am much closer to him than any of my other brothers, though I love them all.'

'When do you leave?'

'In two days' time.'

'Bring Oswiu to me before you go. We need to part without animosity between us.'

~~~

The Holy Saviour led the way around the Mull of Kintyre and up into Kilbrannan Sound between the eastern coast of Kintyre and the Isle of Arran. It wasn't until they reached the southern tip of the Cowal Peninsula, opposite Tarbert to their west, that they entered the sea loch that divided Dal Riada from Strathclyde. The people over there spoke Brythonic and were culturally and ethnically different from those who inhabited Dal Riada and Ulster.

This time Rònan was sent up the mast to watch the eastern shore, but it seemed to be deserted. Oswiu was likewise stationed in the bows to watch the Dal Riadan shore for a possible landing site for the three birlinns to spend the night. However, the shore was rocky and it looked as if they might have to anchor and spend an uncomfortable night on board.

Then Beornwulf called across the water that there was a cove ahead and Oswiu spotted a narrow entrance with a small bay beyond it. The cove had a sandy beach and it was just large enough to accommodate the three craft. They had to enter one at a time, but soon all three birlinns were beached and Oswald sent out patrols just to make sure that there was no-one else nearby. If there was a settlement, then it would probably be Dal Riadan, but he wasn't taking any chances. At the time it didn't occur to him to wonder how Beornwulf knew about the cove.

All three shipmasters set sentries to watch their ships and the campsite, but Oswald also sent out a group of four men to take turns in watching the loch beyond the cove. He had no intention of being taken by surprise. It would be all too easy to bottle them up.

In the event the night passed peacefully and they were about to re-embark when one of Oswald's crew, a sixteen year old newly fledged warrior called Drustan, spotted a thin plume of smoke rising into the still morning air somewhere inland.

Straightway Beornwulf suggested that he accompany Oswald with some of his warriors to investigate. Oswald was immediately suspicious and smiled at the man.

'As our most experienced warrior, I would rather you stayed here and took charge of the defence of the camp. It may be wise to embark a skeleton crew on each vessel and anchor them out in the loch; we risk getting trapped in here otherwise. I'll take half my warriors and see where that smoke is coming from. I'll leave Eochaid and his crew here as well.'

He could tell that Beornwulf wasn't happy for some reason and he had a quiet word with Eochaid and Alaric before he left.

'Watch Beornwulf. I can't put my finger on it, but there's something odd going on. I don't trust him, to be blunt. Keep Oswiu and Rònan safe for me, Eochaid and keep your weapons handy.'

He took thirty warriors with him so that the number of his men left behind still outnumbered Beornwulf's crew and they followed the stream which emptied into the cove inland. The smoke lay roughly in the same direction and he expected to find whoever it was camped beside the stream. They walked beside it as it climbed into the hinterland and when they got close to where the smoke had been seen, Torquill and another young warrior were sent ahead as scouts. It wasn't long before Torquill came running came back to where the others waited.

'Oswald, there's a small loch ahead, perhaps a mile long and a third of that across. The camp where the smoke is coming from is a few hundred yards to the north of where the stream leaves the loch. It's on the loch shore and, from what we could see, at least a hundred well-armed men are there. We got as close as we dared and we could hear what they were saying. The funny thing is they were speaking in our language, not Brythonic, so they must be Dal Riadans like us, mustn't they?'

Oswald's immediate thought was that if there was such a large force of his men in the area, why hadn't Connad told him this? He was uncertain about what to do, until the other scout came back and joined them.

'One of Beornwulf's men emerged about half a mile to the left of where I was lying,' he said breathlessly. 'He ran along the lochside to the camp and I saw him in conversation with a man wearing a polished byrnie and a helmet with gold decoration, a chieftain, I suppose. Then the man with the helmet ordered the rest to gather their weapons and get ready to leave as quickly as possible. They're probably no more than five or ten minutes behind me.'

'Torquill, you're probably the fastest runner. Get back down to the cove as quickly as you can, but walk slowly once you're in view of the others. I don't want you to attract attention to yourself, clear? Good. Then find Eochaid and tell him that we're on our way back with a hundred enemy behind us. He's to warn his men and those of our crew we left behind and then try to kill Beornwulf, if he can. He's a traitor. Signal our two birlinns to come back into the cove. Got all that? Off you go.'

He turned to his men as the young warrior sped off down the stream as fast as he could go, over the slippery rocks and mud that lined the watercourse.

'Archers into the undergrowth. Kill a few of our pursuers to slow them down and then follow us. Stop when you can and repeat the tactic. All I want you to do is delay them.'

The ten men with bows took cover in the gorse and other scrub growing beside a bend in the stream and Oswald led the rest back towards the cove.

A few minutes later, the first of the men camped by the inland loch appeared, led by the man in the gold decorated helmet. A volley of arrows winged their way into the unsuspecting crowd of warriors and several fell wounded or dead. One of the wounded was their leader, with an arrow in his thigh just above the knee. The rest dithered until another volley hit them, then they retreated, dragging the wounded with them. The dead were left where they were.

The archers forced their way through the undergrowth and re-joined the stream beyond the bend. A few hundred yards further on, they stopped again and waited for their pursuers to appear. They didn't. They had obviously learned their lesson and the next thing the archers heard was the sound of men crashing through the bushes as they charged them. They let fly their arrows, bringing down a few and then fled down the stream.

Their attackers were slowed by the undergrowth and Oswald's men were a hundred yards away before they reappeared. They shouted back to the rest of their band and then set off in pursuit. The leaders didn't catch the archers before they reached the cove, but when they emerged onto the beach, they screeched to a halt when they saw what was happening.

~~~

Oswiu and Rònan were bored sitting out in Loch Fyne twenty yards from the entrance to the cove. The ten warriors on board were playing a game of chance, but they wouldn't let them or the other two ships' boys play. The two gazed over the side at the cove. Suddenly their interest was piqued when the saw Eochaid and Alaric talking to Torquill; they knew that he had gone with Oswald and they guessed that something had happened.

They had the presence of mind to go and tell the members of the on-board watch what they'd seen. Some would have ignored them and carried on with their game, but the two boys were liked and the men abandoned their gambling and went to see for themselves. Eochaid and Alaric had wandered over to speak to Beornwulf. A few of the latter's men had gathered around to hear what was being said, but none had weapons to hand, except for the swords they all wore.

Suddenly a seax appeared in Alaric's hand and he cut Beornwulf's throat. The latter's crew were stunned and didn't react immediately. However, the other two crews were ready and immediately grabbed their weapons and shields and attacked the unprepared men from Lorne. Within a few minutes a dozen bodies lay on the sand and the rest of

88

Beornwulf's men had surrendered. They were disarmed and Eochaid beckoned his and Oswald's birlinns into the cove. The one from Lorne was also preparing to get underway, but it headed off back down the Loch, making for the sea. Unfortunately for them, the wind was against them and they made little progress with only enough men for four oars a side instead of the usual twenty.

By the time the two birlinns had been beached Oswald and his men had reached the cove. The men quickly loaded the two ships and piled aboard, whilst archers kept arrows pointing at the unarmed men from Lorne.

Just then the war band from the interior started arriving on the beach and the archers changed their aim and brought several of them down. The late Beornwolf's crew took the opportunity to charge the archers. It was brave but foolish as a volley fired from the two birlinns cut the leaders down. After one last volley the archers on shore ran for the ships as they were pushed off the beach.

The new arrivals also had bowmen and arrows thudded into the shields protecting the archers on board. Unfortunately they managed to kill two of the archers scrambling back aboard, but another volley from the ships forced the enemy bowmen to take cover behind the shields of their comrades. A few more arrows thudded into shields and the hull as the two ships backed water and then turned to exit the cove.

'Whew, that was tight!' Alaric grinned at Oswald. 'It's a good job you had your wits about you. How did you know Beornwulf was a traitor?'

'Someone told me not to trust him; but I'm not sure that traitor is the right word. Those men that chased us were from Dal Riada. I smell treachery; this trap was laid by Connad, unless I'm very much mistaken. Who else could find a hundred men to be waiting for us above the cove where we spent the night? And Beornwulf was selected by Connad, too.'

'How did they know we'd select that cove for their ambush?'

'I didn't think of it at the time, but Beornwulf called across about the cove quite a few minutes before he could have seen it. Obviously his task was to make sure that we camped there.'

'Why didn't they attack at night, then?'

'I suppose that they were waiting until they received Beornwulf's message to confirm that we were indeed at the cove before they moved. We were lucky that they didn't think we'd see their campfires; otherwise we'd have been outnumbered and taken unawares. We owe a lot to Durstan's sharp eyes.'

Alaric nodded and muttered 'bastard', presumably referring to Connad and not Durstan. By now they were rowing hard down the loch through the driving rain and were catching the Seraphim up fast. They eventually overtook her at the junction of Loch Fyne and Loch Gilp. The skeleton crew didn't even try to put up a fight. Oswald put twenty three men from his ship and eighteen from Eochaid's onto her to provide his latest acquisition with a helmsman and one rower per oar. To his delight, Rònan was selected as one of the rowers.

'Where now? I take it we're not heading back to Dùn Add?' asked Eochaid, who had brought his birlinn within hailing distance of the Holy Saviour.

'Not just yet. We need more men, first. That lot back there can make it back in a day or so across country and put Connad on his guard, whereas it will take us days to make it around the Kintyre Peninsula.'

'What about heading for Ulster and asking my father for help?'

'I'd rather not. He's Connad's ally and has given his oath to him as his High King. It would put him in a difficult position. No; I think we should head for Dùn Averty at the end of the peninsula and see if the King of Kintyre will help us.'

'Why should he? He's Connad's vassal, too.'

'Domnall Brecc is Connad's nephew and the son of Buide, who Connad deposed. I'd be amazed if he's friends with the man who killed his father.'

~~~

Acha was surprised to receive an invitation to visit Connad in his hall; she was even more surprised when the slave who brought her the invitation said that she should bring her children with her. She was curious, but not concerned, until she spotted two members of Connad's personal bodyguard following them. She knew then that the invitation did not bode well for her and her family.

The autumnal weather had been benign up until then, with weak sunshine and clear skies. Now, however, it had changed overnight and rain squalls came in from the west with increasing regularity. It had been raining heavily that morning and the ground was muddy and slippery. When one of the warriors following them lost his footing and landed heavily, Acha seized her opportunity and hit the slave accompanying them over the head with the pommel of her dagger.

The second warrior had been too preoccupied with laughing at his companion and then helping him up to see Acha grab the hands of her children and disappear between the huts that lined the main track through the settlement. The two men ran to where she had disappeared but there was no sign of her and the huts provided a maze in which Acha could vanish. It was only after some time spent searching fruitlessly that the two men thought of going back to her hut.

By then it was too late. She had grabbed some food, coins, warm clothing and water skins before making her way to Oswald's hut. She would have liked to have taken her two slaves with her but Oswald had only two horses. She collected them and Gytha before leaving and heading to the south. She rode one horse, with Offa riding in front of her; Gytha rode the other one with Æbbe. By the time the alarm had been raised, they were two miles south of Dùn Add heading for the fishing hamlet at the head of Loch Gilp.

The weather had got even worse. Now there was thunder and lightning as well as heavy rain and soon they were all soaked. However, she daren't seek shelter anywhere. She needed to put as much distance as possible between them and Dùn Add, and quickly. The one good thing about the downpour was that it would make tracking them difficult.

She hoped that, with the money she had on her, she could pay a fisherman to take her to Ulster and King Fiachnae. She had no idea whether he would prove to be a friend, but she couldn't think what else to do. As she rode worry gnawed at her over the fate of Oswald and Oswiu. She smiled wryly to herself. As it had turned out, Oswiu was probably safer with his brother than he would have been had he stayed at Dùn Add.

~~~

'What do we do with these miserable specimens?' Alaric gestured with his thumb at the prisoners. 'We need to get going; we could just throw them over the side to see which of them can swim, I suppose.'

'Tempting, but not very Christian. I don't mind killing men in battle or even to extract information I need, but wanton slaughter is wrong. No, we need to land them somewhere.'

'There's a small settlement at the end of this loch, Oswald,' one of his warriors, who was standing listening to the exchange, told him.

'How far?' he asked, peering into the gloom as dark clouds scudded overhead.

'No more than a mile or so, I believe.'

'Very well.' He dropped his voice so that only Alaric could hear him. 'We'll also drop into conversation with the headman that we are bound for Larne. Word of that will get back to Connad and put him off the scent.'

They beached the three birlinns in the shingle near where several fishing currachs were pulled up onto the shore. At first the few inhabitants were wary and about to flee, until Oswald called out to them that they were friends. Hearing their own language reassured them and they approached him.

'You'll need to pull your birlinns well up onto the shore, Lord. There's a bad storm coming.'

Oswald was about to say that he wasn't afraid of a little rain when a strong gust of wind hit him and nearly blew him off his feet. It was followed by a bolt of lightning which hit the water out in the loch and a tremendous crack of thunder a mere two seconds later. That convinced him that it would be sensible to stay where they were until the storm passed.

There were no more than a dozen or so huts, but everyone managed to cram into one or other of them to shelter from the torrential downpour. Once Oswald had made sure that everyone, even the captives, were safe, he went out again to check that his small fleet were secured on the shore. The tide was coming in and he didn't want to see them smashed to pieces if they somehow floated away.

Satisfied, he was making his way back to one of the huts when a small boy crashed into him, yelling his name. To his amazement he realised that it was Offa. He hugged the seven-year-old to his chest as the boy threw his arms around his neck and cried; then he looked over the boy's shoulder to see his mother holding Æbbe in her arms and Gytha leading his two horses.

Once they had all squeezed into one of the huts he was dying to find out what they were doing there, but there were too many ears listening. Similarly, when Acha asked him what brought him there, all he could do was to tell her that he would explain later.

'It doesn't matter; what does is that we are all safe.'

'For the moment,' Oswald muttered. 'Connad wants me dead,' he whispered in her ear.

She nodded, but didn't reply.

Everyone spent an uncomfortable night, but by dawn the rain had stopped and the wind had died down. To thank him, Oswald made a present of the two horses to the headman and then he released the prisoners.

'Where are you bound?' the headman asked as they prepared to leave.

'To Larne. The shipmaster of one of the other birlinns is the son of the king there.'

'God speed, then.'

As the three birlinns were pushed off the shingle and then headed south towards the Mull of Kintyre and Domnall Brecc's hall, Oswald wondered what sort of reception they'd get.

# Chapter Seven – The Isle of Arran

## 621 - 622 AD

Warriors began to gather on the beach near the settlement at the southernmost end of Kintyre, as Oswald's three ships appeared through light rain that seemed to permeate everything. Although they were rowing against what little wind there was as they rounded the headland, Oswald raised the sail briefly so that they could see that the birlinns were from Dal Riada. The men on shore relaxed a little; however, they remained wary and kept their swords drawn.

'I am Oswald of Northumbria and this is my mother, Queen Acha, currently guests of the King of Dal Riada. The other ships are captained by Eochaid of the Ulaidh and Mægenræd from Dùn Add,' Oswald called across the water.

He didn't feel that he needed to add that, as guests, they appeared to have outstayed their welcome. As they neared the shore he saw what the drizzle had hidden up until then. The settlement was spread up the hillside to a ridge at one side of the bay, but Domnall Brecc's hall was built on the top of an outcrop of rock that rose almost vertically with a steep cliff on the northern side and the sea on the other three sides. At first he couldn't see how one could possibly reach it, but later he discovered that a zig-zag path had been cut into the rock.

The almost flat top of the outcrop was protected by a palisade some twelve feet high with a walkway around it; not that it seemed necessary, given the natural defences. The path ended at a small gateway that was designed to admit one man at a time. As the last few feet of the approach path ran directly under the palisade, the place seemed unassailable.

When he arrived Oswald had noticed with surprise that there were seven other birlinns drawn up on the beach and he came to the conclusion that there must be visitors here. Seven would need some four hundred or so warriors to man them and he doubted if there were more that fifteen hundred in the whole of Dal Riada. Certainly Domnall Brecc could muster no more than four hundred, if what he had heard was correct, and many of those would normally be spread throughout the long Kintyre peninsula and on the Isle of Arran.

Oswald, his mother, Eochaid and Mægenræd were allowed to accompany the guard, who had greeted them somewhat suspiciously on their arrival. Their commander led them up the narrow path to the gate with four of Domnall's men, all armoured and well-armed, at the rear. Oswiu had wanted to go with them, but Acha put her foot down and told him to look after Offa and his sister. He did so, but stared resentfully at her retreating back.

As Oswald had suspected, Domnall was not alone. Fergus of Islay sat at one side of him and a man he didn't recognise on the other.

'Oswald, my Lady, Eochaid, welcome to Dùn Averty. You know Fergus, of course. This is Conmael mac Gilla, the representative of the King of Lorne. Come sit. What brings you to Kintyre?'

'The treachery of Connad and his lickspittle, Beornwulf. The king set a trap for me but, fortunately, we found out what he was up to and left his men, and those Connad sent to ambush us, stranded on the shores of Loch Fyne.'

'And what happened to Beornwulf?' Conmael asked softly.

'My helmsman cut his throat.'

'Good! I'd have preferred that he died more painfully, but I'm delighted he's dead.'

'Why? He was a treacherous dog, but why is a noble from Lorne so pleased?'

'Because he betrayed us at the Pass of Brander. He had been given land by our king and he answered the summons to arms together with his men. He brought about forty, which surprised us, but we later found out that many of them were from our enemy. He'd been bribed by Belin map Neithon to hold back and then attack us from the rear. However, we beat him off and he fled, and we then defeated Belin. We didn't know where he and his curs had fled to. Obviously he sought refuge at Dùn Add -'

'- and was then given a birlinn and the men to make up a full crew by Connad,' Oswald finished.

'It seems that all of us have a grievance against Connad, but that's not why we are here,' Domnall broke in. 'The men of Strathclyde have invaded Arran in two waves, over the Sound of Bute and across the Firth of Clyde from Ardrossan. They have overrun the north of the island and our people – those who survived – have fled to the south.'

'What is your plan?' Acha spoke for the first time since the meeting had begun.

95

Domnall, Fergus and Conmael all looked at her sharply. They weren't used to having women contributing to a war council.

'To land in the south and push the invaders back north to recover the island.'

'May I suggest that it would be better to trap them and destroy them? That way Belin map Neithon will learn a valuable lesson.'

'And how do you propose we do that, my lady? We only have four hundred men between us,' Domnall asked scornfully. 'The enemy have the same number, as far as we can tell.'

'My son has a hundred and thirty more, which gives you the advantage; however, I am not a warrior, so I will leave you men to your deliberations.'

'Thank you my lady,' Domnall said with a nod. 'I'm afraid I can't offer you accommodation here at my hall, but there is a hut near the beach for you and your family to use. This man will show you where it is.'

Oswald watched his mother go with some relief. She was strong willed and her idea had merit, but he was embarrassed to have her overshadow him. He hadn't said anything because he didn't want an argument in front of Domnall and Fergus.

'I take it from what your mother said that you would be willing to help us?'

'My mother doesn't speak for me,' he replied, a trifle more brusquely than he had intended, 'but yes, we have nothing better to do at the moment.' He paused, lost in thought.

'Once you re-capture Arran you will need to replace the inhabitants you have lost or it will be re-taken.'

'Yes, of course. What are you suggesting?'

'Let me keep what I gain as your tenant.' Domnall looked at Oswald sharply, then nodded.

'Very well.'

The three stayed to eat with Domnall and then slept in the hall before going back to tell their men what was intended the next morning.

~~~

It was nearly dusk when Oswald's three birlinns and that of Conmael of Lorne approached the strand of sand gleaming whitely in the gloom. They grounded their keels and then men leapt over the side armed with shield and sword to secure the land overlooking the beach. The others hauled the ships up onto the white sand and set a guard before they too collected their weapons and formed up on the beach.

'There're nine beaches on Arran where it's possible to land,' Domnall had told Oswald. 'There are others, but there are rocks offshore and, unless you know the coast well, they're best avoided. Six of the beaches are in the south, which is the area that my men still hold. We think that Belin's men landed near the main settlement at Brodick and at the end of a small inlet called Loch Ranza. The other beach in the north is at a small settlement in Catacol Bay. It's quite close to Loch Ranza and it's probably your best chance of getting ashore unopposed.'

And so it had proved. Oswald had been placed in command of the four birlinns and their crews. Domnall had found thirty young warriors to bolster his existing crews and, although they were all between fifteen and seventeen and as yet untried, he now had a total of well over two hundred men. They settled down just off the beach for the night and made do with a meal of cold meat, cheese and water. It was now October and decidedly chilly after the sun set, but to light fires would have been foolish.

The next morning they were up before dawn and broke their fast with more cold meat and cheese. Domnall had sent a priest with them and he gave them a quick blessing before they set out. Oswald knew that the priest would encourage the men, but he hoped the man didn't want to deliver a sermon. That would have delayed them, but, thankfully, he didn't. Oswald left Alaric in charge at the beach with the ships' boys, ten of the untried warriors and a few experienced fighters, and led the rest in the direction of Loch Ranza two miles away.

He knew from what Domnall had told him that the loch lay over the shoulder of a mountain that dominated that area of the island. This time he didn't just send out scouts forward, but also a little way up the mountain on their right flank. Initially the going was quite steep and it took them a long time to reach the crest of the ridge that sloped down from the summit a couple of miles inland all the way to the sea.

Torquill had been put in charge of the forward scouts and, two hours after they had set out, he came back to report that there were four birlinns drawn up behind a spit of land that jutted out into the loch near the settlement at its head. Oswald sent for Eochaid and Conmael to hear Torquill's report so he didn't have to repeat it to them.

'The settlement appears to be a blackened ruin, but men are building a hall, huts and a palisade on a flat area immediately below this mountain. It's about a hundred yards from the spit where their ships are

97

and there are women and children with them, so presumably they intend to settle.'

'Thank you, Torquill; you've done well. Any idea as to numbers?'

'We counted about a hundred men and I'd estimate the number of women and children at nearly twice that.'

'How big were the birlinns?'

'They varied from perhaps fifteen oars to a side to twenty. I'd say, with the women and children aboard, there couldn't be more than a hundred and fifty men in all.'

'So presumably there are another fifty in the hinterland, foraging and hunting,' Eochaid added.

'Were the women and children with the men building their new settlement?'

'No, they were at a tented campsite on the other bank of a small river which feeds into the loch. It's several hundred yards away from the new site and not far from the old settlement.'

The body of men followed Torquill back until Oswald and the other two shipmasters could see Loch Ranza below them.

'Good. We'll need to wait until the hunters are back before we attack. We don't want to have to chase isolated pockets of the enemy all over this island. We'll come in from the south east at dawn. That way we'll trap them between us and the sea. We'll leave a few men up here, in case any of them try to flee this way. If they try to escape up the mountain on the other side, they'll still be trapped between us and the sea.'

As soon as it was dark Torquill led them down the way he'd scouted during the day so that at dawn they'd be in position for the attack. It was a difficult path, but the clouds cleared and the nearly full moon lit their way. Because nights were long at that time of year, they had several hours to sleep once they'd got into position, but few did more than doze wrapped in thick woollen cloaks and for the lucky few, wolf and bear skins to keep out the cold.

Conmael had been given twenty of his men to prevent escape up the mountain and now Oswald divided his men once again. Eochaid took his own crew and the remainder of the men of Lorne to secure the settlement, whilst Oswald tackled the more difficult task of attacking the single warriors in the nearly completed fortress near the ships. Thankfully, the palisade hadn't quite been completed and there was a gap twenty feet wide where the rest of it and the gateway would go.

Unfortunately, this was guarded by at least six men, who appeared to be alert.

Oswald gathered his archers and explained what he wanted them to do. His plan was to wait until they were all in view before trying to put several arrows in each at once. However, he was conscious that Eochaid was about to enter the camp of the married men and their families. He wished he had thought to bring a hunting horn with which to co-ordinate their attacks.

He could just make out Eochaid's men moving into position by the first rays of the sun as it crested the mountains to the east. Then he heard the sound of fighting coming across the water and he gave the order for his archers to let fly. Five men crumpled to the ground, but no-one had hit the sixth. For a moment he was frozen in shock before he reacted and opened his mouth to cry a warning. Not a sound emerged, however, as three more arrows from the quickest men to nock a second arrow to their bows punched through his leather jerkin into his chest.

Before the guard hit the ground, Oswald was running towards the gap in the palisade, waving on his men with his sword above his head. It caught the rays of the sun and flashed white again and again and someone called out, 'Follow the white blade!' Soon the cry was taken up and a hundred voices yelled 'Follow Whiteblade!' It was the name he would be known by from then on.

Oswald darted through the gap in the palisade and headed for the doors into the hall, just as they swung open and a man, still half asleep and wearing nothing but his undershirt, peered out. He took one look at the horde of warriors heading for the hall and dashed back inside, pulling the door shut and slamming the bar that secured it into place.

Oswald cursed. It would give the men inside time to put on their armour and arm themselves. Then he noticed that the hall had been constructed with just two small windows at the front. A quick check confirmed that there were none in the side or back walls. The Strathclyde men were trapped inside. Two arrows flew out of the small windows, but both hit shields. Oswald's archers shot back; most of their arrows bristled around the two windows like the quills on a hedgehog, but a few went through the openings and there were no more arrows from inside the hall.

Something of an impasse followed. Of course, Oswald could have used one of the tree trunks lying around ready to be put in place to complete the palisade to break in the doors, but that would mean fighting the warriors inside, now fully prepared, hyped up and ready to fight.

Although he would win, as he had more men, he would suffer a lot of casualties. So he decided on a less honourable course of action to save his men's lives.

The roof of the hall was made of bundles of straw, tightly packed in layers to make it waterproof. The top layer was wet, thanks to the recent weather, but the straw underneath would be dry. He therefore sent men up onto the roof to throw down the top layer and then his archers shot several volleys of fire arrows up onto the dry straw. It was soon ablaze and he could imagine the scene inside as smoke billowed around, making them choke whilst trying to dodge the blazing straw as it dropped onto their heads.

Soon the falling straw had set light to the rushes that were used as a cover for the floor of beaten earth, and even some furniture caught alight. The warriors inside had a choice: be burnt alive, die of asphyxiation, or come out and fight. Most chose the latter and the doors were thrown open as a horde of men, coughing and spluttering, charged out.

The first dozen or so were killed or wounded by the archers, but then the rest were upon them and Oswald's men locked their shields together. Their assailants were weakened and light-headed and were easily cut down as they flung themselves on the shields and tried to wrench them out of the way so that they could get at the men behind. One man pulled Oswald's shield down, exposing his face and a second man thrust his sword at his head, but it struck his helmet and glanced off. Oswald dropped his sword, which was too unmanageable for this type of fighting and pulled his seax out of its scabbard. He thrust it into the mouth of the man with the sword and he fell away with a scream. Torquill, on his left side, killed the warrior hanging onto Oswald's shield and the immediate danger was over.

The hall was blazing furiously now and the intense heat forced Oswald's men to retreat a little way. Their opponents were not so fortunate. There was nowhere to go to avoid being scorched. A few tried to climb the palisade, but the archers, who had retreated to the rear when the hand-to-hand fighting had started, soon picked them off.

Finally, after two thirds of their number had been killed, died in the flames or were too badly wounded to fight, the rest surrendered. As they were disarmed and tied up well away from the flames, Oswald made his way over to the families' encampment. Eochaid splashed across the small river to greet him and the two sat down on a rock.

'How did it go?'

'Very easily, really. We caught them asleep and we were waiting for them as they came out of their tents. A few men put up a fight and they were killed. The rest are our captives. Some tried to run off up the hill, but they were caught by Conmael's men. I don't think anyone escaped.'

'I hope not; I don't want anyone warning Brodick, where the rest of the invaders probably are.'

'I see you had to burn them out?'

'Yes, we still lost a few, but not nearly as many as we would have if I hadn't set fire to the hall to smoke them out.'

'Will you rebuild it?'

'Not there, no. There's room for a fortress on the spit of land where the ships are beached. The encampment is a good site for the settlement, though. The only problem is the water supply, but we can overcome that by building a tank and keeping it topped up with fresh water.'

'What will you do with the captives?'

'That will be up to Domnall Brecc, provided he gives us a fair price for them and for those birlinns.'

'Fergus might want to buy some of them. After all, he's the King of the Isles and needs ships the most.'

'Good point. Perhaps I can get them to bid against each other,' he suggested, grinning. 'For now, we need to bury our dead and treat the wounded on both sides. Once the fire dies down, we can incarcerate the prisoners inside the palisade. It's as good as a stockade once we get the gate and the final length in place.'

'We'll need to send one of those birlinns we captured round to the other beach with enough men to bring ours here.'

'Yes; can I ask you to look after that?'

'What are you going to do?'

'Tomorrow I'll take Torquill and a few of the other scouts to have a look at Brodick.'

~~~

Oswald was to find that doing that was easier said than done. No-one in the three crews knew Arran well, but there were some of the original inhabitants who had been taken as slaves. Most were fishermen who didn't know the interior of the island very well, except for the fact that it was largely uninhabited. All the settlements were on the coast, as the hinterland in the north was quite mountainous.

However, there used to be several huntsmen in the settlement who knew the mountains well. They had all been killed fighting the invaders, but one of them had a son – a boy of twelve called Cormac – who had been hunting deer with his father a few times. He told Oswald that the biggest settlement on Arran was to the south of the tallest mountain – Gaoda Bheinn. He had never been there, but he did know the way to Gaoda Bheinn and he thought that you could see Brodick from there on a clear day.

The next morning was anything but bright and clear. Low clouds hung over the mountain tops and it had turned much colder overnight. However, Oswald was not to be deterred and set off with Torquill, Cormac and three other scouts – Griogar, Iomhar and Ruaraidh.

The six of them made good progress during the morning, following the small river that emptied into Loch Ranza up the valley until it forked. Cormac said to take the left fork and after a further gentle climb, the slope got steeper and the stream petered out in a boggy area. Cormac skirted the bog to the east and shortly they found themselves on a ridge which climbed up into the clouds. Cormac didn't know the name of the mountain they were on, but he was adamant that they couldn't get lost in the mist if they followed the ridge up to the summit and then over the other side and down into a saddle between four mountains, the one to the south east being Gaoda Bheinn. He suggested that they camp in the saddle and set out in the morning to climb Gaoda Bheinn.

That seemed sensible to Oswald. He should be able to work out which was the mountain above the settlement, provided he could judge where south east was from the position of the sun. However, there had been precious little sight of it so far that day. In fact, the weather deteriorated and Oswald woke up in the middle of the night when snow started to land on his face.

By morning the light snow had turned into a blizzard and Oswald realised that they could be in serious trouble. It was about four inches deep, which made walking through it tiring, but the wind was causing it to drift and in places it was a lot deeper. There was no question of climbing to the top of Gaoda Bheinn that day and the priority now was survival.

Griogar and Ruaraidh were in favour of taking the easiest path, which led down from the saddle to what Oswald thought was probably the east. If so, that would eventually lead to the coast and they could then follow that all the way back to Loch Ranza.

'But that is about three times as far as we've come,' Cormac pointed out.

102

'You are the only one of us who knows this island at all. What do you suggest?' Oswald asked him.

'You're not going to leave the decision on which our lives depend to a boy, and a foreigner at that, are you?' Iomhar butted in.

'Why, do you have reason not to trust him?' Oswald asked, his eyes narrowing dangerously.

'Well, no, not really,'

'Good. Then shut up and let's hear what he has to say.'

Oswald realised that, in their current situation, if he let them start arguing amongst themselves, he'd lose control and a wrong decision based on prejudice and fear was likely to follow.

'Well,' the boy began, with a nervous look at Iomhar.

'Never mind about him, just tell me what you think.'

'From what I remember, if we head in the opposite direction up the saddle, we'll reach the highest point in a few hundred yards. We can then drop down into Glen Iorsa and follow that all the way back to Loch Ranza.'

'If that's such a direct route, why didn't we follow it here?' Griogar wanted to know.

'Well, because the climb up to the saddle is very much steeper than the way we came, and it's further that way.'

'I still say that we should follow the route down to the coast,' Ruaraidh said stubbornly.

'Then it's a good job that you're not in charge, isn't it?' Torquill told him with a grin, which diffused the situation.

Still grumbling, the other three picked up their equipment and followed Cormac and Oswald into the driving snow, with Torquill bringing up the rear. The path up to the crest of the saddle was hard going and, once they started to go downhill, everyone saw what Cormac meant.

'Cormac, stop. This route is getting dangerously steep. If someone lost their balance they would slide downhill until they crashed into a rock. Griogar, you brought an axe, didn't you?'

'Yes, but it's only a small one for chopping firewood.'

'That's ideal. You lead and cut steps into the snow. When you get tired, yell and someone else will relieve you.'

The wind had packed the snow against the side of the mountain and Griogar found it relatively easy to cut steps into it. However, reaching down far enough to cut the next step below where he was standing was tiring and his back ached.

'This is fun, but I feel guilty getting all the pleasure myself. Would someone else like to enjoy himself for a bit?' he called up.

With a laugh, Iomhar took over, casting aspersions on Griogar's masculinity as he did so. However, after a quarter of an hour he asked Ruaraidh to spell him. By the time that Torquill and Oswald had taken their turns, the slope was becoming less steep and the snow had stopped falling. By midday, they were down on the valley floor.

They took a brief rest and ate some cold food before pressing on. The snow there was only a couple of inches deep in most places and they made it back to where the river forked just as it was getting dark. Iomhar suggested pressing on, but Oswald said it was too dangerous at night, especially one as dark as this was. It was still overcast and pitch black in consequence.

The next morning Oswald thanked Cormac for probably saving their lives. Iomhar and Griogar apologised for doubting him, but Ruaraidh didn't say anything, just scowled at the boy. Oswald decided to have a quiet word with Torquill, but then changed his mind. Torquill was no fool and he would have already realised that Ruaraidh was bigoted and resentful. He wouldn't be invited to scout again.

The snow had stopped and a little later a thin, watery sun put in an appearance. Oswald returned to find that everyone had been very concerned about them and, consequently, extremely happy to see them all safe and sound. On the final leg of the journey he had made two decisions and once everyone had stopped fussing over him, he sent for Rònan and Cormac. The younger boy arrived first.

'Cormac, I was very impressed with you over the past two days. Am I correct in thinking that you're an orphan?'

When the boy nodded and hung his head, Oswald told him to come and sit beside him.

'There's nothing to be ashamed of,' Oswald told him, putting an arm around his shoulders.

'It's not that, though everyone does seem to act as if it's your fault that your parents were killed, as if I could have fought off a hundred warriors,' he explained bitterly. 'No, it's just that I've nowhere to go and nothing to do.'

'Well, I may be able to help there. My body servant, Rònan, is fourteen and I'm about to free him and let him train as a warrior, so I'll need a new body servant – not as a slave, of course. I'll pay you.'

'You want me to serve you?' the boy's face broke into a broad smile. 'There's nothing I'd like better.'

Rònan was delighted when Oswald told him, but then his face fell.

'I will miss being your servant, though. You were more than a master to me; you were my friend, too.'

'I hope I can still be your friend. Just because you're no longer looking after me doesn't mean that I care for you any less.'

At that the boy looked a lot happier.

'What about Gytha? Won't she be looking after you?'

'No, my mother and my siblings need a servant. You're a free man from today, Rònan. Once we've sorted out this place, I shall start to train the younger warriors properly and maybe recruit some of the other orphans from Cormac's settlement, if they're suitable. You can join them and share a hut with them. They'll probably be glad of your cooking skills!'

The one person who wasn't happy about Oswald's new servant was Oswiu. He'd hoped that he could look after his brother again, once he heard that Rònan had been freed to train as a warrior. Therefore, the news about Cormac came as a bitter blow. Oswiu went in search of him and, without any warning, punched him on the nose.

~~~

Their first winter on Arran was a harsh one. Without supplies from Kintyre they'd have been in danger of starvation. Warriors were not fishermen, however good at rowing they were, and only a few of them were proficient hunters. In any case, game was scarce. The food shortage would have been worse had not Conmael and his men returned to Lorne for the winter with a promise that he would return in the spring.

The few married men, including the priest, who had elected to stay, sent for their wives and children and, as winter wore on, several of the younger warriors married the widows of the settlement men who had been slain by the men of Strathclyde.

Once the hall had been completed, work started on a second hall for the families to share initially. Later, once huts had been built for the married men and a small communal hall for those women who remained unmarried, the original hall in the settlement became the church.

Conmael had taken one of the captured birlinns with him as a reward for his part in the recapture of Loch Ranza. The others Oswald sold, one to Domnall Brecc and the rest to Fergus. This gave him the money to reward his men and to purchase grain, seed and animals from the mainland of Kintyre.

Oswald used the winter well. Once construction work had been completed so that everyone had shelter from the snow, the cold and the driving rain, he introduced a harsh training regime. Most of his men were good fighters, but that wasn't good enough. He wanted them to become formidable. Rònan and one or two other boys from the settlement who were big enough to wield a sword and shield properly were trained separately. Whilst too young as yet to be considered warriors, they would be able to help defend the settlement if it came to that. Oswiu was allowed to join them, not that he would be allowed to fight if and when the time came – he was still far too young – but it made him feel better to be included.

At last spring arrived and Conmael returned. He had expected to find Oswald living in the hall as the chieftain of Loch Ranza. Instead, he was living in one of two separate huts that had been built inside the palisade that surrounded the hall where the single warriors lived. The other was occupied by Acha and her three youngest children, but Gytha was no longer their slave. Acha had recruited an orphaned girl from the settlement called Caitrìona as her servant and Oswald had married Gytha.

Oswald had been attracted to Gytha when he first saw her. As time went on he found that attraction had turned to desire and desire to love. They were married in the new church in the settlement at the end of March. Cormac had stayed on as Oswald's body servant and Gytha had taken Caitrìona's younger sister as her servant to help her look after their home. After two months of marriage, Gytha thought that she might be pregnant, but she wasn't certain, so she said nothing to Oswald, or even to Acha.

Whenever the weather allowed, Oswald took Eochaid, Oswiu and Cormac hunting. The older boy had been furious with Oswiu for giving him a bloody nose, but after Oswald had boxed Oswiu's ears and made him apologise, the two got on much better.

Oswald dearly loved every moment he spent with Gytha, but he found the hut claustrophobic if he spent too long cooped up. Of course, as chieftain of the settlement he was often required to sit in the hall to adjudicate on disputes, try petty criminals and listen to petitions, so hunting restored the balance between duty and enjoyment.

One day in early March the weather was benign enough for him to consider a reconnaissance of Brodick again. This time they made it to the top of Gaoda Bheinn without any trouble. In addition to his usual party of hunters, he had taken Torquill as well. Acha had been dubious about

106

letting Oswiu go along, but as he was now ten years old and Oswald had promised that he wouldn't let any harm come to him, she relented.

The four men and two boys stood on the summit of the tallest mountain on Arran and were stunned by the view. It was sunny but chilly, so the air was crystal clear, not hazy as it often was on hot days in the summer. They could see Kintyre to the west and some distance away to the east, the mainland of Strathclyde. The Isle of Bute, where the men who had attacked Loch Ranza had come from, lay to the north east and the entrance to Loch Fyne due north.

They could see that the southern half of Arran was less mountainous. Domnall Brecc had driven the invaders back towards Brodick and strengthened the defences of the settlements there before withdrawing as soon as winter set in. Belin's men seemed content to maintain their toehold at Brodick for now, but Oswald was certain that they would renew their attempt to capture the island in the spring. He was determined to drive them out before they could reinforce the men they'd left behind to hold the settlement during the winter.

He looked down at Brodick with interest. The mountainside was relatively barren, but halfway down there was a large wood before the trees gave way to pastureland around the settlement. It was too far away for him to make out much detail, but he could count six birlinns tied up along the wooden jetty. At a rough estimate, that meant about three hundred and fifty warriors. Then he noticed two more birlinns on the sea between the mainland and the island. He concluded that reinforcements had started to arrive; he needed to warn Domnall Brecc and prepare his own settlement in case of attack.

'We need to establish a lookout post up here to give us notice in case they head our way.'

The others men nodded, looking worried.

'Do you want someone to stay here and see if any more cross to Arran?' Torquill suggested.

'No, we can always count the number of birlinns later; they won't be doing anything today. The lookouts up here will need to bring food and a tent with them for shelter.'

'Isn't there a danger that Belin's men will come up here and find them?'

'I doubt it. We have never encountered any sign of them in the interior of the island. If they hunt, they must do it down there. No, I expect them to attack us from the sea,' Oswald stated with conviction. 'However, whether they come by land or sea, we will have good warning.'

'May I suggest that the lookouts light one signal fire if they are coming by sea and two if by land?  It won't matter if they know someone is up here, because they'll have plenty of time to make their escape,' Torquill suggested.

'Good idea.'  Oswald wished that he'd thought of the plan.  He was coming to appreciate the young warrior's qualities more and more as he got to know him.

'Perhaps they had better prepare three fires,' Eochaid put it with a glance at Torquill that smacked slightly of triumph.  'Just in case they decide to come by both land and sea.'

Oswald smiled.  'I'm obviously not needed!  Well done, the pair of you!'  He was determined to nip any rivalry between the two of them in the bud.

With that, they turned and started to clamber down the other side of the mountain.

~~~

'The signal fire's been lit!' the lookout on top of the hill above Loch Ranza yelled in excitement.  The two other warriors, who were helping him keep watch throughout the hours of daylight, woke with a start and one of them kicked the boy sleeping nearby hard to wake him up.

'Go and tell Lord Oswald,' one of the men told him.

The boy stared at him, resentful because of the strength of the kick.

'How many fires?' he asked, as if talking to a small child.

The man glared at him and was about to box his ears when the man on watch intervened.

'Good point, lad.  There's just the one so far.  No, wait!  There's a second.'

'So they're coming by land?'

'And by sea.  There's the third.  Well, what are you waiting for, boy?  Off you go.'

'And well done,' he called after the retreating back as the boy flew down the hillside like a mountain goat.  He'd been picked, not because he was the fastest runner, but because he was the most surefooted over the rocky terrain.

Oswald's eyes glimmered with excitement.

'It's a pity we didn't think of a way of indicating how many were coming by sea and how many by land.'

'Does it really matter?' Conmael mac Gilla asked. As he had promised, he had returned the previous week. This time he had brought two large birlinns with him, each with twenty oars a side and a complement of sixty men each. That meant that Oswald now had nearly two hundred and seventy men in total. He was waiting for Domnall Brecc to reinforce him, but no one had arrived to date.

The last report he'd had from the lookouts had been when they had been relieved a few days ago. At that time there were nine birlinns in the harbour, but some were only ten oars a side. His best estimate was that there were five hundred warriors in Brodick. It was not good odds, but the fact that they had split their forces was encouraging.

Oswald was in two minds: whether to try and attack both forces at once, or to ambush the party coming overland and defend the settlement against a seaborne assault until the ambush party returned. He came to the conclusion that to do the former option would risk defeat in two areas, whereas the second had a better chance of success. He just wished he knew how the enemy had split their forces. In the end he assumed that they would divide them equally. He therefore took just over two hundred men with him and left Eochaid and his crew to defend the fortress on the spit of land.

Both Gytha and Acha had urged him to stay and defend the inhabitants, but he knew that success depended on a decisive defeat of the enemy coming overland. Then he could return and trap the enemy between his men and the fortress. Naturally Rònan and Oswiu wanted to come with him, but he told both of them he needed them with his family to defend them for him until he returned. They both knew that, in reality, there was little Oswald could do to keep them safe and it was just his way of letting them down gently, but they accepted it.

Oswald went forward with Torquill, Griogar and Iomhar to find a suitable ambush site, leaving Conmael in charge of the main body. There were two routes that the attackers might choose, but Oswald considered that the steep descent from the saddle, that had caused them such difficulty in the snow, might be usable with care now, though it seemed a poor option for a large body of men.

Oswald didn't want to risk setting his ambush on the wrong route though, so the logical place for it would be on the saddle itself. He hoped they did opt for the steep, but more direct route, as then the enemy would be bunched up waiting for their turn to descend.

He decided to place the bulk of his forces, divided equally, amongst the rocks on the mountainsides to the north and south of the saddle. He detached twenty men under Torquill to cut off any who fled back towards Brodick.  It was few enough, but it was as many as he could afford.

Oswald was only just in time.  His men had had further to travel than the enemy, but the latter had proceeded cautiously, not knowing the countryside, whereas his men had moved twice as fast at a slow run.  They scattered amongst the rocks on the hillsides above the saddle and waited.

Torquill's cut-off party had even further to go as they had to keep out of sight by taking a route behind the mountain to the north and then go over the shoulder into a valley which led south west into the one the men of Strathclyde had taken up from Brodick.  They followed the stream down from the saddle until it met the one flowing down Glen Rosa and then hid amongst the rocks that lined the valley.

Every man was an archer and they planned to pick off those fleeing at a distance rather than get embroiled in any hand to hand fighting, if they could avoid it.  However as they waited, they became more and more concerned.  The sound of intense fighting had reached them some time ago, indicating that the ambush had been sprung, but so far only two men had come back down the valley.  Both had been killed, but there should have been a lot more if the ambush had been successful.

~~~

Eochaid counted the Strathclyde birlinns as they entered Loch Ranza and made for the spit of land on which the fortress sat.  There were four, which probably meant an attacking force of over two hundred men.  However, they didn't seem to be in a hurry to land and launch their assault.  All the inhabitants had crammed into the fortress, abandoning the settlement, and he half expected the enemy to plunder that first, but they made no attempt to do so.  He came to the conclusion that they were waiting for the other half of their men to arrive.  Presumably, the job of this small fleet was to stop anyone escaping by sea.

Eochaid had lined the walkway that ran round the palisade with archers, both warriors and inhabitants who knew how to use a bow.  There was no point in exposing the rest of his fighting men before he had to.

Eventually the man commanding the Strathclyde birlinns must have got bored waiting and they beached them on a small stretch of sand to the north of the fortress.  It was obvious by then that the inhabitants had no intention of fleeing by ship.  The enemy approached the palisade cautiously. The front rank held their shields in front of them and their archers followed behind them. Those in the rear were less well armed and not all even had shields.

Eochaid whispered what he wanted to the most experienced of his archers and the man crouched low as he ran along the walkway briefing his men as he went. When Eochaid yelled 'now', the archers stood as one and released their arrows at high trajectory. By the time the Strathclyde men had shot back, the archers had ducked down again and the arrows thudded harmlessly into and over the ramparts.

Not so the volley fired by Eochaid's bowmen. They had aimed at the less well protected warriors in the rear and many of them were wounded or killed. With that one volley they had reduced the strength of the attacking force by fifteen men. The rest withdrew hastily, taking the wounded with them but leaving the dying where they'd fallen. The archers fired another volley after them and several more were hit. Eochaid counted fifteen corpses in all, as the crows and buzzards flew down to feast on the fresh meat.

Seeing this, some of the attackers advanced again behind their shields to collect the bodies of their dead and Eochaid allowed them to do so. The men of Strathclyde retreated to their ships and for the moment, made no more attempts to attack. Eochaid stood his men down, leaving sentries to keep an eye out for any sign of a renewed attempt to take the fortress, but he was convinced that they were now waiting for the majority of their men to arrive. He prayed that Oswald's ambush had been successful. If the Strathclyde men attacked by night, when he couldn't use his archers, he doubted they could hold the combined force off for long.

~~~

Oswald had waited until all the men were bunched up on the saddle and the descent down into Glen Iorsa by the Strathclyde vanguard had started. He held up his sword so that it caught the sun and flashed the signal to attack across the saddle to Conmael, who was leading the other half of the ambush party. Almost as one, both groups rose from their hiding positions and charged downhill. The slopes were steep and covered in rocks and boulders. They leaped from rock to rock and slithered down the scree and Oswald was surprised to learn later that only three men had broken their legs during that wild charge. They hit the unprepared men of Strathclyde with such momentum that they drove

111

great gaps into their ranks, dividing them into small groups, before the fighting started in earnest.

Some fifty men had been killed or badly wounded by the initial charge, which reduced the odds to almost even. However, the enemy started to fight back. There was no formation and the battle deteriorated into a series of hand-to-hand fights. Now the rigorous training regime that Oswald had insisted on during the winter began to display benefits.

He and five others had surrounded a small group of their foes. Whenever one of the latter tried to thrust sword or spear at Oswald or his men, they countered swiftly with their shields and caught their opponent unbalanced with their return thrust. The group of eight was soon whittled down to four, but one of these was a big man with a two-handed battle axe. He had already brought it down on the head of one of Oswald's warriors, cleaving through his helmet deep into his skull.

He batted away Oswald's sword and brought the axe slicing round in a swing that would have cut deeply into the side of anyone in its way, chain mail armour notwithstanding. Luckily, everyone managed to get out of its way, but it afforded the opportunity for another of the Strathclyde men to score a hit in the leg of the man to Oswald's left. Oswald feinted towards the belly of the axeman and, when he brought up his axe to knock the sword away, he changed the direction of his lunge and the point entered the big man's groin. He screamed in agony and the man who had been wounded in the leg finished him off with a chop into his neck.

As he fell dead, his companions lost heart and surrendered. However, Oswald had given the order for no quarter. They couldn't hurry back to Loch Ranza if they were encumbered by a load of captives. This was, therefore, a fight to the death. Besides, the elimination of so many of Belin's fighting men would seriously weaken him and keep Dal Riada safe for years to come.

He wasn't proud of his decision and he repented it for years afterwards, but it was the right one strategically. It took them moments to cut the rest of the group down and then Oswald turned to seek his next opponent. One of the others took advantage of the pause to bind up the leg of the man who had been wounded. Fortunately it was only a flesh wound and with rest would soon heal, once it was stitched up.

Oswald caught sight of a man wearing a gleaming byrnie and a helmet with a faceguard representing a man with a golden beard. That, coupled with the circlet of gold around the helmet, indicated that he was a man of importance and wealth; most probably the man commanding the Strathclyde men on Arran. As Oswald made his way towards him he saw him kill another of his men and he determined, not only to kill him, but to humiliate him first.

As Oswald strode towards the Strathclyde leader, a warrior with a spear tried to stop him. Oswald blocked the spear point with his shield and then dug the point of his sword into the man's belly, twisting and pulling out a handful of slimy grey intestines with it. After that, no-one else got in his way.

The man with the gold-embellished helmet saw him coming and braced himself with his small round shield held in front of him and his sword held ready. Oswald noticed with interest that it was a good six inches longer than his own blade and that the man was about four inches taller. Oswald smiled grimly; he detected an air of overconfidence in his foe.

He allowed the man to make the first move, shoving his small shield, called a targe, towards Oswald's face whilst aiming a cut at his unprotected legs. Oswald leapt in the air and the sword sliced the air under him. He had timed his jump perfectly and his leather clad feet came down on the flat of the blade. His surprised opponent was dragged forward; had he thought quickly enough, he should have released his sword to keep his balance and pulled out the seax hanging from his belt.

As he lurched forward, Oswald held the point of his sword steady and it cut into the side of the man's neck, opening up a long, deep cut which bled copiously. He could just as easily have moved the point two inches to the left and the man would have been dead and he knew it. Behind the gilded face mask, Oswald could see the fear in his eyes. He knew he was being toyed with.

Whilst the battle raged around them, the two men circled each other warily. Oswald knew that the man was desperate to finish this before he lost too much blood and became weak, but Oswald was in no hurry. His opponent was the invader and he wanted him to pay.

The Strathclyde leader tried a feint at Oswald's eyes and then moved the point of his sword downwards, hoping that Oswald would follow with his shield to protect his abdomen and thighs. He didn't and as he'd expected, his foe went for the eyes again at the very last moment. This time Oswald moved his shield to counter it and thrust his own sword into the man's groin. He was now seriously wounded and could hardly see for the pain. The point of his sword drooped and he no longer had the strength to hold up his shield. With a long, powerful sweep of his sword Oswald cut into the man's neck. He felt the jar up his arm as it cut

113

through the spine and then the head with its magnificent helmet went spinning away to hit the ground several yards away.

The heart went out of the men of Strathclyde when they saw that their leader had been killed. They tried to slip away down the path they had come, but Oswald's men moved quickly to pen them in. After more than half of them had been killed, Oswald called a halt to the slaughter and the remainder were disarmed and roped together. Leaving ten men to guard them, he sent another man to collect in the cut-off party. He could ill afford the ten guards, but he couldnn't bring himself to kill the captives in cold blood. Trying to overcome his lethargy, a reaction as the adrenalin, which had been coursing through his veins up to that moment, drained away, he headed back towards Loch Ranza with the rest. He had lost comparatively few men compared to the enemy; even so, his force had now been reduced to less than one hundred and fifty and some of those had flesh wounds. He only hoped they would be enough when they got back to the settlement.

~~~

Late in the afternoon Eochaid, with a sinking heart, saw another six birlinns enter the loch. His first thought was that Oswald had been fooled and that this was the rest of the Strathclyde men from Brodick. However, he then recognised the emblem on their sails as that of Domnall Brecc and breathed a sigh of relief.

The enemy obviously didn't know what to do. Their first instinct was to launch their birlinns and try to escape, but they were outnumbered and trapped in the loch. Four of the new arrivals remained near the entrance to the loch in case the attackers tried to escape, whilst the other two came in and beached near the fortress. Eochaid went out and greeted the king and together they led their men, now numbering over two hundred, towards the enemy. When the other four ships, seeing that the enemy ships had remained on the beach, came in to disgorge another two hundred and twenty warriors, the Strathclyde men quickly decided to surrender.

Thus, when Oswald eventually arrived with his exhausted men, they found that they needn't have practically killed themselves getting there. It was just as well, as they were in no condition to fight.

'Describe this leader to me, Oswald,' Domnall Brecc asked later that evening at the feast which had been hastily organised by Acha to celebrate their victory.

He frowned when Oswald had done so.

'I'm almost certain that it could be none other than Eònan, one of King Belin's cousins. He's been after a kingdom of his own for some time. He was the one who tried to invade Lorne and was defeated at the Pass of Brander. I don't suppose for one moment that Belin will grieve for long. Eònan was ambitious and resented being the son of the younger brother. He could well have tried to topple his cousin in due course, had he failed to secure a kingdom elsewhere. Some think it's Belin who was the aggressor, but I think it was only Eònan. He had been held in check by the old king, but Belin's too young and inexperienced. No, I think you have done everyone a favour by killing him.'

A little later Domnall heard someone call Oswald 'Whiteblade'.

'What's this "Whiteblade"?'

'Oh, nothing.' Oswald blushed and then explained. 'Twice now the sun has reflected off my sword as I gave the signal to attack, apparently making it seem as if it was flashing with a brilliant white light, like a halo is supposed to around the heads of our Lord and the saints. The men said it was a sign from God that we would prevail. Since the first time, when we captured this settlement, they have called me Whiteblade. They did it again today but they'll soon forget about it.'

But they didn't.

# Chapter Eight – Return to Bebbanburg

## 623 AD

Oswald was delighted when, the following December, Gytha gave birth to a son, who they called Œthelwald. He wasn't the only happy one; Acha was pleased to become a grandmother and to see that her eldest son now had an heir, though as yet, he hadn't much to inherit. Oswiu and Offa found it hard to think of themselves, at ten and eight respectively, as uncles, but perhaps the most thrilled was six year old Æbbe, who went round telling everyone proudly that she was now an aunt.

Domnall had confirmed Oswald as chieftain of the settlement in Loch Ranza, but he had installed one of his own nobles as Lord of Arran in Brodick. However, that suited Oswald for now. Connad seemed to have forgotten about him, or if he hadn't, he seemed content to let him be. Oswald and his family were living in peace and the settlement was becoming prosperous.

Most of the warriors who had sailed with him and Eochaid had elected to stay and all but a few had now married. Half of those who had been killed the previous year had been replaced by newly trained youths, including Rònan. The lad was now sixteen and had surprised everyone by marrying one of the prettiest girls in the settlement who was a year older than him. Her first husband had been killed in the battle with the men of Strathclyde and Rònan had vowed to have her as his wife as soon as the period of mourning was over.

At first she wasn't interested in a boy younger than herself who, she suspected, was still a virgin, but his persistence and the fact that he was a close friend and companion of Oswald, eventually won her over. They had married in March and he had vowed that she would give birth to a son by the end of the year. His lovemaking was no less persistent than his courting and by May his wife had morning sickness.

The only one who was discontented was Oswiu. He would soon be eleven, though he looked a year or two older and Acha had decided to ship him off to be educated on Iona this coming summer. His brothers had become novices when they were twelve, but she knew that Oswald had decided to start Oswiu's warrior training early, in view of his size and the promise he showed when practicing with Rònan. In the two years on Iona, he would learn to read and write and the gaps in his religious education would be filled. The local priest was a good man, but his knowledge of the scriptures was rudimentary. Even Oswald knew more than he did about the life of Christ.

However, something happened in early May which upset the pastoral idyll. Life had been equally uneventful in Ulster for the past year. The Uí Néill were busy fighting amongst themselves and Fiachnae mac Báetáin was getting bored; more importantly, so were his warriors.

He had met a shipmaster who claimed that there were more islands to the north of Britain where there were easy pickings. Moreover, the man had sailed up the east coast of Britain to get there. He had even beached his ship for the night near a place called Bebbanburg.

Oswald had also heard of the islands. They were called the Orcades and, along with Skye and the Outer Hebrides, they had been part of Dal Riada over a century ago. Gradually the Picts had ousted the Dal Riada Gaels and an uneasy truce had existed between the Picts and Dal Riada ever since. When he heard this, Fiachnae became doubtful in case it created problems between Dal Riada and its neighbours; however, Oswald felt that anything that upset the treacherous Connad was to be encouraged.

It was eventually agreed that Oswald and Eochaid would take the two largest of the four birlinns they now had and would accompany Fiachnae and his six ships to raid Skye, the Orcades and down the east coast of Pictland until they reached Bebbanburg. They would then attempt to take Edwin's capital before Fiachnae headed for home, whatever the outcome.

When Gytha heard of Oswald's plan, she went to Acha and both women tried to dissuade him.

'Oswald, you know that this is a madcap scheme. Fiachnae is likely to get killed and take you and his son with him. None of you knows the waters to the north, or down the east coast and I'm told that there are fierce storms which will sink even the stoutest ship.'

Oswald laughed. 'Mother, we are all experienced sailors and Fiachnae has hired the shipmaster who has already done this route as our guide. Nothing will go wrong and at best, I'll re-take Bebbanburg and kill Edwin.'

'Oswald, you are barely nineteen and think you know it all, just because you've won a few battles and managed to sire a son; something most men in the world have done. If you go, you'll do it without my blessing.'

117

Oswald's eyes narrowed. Acha had foolishly made this a contest of wills between her and her eldest son. She had lost last time and she would lose this time as well.

'Very well. I would have liked your good wishes for the success of this venture, but if that's the way you feel, there's nothing more to be said.'

'Oswald, I didn't mean-'

'Don't demean yourself by taking back your threat, mother. What's been said cannot be unsaid.'

As he left, he turned in the doorway.

'Oswiu has asked to come with me and, as this will be the last chance of a voyage for him before he leaves for Iona, I have said yes.'

Without giving his mother a chance to object, he went out of the door and closed it gently behind him.

Oswald took his birlinn and that of Eochaid, leaving the other two and their crews to defend the settlement, now called Duilleag Bán na Cille – literally, the settlement of Whiteblade. Fiachnae had brought six craft with him, so in total they had over five hundred men. Naturally, Oswiu was ecstatic to be taken along and sat in the bows watching the sea ahead of them and yelling excitedly when he spotted a pod of basking sharks.

Normally Oswald would have hunted them, as they produced oil for lights and torches and their flesh was edible if other meat was in short supply. This time, however, he ignored them and continued to follow the rest of the fleet around the Mull of Kintyre and up the coast. That night they beached the fleet on Iona. Oswald and Oswiu went in search of their brothers and found, instead of the mischievous boys they used to be, two serious young monks and an equally serious novice. Oswald enjoyed seeing his brothers again, but he was glad that Oswiu, who he now realised was his favourite brother, wanted to be a warrior like him and not a priest. He hoped that his two years on Iona wouldn't change him.

He asked to see Aidan and was disappointed when he was told that he wasn't there anymore. He was now Brother Finnian's acolyte and he was away with him somewhere in the land of the Picts, trying to convert them to Christianity. Oswald knew that the Picts were a savage race and prayed in the chapel that evening for Aidan's safety.

The next day they sailed on north past Coll, Tiree and several small islands before reaching Skye. They beached the birlinns on a deserted stretch of silver sand and camped for the night. Skye proved to be something of a disappointment. The interior looked mountainous, similar to Arran, so Oswald suspected that the settlements all lay on the coast. In the main, these were small fishing hamlets, but a few had sheep and the odd cow grazing on pastureland close by. With the crews of eight birlinns to feed, they took the livestock and what grain they could find, but left the people alive and the settlements unburned.

The only sizeable place was on the east coast of the island, a place called Port Rìgh – the port of the king. The man who called himself King of Skye lived in a hall surrounded by a palisade on a flat topped hill at the southern end of the bay, where there was anchorage for a number of fishing craft, three birlinns and two trading ships. The palisade didn't provide much of an obstacle to several hundred warriors and the King of Skye died with his men.

The Picts were a poor people; even the king's bodyguard had no body armour and only one or two had helmets, probably captured in battle to judge by the dents in them.

The king's hall didn't yield much in the way of treasure, but there were two small chests of silver and some simple pieces of jewellery which had belonged to his two wives. Fiachnae took the younger women and children they captured as slaves and sent them to the markets in Ireland in the three captured birlinns. Unfortunately, even with skeleton crews, this took away a hundred men.

The rest pushed on north to the Orcades. They discovered a small archipelago of islands with settlements similar to Skye. The main town had even less to offer in the way of plunder than Port Rìgh and after stocking up on food, they turned south along the east coast of the mainland.

They were now in what was called the German Ocean and the settlements they came across got steadily more prosperous the further south they sailed. By now it was mid-summer and Fiachnae began to talk about turning around and heading back.

'My warriors and I didn't come all this way just for a few bags of silver and a share in whatever the slaves from Skye will bring,' Oswald told him vehemently. 'I came because you dangled the bait of retaking Bebbanburg in front of me. Now you've whisked it away. You say that you're worried about the return journey, as it's taken us over two months to get this far. That's true, but it is still only July. We won't be raiding on the way home, so it'll take us a lot less time and we'll be back long before the winter storms start.'

'How dare you talk to my grandfather like that!'

Oswald was surprised to see that the outburst had come from Congal Claen, now fourteen, who sat beside Fiachnae. He no longer seemed the petulant child he had been when Oswald had first met him two years ago.

119

He had an air of confidence, almost haughtiness about him. Perhaps Eochaid's disinclination to become king after his father had a lot to do with the boy's transformation. He would now be the heir presumptive. Oswald hoped that Fiachnae was destined to live for a long time yet; he didn't think he and this arrogant puppy would get along too well.

'Hush, boy,' Fiachnae chided him. 'Oswald has a point. I did promise him that we'd have a crack at capturing this place called Bebbanburg. How much further is it?'

'Well, where we are now is called the Kingdom of Fife. Goddodin, the northernmost part of Northumbria, starts across the other side of the wide estuary you can see to the south of here. From what I remember, Bebbanburg is a day's sail further on.'

'Very well. We'll carry on for three more days, to allow for some raiding on the way.'

Oswald wasn't happy about plundering what he hoped would become his kingdom, but he supposed he could live with that if it meant driving Edwin out of his home. If they succeeded, he and his crew wouldn't be returning to Arran, but would try and rally the Northumbrian nobles to his cause. He could then send for his family once he was firmly in control; but first they had to capture the fortress on the coast. That wouldn't be easy, even with several hundred men.

He thanked Fiachnae and as he turned to leave he caught Congal's eye. The boy was staring at him intently. He could sense the pure venom in that look and despite himself, he shivered. He didn't know why the boy should hate him, but it was obvious he did. He would have to be careful; he didn't trust Congal at all; he didn't seem to be the kind of person that held his honour in high regard. He believed that Congal might stoop to something underhanded in order to harm him and for some reason, he became worried about Oswiu.

~~~

Aidan had been delighted when Ségéne mac Fiachnaíhe, the new Abbot of Iona, had agreed that he could accompany Finnian when he left Iona for the land of the Picts.

'Brother Brendan will be sorry to lose you; he says that you'll make a good healer one day. However, our primary task is to convert the heathen and Finnian thinks that you have the making of an effective missionary as well.'

'Thank you, Father Abbot. Who will be taking over from me as assistant to the infirmarian?'

Ségéne was about to chide him for his impudence in asking something that was not his concern, but he realised that Aidan was only worried that he might be leaving Brendan without a suitable apprentice to train.

'Osguid has asked to be considered and both Brother Brendan and I think that he has the interest and the ability to learn.'

He nodded, well satisfied. Osguid would make a good infirmarian in due course.

Aidan was not looking forward to the sea journey from Iona to Loch Linnhe into the north-east of Lorne, where they would start their journey through the Great Glen into the heart of the Land of the Picts. The last time he had been on a sea voyage he had been violently seasick; this time he avoided getting drunk first and he was pleasantly surprised that, far from feeling ill, he actually enjoyed it.

He knew that the Land of the Picts was a confederation of various kingdoms, some small and some nearly as large as Dal Riada. They were making for the relatively large Kingdom of Ardewr whose queen was a Christian from Lorne. She had tried, and failed, to convert her husband – King Murchadh – and the people of Ardewr still worshipped the ancient Celtic pantheon of gods. Finnian was hoping that, with Queen Genofeva's help, he and Aidan would succeed.

As they walked up the Great Glen the few people they encountered were suspicious, but they left them alone. When Finnian said that they were on their way to see Queen Genofeva, most grudgingly gave them a little food and if they were lucky, a place to sleep for the night. Aidan's language was Gaelic, but gradually he learned to make himself understood in the Brythonic language spoken by the Picts. Finnian spoke both well.

Eventually, after a month or so, they arrived at the king's hall. Although there were a significant number of huts built along the lochside, the hall itself was a big crannog built out into a long stretch of water that the locals called Loch Ness. The structure was made of timber built onto a wooden platform which was supported on piles driven into the bed of the loch. The only approach to it was along a narrow walkway, which meant that it was practically unassailable, even by boat. There was a ten feet tall palisade around the platform with a narrow gateway leading onto a jetty to which several small boats, mainly currachs, were moored. Both monks were impressed. It was a remarkable feat of engineering.

The two sentries at the shore end of the walkway crossed their spears to stop the two monks. One of them yelled something to a boy who was sitting on the walkway fishing; he immediately abandoned his crude rod, fashioned from a stick with a catgut line and ran along to the hall. A few minutes later, a man dressed as a druid came out of the door of the circular building and walked towards them, followed by the boy, who recommenced his fruitless attempt to get one of the abundant fish in the loch to take the worm speared onto the small curved bit of bone he was using as a hook.

Finnian's heart sank when he saw that he was going to have to deal with a druid. They, quite rightly, feared the Christian missionaries since, if they were successful in converting the people, the druids' power and influence was at an end.

'What do you two dogs want here?' the druid asked them belligerently.

'We have come a long way to see Queen Genofeva,' Finnian replied mildly with a smile.

This seemed to enrage the druid and he started to swear and curse them. When he had finished, Finnian was still smiling at him benignly, which enraged the man even further. Aidan looked at the two of them and started to giggle. The more annoyed the druid became, the broader Finnian smiled. Much to his surprise, one of the sentries started to grin. When the druid finished by saying that Genofeva wasn't there, the sentry contradicted him. It was evident that he didn't like the druid, because he shouted at the boy again and told him to fetch his mother. The boy, who looked to be about thirteen or fourteen, got up with a sigh and ran back to the hall.

The druid started to yell at the sentry, who gave back as good as he got. This surprised both monks, as normally the Picts respected their druids. The other sentry, who was younger, said nothing, but looked as if he wished he wasn't there.

When the boy re-appeared, he was followed by a striking looking woman and a man dressed in a fine woollen tunic dyed crimson who wore a sword at his waist. The woman's dress was a shade of mid-blue that matched her eyes and as soon as they saw the gold crucifix around her neck, they knew that this was the queen. Both monks and the two sentries bowed low at her approach.

'Why did you say I wasn't here, Uisdean?' she demanded abruptly, ignoring everyone else.

'I didn't think you wanted to be troubled by these itinerant beggars, Lady,' he replied dismissively.

'Well, you were wrong, as you so often are.'

She turned to Finnian and Aidan with a smile that lit up her face. Unlike the swarthy dark-haired Picts, Genofeva was blonde haired and had a fair complexion. Aidan realised with a start that the boy, who had abandoned his fishing and followed the queen, looked like her, although his hair was more of a bronze colour and his complexion was also slightly darker. He had to be her son.

'Welcome to Crannog Ness. It's been a long time since I had the pleasure of entertaining members of my own faith. I'm Genofeva, this is my husband's brother, Sionn and this little brat is my eldest son, Ròidh.'

Finnian nodded to both and the boy gave him a cheeky grin as they were introduced. Then the monk explained who they were and what they were doing in Ardewr. When he said that they were there to spread the word of the one and only true God, Uisdean hawked and spat at their feet before cursing them again.

'That's enough, Uisdean. Don't let us detain you. I'm sure you must have something useful to be doing, though I can't imagine what.'

The druid glared at her before rudely pushing past the two monks and going into the settlement.

'I suppose his reaction is natural; he's afraid that you will succeed in converting my husband, King Murchadh. I've been working on him for a long time and he's not as opposed to the idea as he once was.' She smiled at Sionn and Ròidh. 'Both of these two are ready to accept Christ as their saviour, but there has been no-one to baptise them, which is one of the reasons I'm so glad to see you two.'

Murchadh had returned from hunting in a good humour, having killed a boar, two hinds and a stag over the past two days. His mood soon changed, however, when Uisdean rushed up to him and whispered in his ear. He strode purposefully along the walkway and burst into the hall. His wife sat with an elderly monk on one side of her and a much younger one, scarcely more than a boy, on the other. His brother sat next to the older monk and his son was talking animatedly to the young one.

Their conversations ceased abruptly when he burst in, glaring at the five of them, whilst Uisdean stood, looking smug, at his elbow. Before he could say anything, Genofeva rose to her feet and went to greet him with a kiss.

'Did you have good hunting, husband? We are fortunate to have guests for a while; this is Brother Finnian and Brother Aidan, who have walked all the way from Iona to visit us.'

'They walked over the sea then, did they, like your Christ is supposed to have done?' Murchadh laughed uproariously at his own joke and the rest dutifully joined in, all except Uisdean, who seemed quite upset at the king' change of mood.

'With your permission, they will baptise Sionn and Ròidh in the loch tomorrow.'

'If that's what they want, then I'm not going to interfere.' He paused and then rounded on the druid.

'It's no good scowling like that, Uisdean. You look like a spoilt child. I've told you before, I have an open mind about this new faith. It's spreading and the old religion is shrinking. There must be a good reason for that.' He drew a deep breath before continuing. 'You told me that my wife had brought lepers and beggars into my hall, but you lied. How much else of what you say is lies? Tomorrow, before the baptism ceremony, I will hear what you and these two monks have to say. If I believe them, then I will join my brother and son and be baptised, too. If they fail to convince me and I side with you and your fellow druids, they will be driven out of here and there will be no baptisms.'

Aidan didn't sleep well, worrying about the morrow, but Finnian snored away as if he didn't have a care in the world. The next day was dank and dismal. Low clouds obscured the tops of the hills on both sides of the loch and a fine drizzle made the loch look dark and forbidding. Finnian and Aidan made their way along the walkway to the hall from the small hut they had been allocated in the settlement. Uisdean and five other druids were already there, but there was no sign of the king and his family. Slowly a number of warriors and men who looked as if they might be members of the king's council drifted in, shook their damp cloaks in front of the fire in the central hearth and stood around talking.

Aidan, having nothing better to do, studied the way the hall was constructed. The walls were made of wickerwork panels pegged to short upright posts which appeared to be the tops of the piles driven into the loch bed. Other, much taller, posts were arranged in the shape of an octagon around the central hearth.

The roof supports were also tree trunks, which were secured to the wall posts and the tops of the central posts forming the octagon. They protruded to the centre of the roof, where the ends were secured to a ring made from thin saplings tied together. This central hole allowed the smoke – or most of it – to escape. A shallow conical structure was fastened to upright posts a foot high tied to the ring of saplings in an effort to keep the rain out whilst letting the smoke escape, in which it was only partially successful. Aidan presumed that it worked better if the wind blew to draw the smoke upwards, which it wasn't doing that day. Consequently, there was a blue, smoky haze in the hall.

The leather curtain which hung in front of a screened off section of the hall was suddenly pulled aside and the king and queen entered the main body of the hall before taking their places on two chairs set on a slightly raised dais. Sionn and Ròidh went and stood on either side of the dais and a slave came in cradling an infant in her arms and accompanied by a six year old boy who looked like Ròidh. These were obviously Murchadh's other two sons and Aidan wondered whether they too would be baptised today if Finnian was successful.

Uisdean started by reminding everyone about the heroes of Celtic legend such as Bran and Cu Chullain and the pantheon which they and their forebears had believed in for centuries. He went on to describe the joys of the afterlife in the Otherworld when they died and warned them that they risked being cast into the outer darkness if they failed to believe.

It was unfortunate that Murchadh's baby son interspersed the oratory with lusty cries and eventually wails of distress. Others also felt like crying out, but from boredom not because they were hungry. Uisdean spoke for so long, telling everyone what they were already all too familiar with that even his fellow druids grew impatient. When Murchadh yawned long and loudly, Uisdean took the hint and drew his speech to a lingering conclusion.

By now the mist had cleared and Loch Ness was bathed in sunshine with scarcely a cloud in the sky. Finnian therefore suggested that they leave the smoke filled hall and go outside. They re-convened by the shore of the loch south of the settlement and four slaves produced chairs from one of the huts for the king and queen to sit on.

'What Uisdean has told us at such great length undoubtedly has its basis in fact.' Finnian began. 'No doubt Cu Chulainn did battle his foes on the island of Labraid and win, but the trouble with sagas and stories passed down by word of mouth is that each bard tries to outdo the last person to tell the tale and what were feats of valour become embellished until the heroes become deities and their powers magical.'

At this point Aidan passed Finnian a Bible produced on Iona, with beautiful calligraphy and illustrated capitals. He held this up, opened at the beginning of the Gospel according to Saint Mark.

'This is the word of God, the one and only true God and of Jesus Christ his only begotten son. This was copied without embellishment or alteration of any kind from an original held in the monastery on the Isle of Iona. This gospel was written by Mark at the dictation of Saint Peter, who was Christ's greatest friend and disciple. We therefore know that it has not been exaggerated over the centuries, since the events it speaks about actually happened.'

He then changed tack and tried to relate the beliefs they grew up with to those of Christians.

'What you call the *Otherworld* we Christians call *Heaven*, but that is reserved for those who lead a good life; that is, those who are men and women of honour. Those who lead evil lives will burn in Hell and suffer for all eternity.'

This made several of his audience glance about uncomfortably.

'However, for all those who truly repent and mend their ways, God is forgiving and will absolve you from your previous sins.'

The relief amongst his listeners was almost palpable. Finnian then went on to explain about Christ's message to the world, the miracles he performed and the ultimate sacrifice he made by being crucified.

Unlike Uisdean's bored audience, the Picts hung on his every word and Aidan realised what a great orator his mentor was. He vowed there and then that he would strive to emulate him. It wasn't enough to believe in Christ and to know the scriptures; you had to fire those you sought to convert with unbridled enthusiasm for the Faith and carry people with you.

That afternoon the two monks baptised, not just Sionn and Ròidh, but Murchadh and over half his people as well.

~~~

Oswald and Oswiu stood in the bows of the Holy Saviour and gazed at their birthplace across the two miles of sea that separated them. Oswald had forgotten how impregnable it looked. It stood on an outcrop of basalt rock that dominated the land on three sides, with the sea on the fourth. The top of the outcrop sloped down to the north and south and steep paths ascended to the two gateways set into the tall palisade that ran around the wooden buildings inside. In the centre was a tall tower from which a sentry kept watch.

The fleet beached their birlinns to the south of Bebbanburg. That evening, whilst the men ate and drank, Oswald, Eochaid and Fiachnae sat

126

and discussed what to do. Congal Claen came and joined them uninvited, much to the annoyance of Oswald and his friend, but as the king said nothing, they didn't feel that they could object.

'How do you propose to attack that place? It looks bloody impregnable,' the king asked, clearly annoyed. He thought that he'd been brought on a fool's errand.

'I told you that you were wasting your time coming this far south, Grandfather. We should have headed home days ago,' Congal added, earning him a glare from Oswald and his uncle.

'We have more men than Edwin has here,' Oswald pointed out. 'If we start to plunder the local area he'll be forced to come out and fight us.'

'How many men will he have in Bebbanburg and the surrounding area?'

'No more than fifty in the fortress and perhaps another two hundred within a day's ride.'

'Very well. We'll plunder the area for two days. If he hasn't come out to fight by then, we leave and sail home,' Fiachnae decided.

'But Grandfather,' Congal started to object.

'Quiet, boy. I've made my decision. You shame me by querying it.'

Congal looked mutinous and glared at Oswald, but he held his tongue.

Raiding around the local area produced some worthwhile plunder and a few slaves. Oswald hated doing this to his own people, but agreed to give up his share of what they had looted in Northumbria in return for the release of the slaves. It salved his conscience, but his crew wasn't happy with the loss of their share.

Edwin stayed secure inside Bebbanburg's defences and didn't attempt to interfere with them, so from Oswald's perspective, returning there had been a disaster. Word would get about that he had been with the raiders and that would make it difficult for him to return in the future. When they sailed away, he was depressed and nothing Oswiu or anyone else could say lifted him out of his dejection.

# Chapter Nine – Dùn Add and the Land of the Picts

## 626 AD

After the debacle at Bebbanburg, Oswald was content to remain on Arran and he settled down to develop his community at Duilleag Bán na Cille. Oswiu had been shipped off to Iona soon after he had returned and Oswald was surprised by how much he missed his brother's company.

Eochaid had also left after a year to return to Ulster at the request of his father. One of the branches of the Ulaidh – the Dál Fiatach – had renounced their allegiance to Fiachnae and had elected their own king. The cause of the rift had been Congal Claen, who had taken a fancy to a girl of the Dál Fiatach and, when she had refused his advances, he had abducted and raped her. Inevitably, war broke out between the two branches of the Ulaidh, the Dál nAraidi being the one that Fiachnae, Congal and Eochaid belonged to.

The internecine warfare amongst the Ulaidh should have given the Uí Néill the opportunity to seize all of Ulster, but they were still fighting amongst themselves as well. Eochaid didn't want to leave Oswald after the many years that they had been close friends, almost brothers, really, but he felt that he had a duty to aid his father and sailed in the Gift of God with those warriors who were single and wanted their chance at glory. Oswald watched the birlinn sail down the loch and didn't turn away until it had disappeared from view.

He was glad that Rònan was still with him. With Alaric, he was his closest friend now. The Pict was no longer a boy; he came home to find out that he was the father of a baby girl and a year later his wife presented him with a son.

By the time that Oswiu, now thirteen, returned in 625 AD, Oswald thought that he had resigned himself to living his life out on Arran, but Oswiu brought news that changed everything. Domnall Brecc had fallen out with Connad again and this time it was serious. Fergus of Islay had sided with Domnall and Brennus, King of Lorne, was trying to mediate. Oswald was tempted to stay out of the dispute, until Oswiu told him that one of the charges that Connad had made was that Domnall was harbouring fugitives from his justice, namely Oswald and his family. Apparently Oswald and Acha were accused of plotting to kill Connad.

Oswald now had no choice; he prepared the Holy Saviour and the Seraphim. Oswiu was still too young to be a warrior and, in any case, he hadn't yet started his training, so Oswald offered to take him as a ship's boy again. He could see that Oswiu was disappointed, but he nodded. At least he'd be the senior this time, as the other two boys were eleven and twelve.

He had no trouble filling both ships with warriors, but he made sure that he left enough behind to man the fort adequately. There had been no more attacks on Arran from Strathclyde, but a war within Dal Riada might tempt Belin to expand his territory. He left Alaric behind this time as his deputy. He'd been training Rònan to be a helmsman; he would now take his place on the Holy Saviour.

Gytha couldn't keep the tears from her eyes when Oswald said farewell to his family. She was now expecting their second child and Œthelwald, now three, joined in weeping because his mother was upset. Acha gave them a look of scorn and bade her sons come back safely without emotion. Both twelve year old Offa and his ten year old sister managed to remain equally stoic. Perhaps Oswald wouldn't have been so keen to escape from the emotional leave-taking had he known that it would be the last time he would see Gytha.

In August 625, the two birlinns rowed down Loch Ranza and then hoisted their sails as they turned to run down the Kintyre peninsula to Dùn Averty. Oswald found his mood improving as the sea breeze invigorated him. Life with Gytha was very pleasant and he loved his son but, if he was honest, he had missed the adventure and the danger of life as a warrior.

~~~

Aidan had stayed at Loch Ness with Finnian after the mass baptism, whilst a messenger was sent to Iona to ask for a bishop and priests to carry on their work. Finnian was anxious to press on north- eastwards to the end of the Great Glen and then eastwards into the adjacent kingdom of Pentir. However, tragedy struck before the new bishop could arrive.

Uisdean had never accepted his king's conversion to Christianity. He believed that it was a phase and that eventually he'd return to the old religion. The chief druid did everything he could to undermine Finnian and Aidan until eventually Murchadh threatened to exile him and his fellow druids. He would have done so long since but a third of his people had stuck with the old religion and they would oppose any attempt to get rid of their priests.

Finnian had asked Murchadh for his help in building a church for his congregation to worship in. This had incensed the druids, who worshipped in the open at a sacred grove. Uisdean had arrived at the chosen site as work on the small church started and remonstrated with Finnian and Aidan. Both monks remained calm but the chief druid got more and more angry, not helped by the unruffled way in which Finnian responded to his increasing rage. Finally, Uisdean lost control and pulling out the sacrificial knife he used to kill animals on the altar in the sacred grove, he plunged it into Finnian's chest.

It slipped between two ribs and pierced his heart, killing him instantly. As Finnian collapsed, Aidan caught him in his arms, crying out in horror. That saved him, as Uisdean was intent on killing him, too, but he couldn't stab him with Finnian's body in the way.

Before Uisdean could do any more damage, Sionn drew his sword and would have killed him there and then but Ròidh, who had been standing by his side, barrelled into him, knocking the much larger priest off his feet and began to pummel his face. By the time Ròidh was dragged off him, he had broken Uisdean's nose in two places and knocked out several teeth. The druid's face was covered in blood and one of his eyes had been so severely damaged that he could no longer see out of it.

'I'm glad I've never annoyed you,' his uncle told him as two men hauled him, still struggling and spitting in fury, off the cowering druid. 'You'll make a fine warrior one day, Ròidh.'

The boy's answer, when he'd calmed down, surprised him.

'I don't want to be a warrior; I want to be a monk like Finnian and Aidan.'

'But you are my brother's heir.'

'He has other sons. Ardewr won't lack for kings, or warriors either, but it does need monks to spread the word of God. No-one else knows yet, but I planned to go with Finnian and Aidan when they left. Now Aidan will need a companion and assistant more than ever,' he said sadly.

'I think you had better talk to your parents, or were you planning to sneak away?'

'Of course not!' the boy retorted, affronted that his uncle thought he might. 'But I was going to wait until the new bishop got here first.'

The murder of Finnian, who was much respected, even by those who were still pagans, had shocked everyone. They were used to violence and sudden death, but the murder of an unarmed man was not to be tolerated. Uisdean was tied up and held prisoner overnight. His fellow druids were confined to their hut with guards outside, just in case they tried something.

The next day Uisdean was dragged before the king for judgement. The pasting that Ròidh had given his face was now much more evident. His damaged eye was completely closed up and had turned various shades of blue and purple. His face, now cleaned of blood, was badly swollen and when he opened his mouth, the front teeth were noticeably absent.

'Do you have anything to say for yourself, Uisdean, before I pass sentence?'

'You cannot try me; I am a druid and your high priest. I demand to be tried by my fellow druids. They will support me in ridding this land of this follower of the false gods.'

'Do you intend to kill me too, as I am also a follower of the Christ? And my son, wife and brother and the majority of the people of this settlement?'

'No, of course not, Lord King. Without the lies of the monk Finnian you will all return to the true faith. My only regret is that I didn't kill the young monk, too.'

'You are condemned out of your own mouth. My decision is that you will be taken out into the loch, tied in chains and thrown into the waters. Let your gods save you if they can.'

The roar of approval that greeted this pronouncement left Uisdean in no doubt of the lack of support he now had. He didn't struggle when he was shackled and pushed into a currach. At least he could die with dignity. He had no illusions that somehow he would survive the punishment.

On the day after Finnian was buried under where the altar would be placed in the church, Aidan was surprised when there was a crowd of people outside his hut asking to be baptised. Over the coming days more people came to join the Christian faith until there were only a handful left who hadn't converted to Christianity. Even a couple of the younger druids had come to discuss religion with him and had eventually been baptised. The other three left Ardewr and were not seen again. It was rumoured that they had journeyed north into the Kingdom of Caith.

Aidan and Ròidh became close friends and the boy spent most of his time with the young monk. Often they went off fishing together, if they weren't busy helping build the church or ministering to the people. After a while Ròidh announced flatly that he would be leaving with him when Aidan moved on to Pentir.

'What makes you think I'm going to Pentir? Come to that, why do you think that your parents would let you come with me?'

'You are, aren't you? As soon as the bishop arrives, I mean. My parents won't stop me. I turned fourteen this summer and I should've started to train as a warrior, but I refused. They know I want to become a monk like you and Finnian. They weren't happy about it at first, but they know I've made my mind up. Since I attacked Uisdean, which I now know was wrong of me, my father has seen me in a new light. I am no longer a boy in his eyes, but a man and able to make my own decisions. My mother is less reconciled to the idea, but she'll accept it in time.'

'I see. Well, if you're sure, I can't think of anyone I'd rather have with me as a companion. However, you'll have to travel to Iona to serve your noviciate before you can become a monk, if that's what you want.'

'Will you be going back to Iona?'

'At some stage, yes, I suppose so, but not until my mission in Pentir is over.'

'Well then, I can wait until then, can't I?'

Two weeks after that the new Bishop of Ardewr arrived with three priests. He was a kindly, if somewhat elderly, man with a wicked sense of humour and Aidan knew instinctively that he was right for the task in hand. He and Murchadh got on well together from the start and Aidan prepared to leave. He waited until the bishop had consecrated the newly completed church and then spent the night there, keeping a vigil by Finnian's grave, before he and Ròidh set out early the next morning, travelling north-east up the Great Glen towards the mouth of the River Ness and the border with Pentir. Neither had said goodbye. Both wanted to avoid the emotional scene that it would entail; besides, they would return one day on their way back to Iona.

~~~

When they got to Dùn Averty they found that Domnall Brecc had already left, so Oswald continued on around the Mull of Kintyre and headed north-west towards Islay. He was impressed when they sailed into the broad bay in front of the king's hall. There were fourteen birlinns and several currachs drawn up on the shore. The latter were really little more than large fishing boats which could hold a dozen men, at best.

Although some of the birlinns were quite small, perhaps only ten oars a side, it meant that King Fergus was hosting some seven hundred warriors or more. He had been told that Dal Riada was able to field some fifteen hundred men in total, but that would include those needed to guard the settlements dotted around the mainland and the isles. He therefore suspected that the force the three kings had assembled probably outnumbered the number of warriors the High King – Connad – could muster.

However, although it was comforting to know that his side was superior in terms of manpower, Oswald worried that any battle between the two factions could seriously, perhaps fatally, wound Dal Riada as a whole. Normally, the Ulaidh could be counted amongst the warriors of Dal Riada, but now they were as divided as those in Caledonia.

He had got used to the epithet *Whiteblade*, but it still came as something of a shock when hundreds of voices yelled it out in acclamation when he walked into the overcrowded hall. That night he voiced his concerns. He was listened to, but the night was devoted to feasting and drinking and it wasn't the time for a strategic discussion.

It wasn't until the following afternoon that the three kings and other leaders present felt well – or sober – enough to discuss how they were going to remove Connad from the throne. He personally controlled the area south of O Ban in Lorne to the northern end of the Kintyre peninsula.

Connad was said to have improved the fortifications of Dùn Add and planned to defend it with the hundreds of men he had mustered.

'When I was last there it couldn't have held more than a hundred warriors and even that would mean expelling all the non-combatants,' Oswald observed.

'What Whiteblade says is true,' Brennus of Lorne said. 'However, since then Connad has built another palisade around the Dùn and it can probably now hold four hundred men.'

'What about supplies?' Domnall asked. 'For how long could they hold out?'

'We can't afford a long siege, Domnall,' Brennus stated. 'I'm already nervous that I haven't left enough men behind to defend the Pass of Brander.'

'Connad isn't exactly a popular king,' Oswald pointed out. 'Perhaps we can persuade many of his men to remain neutral when we attack.'

'And how exactly do you propose to do that, Whiteblade?' Brennus sneered.

'By getting inside the fortress and talking to his men,' Oswald replied calmly, refusing to take offence.

'Who would be foolish enough to risk their life by doing that?' Fergus asked sceptically.

'Over half my crew originally came from Dùn Add and they've still got family there. They would risk much to prevent senseless bloodshed just to keep a tyrant on the throne. I will ask for volunteers to sneak into the fortress.'

'And who would lead them on such a madcap adventure?'

'I will.'

~~~

Aidan and Ròidh got up after a wet night under a tree and ate the rest of the trout that Ròidh had caught the previous evening by what he had termed 'tickling' them. This consisted of waiting patiently until he could get his hand under one and flipping it onto the bank. He had caught four that way, two of which they'd eaten the previous night with some hard bread they'd brought with them, and two the following morning to break their fast. They still had some cheese left, but Ròidh said that, as they had just passed the end of the loch and were now walking along the river, it should only be a few more miles, according to those who had been there, before they reached the sea. In contrast to the previous evening, the weather was sunny and hot and their clothes steamed slightly as they slowly dried out.

The landscape when they got to the coast was not what Aidan was hoping for. Ròidh had never seen the sea before and was initially disappointed by the meagre expanse of water. It wasn't what Aidan was expecting, either. Later, they discovered that what they were looking at was an inlet about twice the width of the loch they had just left behind and that, as this went eastwards, it expanded into the Moray Firth before it joined the German Ocean.

There was a small settlement at the junction of the firth and the river they were following. As they approached, about twenty men and youths appeared, brandishing spears, daggers and axes more suited to chopping firewood than cleaving an enemy in two. Aidan was nonplussed; previously when they had encountered a hostile reception, Finnian had calmed the situation and charmed the inhabitants into giving him a hearing. Aidan found that he opened his mouth, but he just couldn't think of what to say.

Luckily Ròidh wasn't so tongue-tied and introduced himself as the eldest son of the king of the neighbouring Picts. He went on to explain, as weapons were lowered, that Aidan had been entrusted by his father with the task of journeying to see their king, Necton and asked with a smile if they might stay the night and purchase a small quantity of food.

'Prince Ròidh, you and your friend are more than welcome to stay here. My son has room in his hut for your friend and I would be honoured if you would stay with me and my wife.'

That put him and Aidan in a difficult position. To refuse his offer would be the height of rudeness, but they didn't know these people. They might be trying to separate them in order to overpower them more easily.

'You are very kind to offer us such hospitality, but we wouldn't want to put you to the trouble. I can see an upturned boat over there which you are repairing. That will provide sufficient shelter for our needs, but we would be grateful if we could purchase some fish and bread from you.'

The headman looked put out, but he nodded.

'I think it would be more suitable to offer King Murchadh's son a better place to rest your head, but if that is your wish…. However, you will both join us for a feast in your honour tonight, I hope?'

'We would be delighted to. Thank you,' Ròidh said quickly, in case Aidan was about to decline.

The next day they set out later than they had intended with sore heads and bloated stomachs. Aidan felt a little guilty about eating so much food as the inhabitants were evidently poor, but Ròidh said that their visit would be talked about for ages and they would be devastated if he thought that they couldn't afford to lay on such a feast.

'How far is it to King Necton's hall?' Ròidh had asked the settlement headman before they left.

He looked at the other men helplessly.

'I'm sorry, Prince Ròidh, but none of us have been there, nor have we ever met anyone who has. All we know is that it is inland and I presume it is some distance away; perhaps many days' walk.'

That contradicted what they had been told previously. Murchadh had been certain that it lay on the coast. Both Ròidh and Aidan thought that they would rather rely on the king's knowledge than the vague thoughts of people who had never been further from their home than a few miles out to sea.

'Thank you for your help yesterday,' Aidan said as soon as the pair were out of sight of the settlement. 'Although I have seen Brother Finnian charm his way into people's hearts so many times, I fear I lack the skill myself.'

Ròidh smiled at his companion. 'You just need confidence in yourself. Next time I'll hang back and let you do the talking.'

'Oh!' Aidan was about to object when he realised that Ròidh was right. He mustn't depend on the boy's father's status if he was to have any chance of success as a missionary. The boy was meant to be his assistant, not the other way around.

'You're right, of course. I'll do the talking next time.'

Although Aidan was the older by eight years, he'd tended to defer to his young friend because of his royal status. Now he realised that that wasn't appropriate. He would have to think of Ròidh as a potential novice monk, nothing more. It wouldn't help Ròidh if and when they arrived back on Iona if he was anything more than Aidan's assistant. There were other monks and novices with royal blood in their veins and they were treated no differently to anyone else. As monks, the king's son was regarded for his piety and usefulness to the monastery, the same as the fisherman's son.

Aidan therefore began to teach Ròidh to speak and then read and write in Latin. The two were already helping each other to improve their skill in each other's languages, but that exchange of knowledge put them on an equal footing. Teaching Latin and improving the boy's knowledge of the scriptures, as well as being older, established Aidan as the senior of the two, despite Ròidh's upbringing and natural tendency to take charge.

'Good evening, I'm Brother Aidan from the Holy Island of Iona and this is my assistant, Ròidh. We would be grateful if you could offer us hospitality for the night. In return, I bring news of the outside world and will tell you of the miracles performed by our saviour Jesus Christ,' he began, when confronted by the suspicious inhabitants at the next settlement.

One of the boys picked up a stone and threw it at Aidan. With a great deal of luck, Ròidh managed to catch the stone, which must have stung his hand, but, if so, he gave no sign. He hefted it in his hand and made as if to throw the stone back at the boy, who ducked nervously. Ròidh dropped the stone and smiled and the inhabitants laughed. It broke the ice and they spent another comfortable night.

This time there was no feast, but they joined the headman and his family, which included the humbled stone thrower, for a modest meal of fish and bread washed down with a particularly nice mead made from the product of bees kept to produce honey for the settlement. It was the first time Aidan has seen wild bees kept and used in this way and he decided to suggest it to the abbot when he returned to Iona.

Aidan told the sceptical family about the life of Christ in the Brythonic tongue, with occasional help with unfamiliar words from Ròidh, and told them about a few of the parables and miracles from the beautifully illustrated Bible he had inherited from Finnian. This often necessitated a translation from Latin into Gaelic and then into the version of Brythonic spoken by the Picts, but the listeners didn't seem to mind. There were no druids locally and the deities they prayed to were those that they believed controlled the sea, the weather and the abundance of fish in the sea.

Aidan deliberated whether to spend longer at the settlement, but there were too few people there to make it worth his while to devote the time necessary to turn them into Christians. His task was to convert the king and establish a base upon which others could build. Nevertheless, he felt guilty about leaving behind the headman and his family with their interest unsatisfied. They hadn't gone far, following the ill-defined path along the coast, when they heard the sounds of pursuit. Fearing for their safety, they hid in the undergrowth and were amazed to see Varar, the headman's second son, hurtle passed them, looking for all the world as if he was intent on catching them up.

The previous evening all of them had been interested in what Aidan had to say, but Varar was the most spellbound and the one who asked the most questions.

'Varar, where are you going?' Aidan called after him and he and Ròidh stepped out on the track.

'Oh, there you are. I was frightened that I had taken the wrong track and I'd missed you.'

'So you were chasing after us. Why?'

'Because I want to hear more about this magical god called Christ. My father has agreed that I can travel with you to the king's hall and then return to my settlement to tell them what I have learned.'

Aidan thought quickly and could see no reason not to do as the boy asked. As they would be returning that way on their way back to Iona, he decided that he would be happier if Varar wasn't left to fend for himself, as he would be if he sent him back now on his own.

He was roughly the same age as Ròidh and the two quickly became friends, despite their very different social standing. They continued along the coast and usually found a fishing hamlet at which to spend the night. As Varar was the son of the headman of a settlement like those they stayed at, he helped allay the suspicions of the people along the way.

137

Aidan continued to preach as he went, gaining in confidence all the while. Occasionally they would encounter local pagan priests at these settlements, but they weren't either clever or well-educated and Aidan, or even the two boys, could in time defeat them in debate. Of course, this didn't endear them to the priests and more than once they were threatened physically.

On one occasion Aidan was knocked to the ground as he repeatedly demolished the so-called evidence the priest produced for the existence of his false gods. Ròidh immediately went to stand over Aidan to protect him from further blows and to threaten the priest, but Varar rounded on the headman and accused the priest of dragging the headman's honour in the dust by violating the laws of hospitality. Picts took their honour very seriously and the headman had the priest forcibly ejected from the circle in which the settlement elders sat. He apologised but Aidan assured him that he had nothing to apologise for.

Later that night, the priest, whose name was Cenioch, had crept into the hut which had been allocated to the three travellers, and went to stab the blanket-covered bodies as they slept. When he pulled back the covers from the first body he found a sack of wool underneath. The headman then entered the hut, followed by Aidan and the boys. Varar had kept watch on the priest's hut and had gone to summon the headman and the others when he saw him make for the guest hut.

The man was confined until he could be tried and then Aidan spoke eloquently in his defence. He told them of Christ's pronouncements about forgiveness and the man was allowed to leave the settlement after being sentenced to banishment for life. His wife and baby son were given to another man and he was escorted five miles inland to make sure he didn't try to follow Aidan when he left the next day.

The rest of the journey to King Necton's capital was comparatively uneventful. However, when they arrived at Elgin, situated at the confluence of the Spey and Findhorn Rivers five miles inland from the coast, the three got a shock. When they were shown into the king's hall, there, standing next to Necton's throne, were two priests, one of who was Cenioch, the man who had tried to kill them two weeks previously.

~~~

Oswald made his way carefully down the coast from Loch Melfort, where he and his three companions had landed, towards Dùn Add, some ten miles to the south. He had chosen Rònan, Alaric and a man called

Fáelán, who had been born in the settlement of Dùn Add and who had been in his crew since the beginning. Fáelán had quite a few kinfolk still living in the settlement so Oswald hoped that they would help him.

They reached Dùn Add at twilight, when there was just enough light for him to see the outer circular earthworks and palisade that Connad had constructed, both to improve the fort's defences and to accommodate a lot more warriors inside.

However, it seemed that most chose to sleep with their wives and families in the settlement, as several hundred left the fort a few minutes later and made their way to the scattered huts to the south and west of the fortress. As the last group exchanged ribald comments with those left on watch, the gates slammed shut. It seemed that Connad had no inkling that the three rebellious sub-kings had anchored their fleet only ten miles away.

Oswald was disappointed to see that, in an act of petty revenge, Connad had demolished the hut that he and Rònan had built. His mother's hut was still there, but another family now lived in it. Thankfully, Fáelán's family were delighted to see him again. He had been little more than a youth when he left and he had settled down on Arran and married a local girl. He had two daughters, one only newly-born and so they all had a lot of catching up to do.

After they had eaten, Oswald, Rònan and Alaric left them to carry on talking and went to reconnoitre the new defences. Whoever had designed them didn't know his trade. The ditch offered more opportunity to approach unseen than it hindered an assault. It ran close to some bushes which Connad had neglected to clear away and, once in the ditch, attackers moving quietly on a dark night should be able to travel along it undetected.

The palisade had been built on the bank thrown up by the men who had dug the ditch, but they hadn't compacted the soil enough and so the palisade wasn't as firmly anchored into the ground as it should have been. Furthermore, it had been set a foot back from the top of the earthworks and, as it was only ten feet tall, two men standing on the narrow ledge below it could lift a third man up enough so that he could pull himself over the top.

They froze as a sentry walked past along the parapet and then made their way back to Fáelán's hut.

'It should be an easy matter to scale or pull down the outer palisade and capture the outer defences,' Oswald told everyone. 'However, that still leaves the original palisade and the hall within.'

'Connad has also improved that,' Fáelán's father told them. 'There are four towers, one by the gate and three around the perimeter. They are manned by archers all day and they have a clear view from the top into the outer area and beyond.'

'Then we must attack on a dark night,' Oswald told them. 'My main worry is the warriors in the settlement. We daren't be caught between them and the defenders of the Dùn.'

'Leave them to us,' Fáelán told him. 'I've already discussed it with my father and uncles. We'll talk to all those we feel we can trust tomorrow and persuade them to keep anyone loyal to Connad from interfering. Mind you, I suspect that, given the right circumstances, few would side with him. He's unpopular, but people are scared of upsetting him. If they feel that he is about to be toppled, they'll be quick enough to join the winning side.'

'I hope you're right. We'll leave here before first light tomorrow and schedule our attack for two nights hence. Will that give you enough time?'

'Yes, that gives us to two days and one night to prepare everyone; it should be more than enough.'

~~~

Aidan looked at Cenioch warily and clasped his stout stick so firmly that his knuckles were white. The pagan priest had chosen a sword as his weapon and stood leering at Aidan like a buzzard about to rip its beak into a juicy piece of carrion. Cenioch had obviously predisposed Necton towards his version of events and Aidan suspected that he would have been executed without a fair trial had it not been for the two boys. As one was the son of a king who was an ally and the other the son of a local headman, their word carried more weight than would normally have been the case for underage boys.

The other priest had, of course, supported Cenioch, as did many of the warriors present. Necton was in a difficult position. He didn't want to upset the boys' fathers – and if he executed Aidan, he would probably have to dispose of them, as well, or they would cause trouble – but he needed to keep his own people happy. In the end he decided on a fight to the death, in the belief that the gods – or the one true God, as Aidan and his acolytes insisted on – would protect the one who was telling the truth.

140

'Let me fight for you,' Ròidh insisted. 'At least I've had some training in how to use weapons; you haven't. Neither has Varar, nor Cenioch, come to that.'

'No, I'm the one who is accused. God and his Son, Jesus Christ, will protect me.'

After a cloudless night the day dawned cold, but it soon grew unseasonably warm for October. Just before the sun reached its zenith, the accused and his accuser took their places inside the ring of warriors. The men all carried spears or swords with which to prod an unwilling combatant back into the fight, if one backed off too far. When King Necton gave the signal, the men started to cheer and the two boys watched helplessly as Aidan just stood there, clutching the wooden cross suspended from a leather thong around his neck in one hand and his staff in the other, and gazing skywards as if for heavenly inspiration.

Cenioch moved towards him cautiously. If he had rushed at him, Aidan would have been dead, but the pagan suspected a trap. Then suddenly, he and all the men watching the fight became aware that the sky was getting darker and a shadow started to pass over the ground. They looked up expecting to see a solitary cloud, but instead it looked as if something was swallowing up the sun. Everyone wailed in terror, thinking that the end of the world had come; even Ròidh and Varar were terrified, but Aidan called to them that it was just a solar eclipse and nothing to worry about.

He strode towards the cowering Cenioch and knocked the sword out of his hand with his staff as the world faded into blackness. As he brought the solid length of wood down on the priest's head, knocking him senseless, the moon started to move away from the sun and the world gradually grew lighter again. Even when the sun was fully revealed once more, everyone was still in a state of shock. They clearly believed that the Christian God had been responsible for coming to Aidan's rescue. Both Ròidh and Varar looked at him in awe.

'Did you make that happen, Brother Aidan?' Ròidh asked in a voice that was barely a whisper.

Aidan chuckled. 'No, of course not. It's a natural occurrence that happens every so often. It's called an eclipse. I read about them on Iona and Finnian once told me that he had been trying to convert a settlement in Ireland when it happened some time ago, though he said that was a partial eclipse and so not as impressive. I saw the moon approaching the sun and prayed that it would be an eclipse, so I was expecting it.'

Gradually everyone recovered their self-confidence. The king was one of the first and seemed annoyed that he had been seen to be afraid of the sudden darkness.

'You must kill Cenioch,' Necton told him, kicking the unconscious body in the ribs. 'It's our law that a fight to the death means exactly that.'

'And it is God's law that thou shalt not kill,' Aidan told him. 'God's law overrides whatever law man makes.'

'That's ridiculous; men are killed by other men all the time. What sort of a god would forbid killing? Our enemies would wipe us out!'

'God's law means that you must not kill unless it is absolutely essential to save life. But executing Cenioch is not an act of self-defence. It would be an act of wanton murder.'

'Very well. I respect the fact that your religion doesn't allow you to do so, but mine expects it,' and he gestured to one of his bodyguards, who immediately thrust a spear into the comatose priest.

'He has shamed me. I believed him and not you, but you have proven him to be a liar. No-one does that to me and lives.'

He looked Aidan up and down and seemed to reach a decision.

'You say that Murchadh and his people have converted to this new faith? I suspect that it's all because of that wife of his. He always was a fool for a pretty face. It seems to me that your god of love and peace has been created for women and not men, but your demonstration of power over the sun has persuaded a lot of my men to fear you and to be ready to listen to you. I've decided that you may stay with us for one month. During that time you can explain this Christ and his teachings to those willing to listen and I will debate your faith with you. If, at the end of that time, I believe in this Christ, I'll be baptised and so will my people. You can stay with us and be our priest.'

Aidan shifted from one foot to the other uncomfortably.

'I'm grateful to you for the month and I'm confident that I can convince you in that time, but I cannot stay after that. I'll send for a more experienced priest, a man we call a bishop and he will serve you and your community. My calling is different. I must go on to spread the word to other nations.'

'I see. Well, I'll decide if I'll let you go after I've met this bishop. If I don't like him, I'll kill him and you'll have to stay.'

Aidan was shocked at Necton's ultimatum, but there was little he could do but pray that whoever Iona sent was to the king's taste.

~~~

Oswald was chosen to lead the assault on the outer perimeter. In the event no fighting was necessary. Fáelán's father was on duty that night and he and his family and friends had volunteered for the first watch. They opened the gates and Oswald's men ran in.

The space between the two palisades was occupied by two warrior's halls – one for married men on duty for the night and one for single men whose home it was permanently. There were also stables, pens for sheep, a granary and other storage sheds. It was obvious that Dùn Add could have withstood a long siege.

The attackers numbered two hundred men in all. Half made for each hall, Oswald leading one group and Fáelán's father the other. The latter was hoping to convince the married men not to fight for Connad and thus to avoid any bloodshed. His men quietly gathered up all the weapons they could find amongst the sleeping men and barred the door. When Connad's warriors awoke they found themselves faced with a line of armed men around the walls.

'You all know me. I'll come straight to the point. The other kings of Dal Riada have become fed up with Connad's deviousness and lack of leadership and have decided to depose him. He's afraid of his own shadow and sees plots where there are none. We grow weaker whilst our enemies grow stronger. When was the last time he stirred out of his hall? Never. The other kings have elected Domnall Brecc to succeed him. He plans to extend our territory northwards into Torridan and the Isle of Skye and eastwards into Cowal, driving out the Picts and the men of Strathclyde. These places used to be Dal Riadan before Connad cravenly gave them up without a fight. Now who'll support Domnall as High King of Dal Riada?'

There was a general murmuring before one man shouted out, 'But we are oathsworn to Connad. Whatever we think of him, he is our leader.'

'He has been deposed by the vote of his fellow kings, so you can choose to follow him into exile, if he is allowed to live. If he is killed, you are free of your oaths. I suggest we wait and see.'

This was greeted by a general mummer of assent.

'Now, if you give your oaths that you will remain here, I'll leave a few men to guard you whilst we storm the inner palisade.'

Meanwhile, Oswald was having less success in the single warrior's hall. He and his men approached quietly, but, as luck would have it, a group of four were still awake playing a game of chance and drinking. In their partially inebriated state, they were at first unaware of the

143

intruders. The noise of snoring had muffled the opening of the door and the soft footfalls on the straw-covered floor of beaten earth, but then one looked up and gave a cry of alarm when he saw men collecting weapons near the door.

That woke the others, or many of them, but Oswald had reacted swiftly. A few who had grabbed weapons near the door died swiftly, but the rest retreated to one end of the hall facing Oswald's men. The latter were fully dressed in chainmail byrnies or leather jerkins and wore helmets, whilst the former were wearing little and armed in the main with just a sword or seax. Oswald gestured and his archers moved forward, covering the confused men with their bows.

'Now, you have a choice: die here and now, or lay down your arms and live,' he told them. 'Connad has been deposed by vote of the other kings and Domnall Brecc is now High King. You can lay down your lives for a man who at best has a life of exile to look forward to, or you can swear allegiance to Domnall. Which is it to be?'

'We are sworn to Connad, Oswald. We can't betray him just like that,' one of the men facing him holding a spear declared.

'I understand that; then I suggest you lay down your arms and await the outcome of the assault on the king's hall. If Connad is killed, you are freed of your oath to support him.'

'And if he isn't – if he escapes or is taken prisoner?'

'Then you will have to make a decision, won't you? For now, you need to put down your weapons. You have until I count to twenty to do so. One, two...'

The young man holding the spear evidently reached a swift decision. He hefted his spear and threw it at Oswald. It was aimed at the unprotected space between the bottom of the face mask on Oswald's distinctive helmet and the neck of his byrnie. The distance was a few yards only, but it was aimed in haste and it glanced off the side of Oswald's helmet before clattering to the floor. Immediately six archers put arrows into the torso of the thrower and he died instantly. The remainder of the men stood in shock at the sudden death before one threw his sword down, then several followed suit. Five minutes later they were all disarmed and Oswald left them under guard whilst he re-joined the rest of his force outside.

Evidently the sentries on the inner palisade had realised that something was happening below them, as they called out a challenge when Oswald and about eighty of his men re-appeared outside the warriors' hall. Although it was dark, there was enough moonlight to be

144

able to see shadowy figures and when there was no response to the challenge, a few arrows whistled down towards them. Realising that they were easy targets, Oswald withdrew his men out of sight behind the buildings and waited for the three kings to join him.

'Well done, Oswald,' Domnall congratulated him warmly and threw his arm around the younger man's shoulder.

'Yes, great; but what do we do now?' Brennus of Lorne muttered grumpily.

Oswald sometimes thought that nothing would ever make the man happy.

'Well, we can starve them out,' suggested Fergus of Islay and the Isles.

'I have another idea,' Oswald put in.

The others looked at him in surprise. This was meant to be a council of the kings, but they had forgotten that Oswald was still there.

'Very well,' Domnall said, to break the disapproving silence. 'Let's hear it.'

'This outer palisade runs around three sides of the inner one, but the short escarpment on the north side is only defended by the inner palisade. Because we are all inside the outer defences, that's where they are watching. I suspect that the north side is poorly defended, if at all.'

'So?' Brennus asked contemptuously. 'As you said, the palisade is constructed on top of a cliff face. It may be only a short pitch, but it effectively makes the defensive wall more than forty feet high. I agree with Fergus; I say we starve them out.'

'Cyning,' Oswald turned to Domnall again, 'I have men who are expert climbers. They can scale the cliff easily. Indeed, when I lived here, I used to train warriors by getting them to do just that, but at another outcrop a mile away.'

'Fine, so you can get to the top of the rock, but how do you get up the sheer face of the palisade?' Fergus demanded to know. 'There is only a ledge six inches wide between the top of the climb and the bottom of the timber wall.'

'That's just it. The top of the escarpment is rock with a covering of turf no more than six inches deep. When it was built, they dug into the rock in just three places and sunk the timbers in by no more than a foot. The rest of the timbers are lashed to those three uprights and consequently aren't very strong. If we can loop ropes around the top of the timber poles in the centre of a run between the embedded uprights, there is a good chance we can pull it down with horses. My men can then climb up and enter the defences that way.'

145

'How do you know all this?  You weren't here when the palisade was built, were you?'

'No, but Fáelán's father and uncles were.  They helped to build it and they told me how it was constructed.'

Evidently Brennus was suspicious of Oswald, for whatever reason, so the three men were sent for to attest to the truth of what Oswald had said.  This annoyed Oswald more than a little and he decided that he would never trust the King of Lorne.

It was too late to make an attempt on the north wall that night and the next day was spent in futile negotiations with the Bishop of Argyll and the Isles, who looked after the spiritual welfare of both Connad's and Fergus' people, as mediator.

'Your three sub-kings propose that you resign the high kingship of Dal Riada and content yourself with the rule of Dùn Add and its territories.  Domnall Brecc has been elected to replace you as High King, but he will rule from a new Dùn to be built in the north of Kintyre,' the bishop told Connad somewhat pompously.

'Never!' Connad roared at the unfortunate cleric, who was by nature a rather timid man, if one full of his own self-importance.  'Go back and tell Domnall Brecc and his traitorous fellow sub-kings that I will have the heads of all three of them and that treacherous swine, Oswald, before this is over.  I have an army gathering near Loch Fyne and I have sent to both my friend Fiachnae mac Báetáin and my fellow king, Belin map Neithon, to come to my aid.  Then we will see who is master of Dal Riada.'

Connad was always thought of as clever and devious, but it wasn't very bright of him to mention having sought help from Strathclyde, who had always been enemies of Dal Riada.  When this was relayed to the inhabitants of Dùn Add and the warriors being held captive in the two halls, they were furious.  Few now considered themselves bound to Connad and most warriors, except a dozen who still held fast to their oath to him, now swore loyalty to Domnall Brecc and his two fellow kings.

Fiachnae had his own problems in Ulster, but in any case, he felt bitter about Connad's failure to help him in his time of need, so he was hardly likely to side with him.  Besides, he was a long way away.  It now became imperative to dispose of Connad before Strathclyde could invade.  If he was dead and Dal Riada was firmly under Domnall's control, Belin's excuse for an invasion would disappear and he was too canny to take on a united Dal Riada.

That night Oswald and a dozen of his best climbers, including Rònan and three boys, scaled the steep escarpment.  As Oswald suspected, there

146

was no sign of a sentry on that side and the men lifted the boys up on the shields that they had carried on their backs. They attached a loop of rope to three of the upright timbers in the section between two of the posts that had been sunk into the ground, then cut the bindings at the top, middle and bottom of the posts where they joined the sunken uprights, after tying the section in place with thin twine. That done, they moved to one side whilst the horses were fastened to the other ends of the ropes.

More men swarmed up the rock face to join the others on the narrow ledge either side of the section of palisade that was to be removed, until it couldn't hold anymore. By then, there were forty men in place. When Oswald gave the signal by flashing his blade so that it caught the moon's light, the horses pulled the section of palisade away and it crashed to the bottom of the escarpment. Oswald led the way into the fort with his forty men close at his heels, whilst the boys threw down ropes to help the less able climbers ascend the rock face.

Oswald's object was to reach and open the main gate. The other three sides of the palisade were packed with men and those with bows started to shoot down at Oswald and his running men.

'Shields up!' Oswald yelled just as the first volley was loosed. Only two of his men, slower than the rest to react to his command, were hit and they only suffered flesh wounds. They reached the gate and easily overcame the six men guarding it at ground level. Those on the parapet above hurled down rocks which smashed into the mass of warriors below. Luckily only three were crushed to death, but four others suffered broken arms or legs. However, by then Oswald had reached the gate and he and his men quickly removed the two locking bars.

Once the gates were thrown open, Oswald and his men were knocked out of the way by the hundreds of men waiting outside. Another man died in the crush and several suffered fractured ribs, but they were in and now a short one-sided battle started between the six hundred attackers and the men of Connad's personal bodyguard.

Oswald battled his way to the doors of the king's hall, suffering only a minor cut to his arm on the way. Inside, he found Connad cowering behind his throne. The four men beside him took one look at the scores of men flooding into the hall behind Oswald and threw down their arms.

'Cowards!' Connad screamed, waving his sword and cutting one unarmed man down from behind. 'Protect your king!'

The other three quickly picked up their discarded swords and hacked their erstwhile master to death, before once more throwing the bloodied blades to the ground.

'So dies a dishonourable man, treacherous to the last,' Domnall Brecc said quietly, clapping Oswald on the shoulder in congratulation.

# Chapter Ten – The Battle of Leithet Midind

## 627 AD

If Oswald thought that he could now enjoy some time with Gytha and have a well-earned rest, he was sadly mistaken.  First came news that Edwin, the man who had replaced his father as King of Northumbria, had married a Christian princess, Ethelburga of Kent, who had brought Paulinus, a Roman Catholic bishop, with her.  Far from pleasing the Christian Dal Riadans, they were dismayed as the Celtic and Roman churches vied for supremacy in Britain and Ireland.  In the main, the Roman faith held sway in the southern half of England and the Celtic Church in the North, in Wales and in Ireland.  Edwin had been baptised by Paulinus, who had now been made Bishop of Eoforwīc.

The alliance with Kent depressed Oswald and his dream of one day reigning in Northumbria seemed as far away as ever.  However, Kent and Wessex were rivals for the control of Sussex and the Jute Kingdom of Hampshire, so the alliance hadn't pleased Wessex either and eventually the King of Wessex went to war with Edwin.  Oswald didn't pay much attention to two other developments, though in due course they were to have far-reaching consequences for his life:  Penda had been elected King of Mercia and Cadwallon returned from exile to seize the throne of Gwynedd in Wales.

As well as being High King, Connad had ruled one of the Dal Riada sub-kingdoms.  However, after his death the three remaining Dal Riadan kings in Caledonia decided to divide up that kingdom between them.  Now that there was no king at Dùn Add, Domnall would move there instead of creating a new capital.  From there he could continue to rule both the Kintyre peninsula and the territory between it and Dùn Add, as well as Dal Riada, as High King.

The sour faced Brennus gained the land between O-Ban and Dùn Add and the land between Loch Awe and Loch Fyne.  In return, he promised Domnall his help when the latter invaded the Cowal Peninsula to the south of the sea loch. This would mean war with Strathclyde, but Domnall was intent on re-establishing Dal Riada's traditional borders.

Fergus would retain the Isles, but Domnall promised him help as well, this time to take the sparsely populated Isle of Skye and the smaller islands surrounding it. However, Domnall's first priority was to re-establish Dal Riadan control over their original homeland in Ulster. The Dal Riadans belonged to a tribe called the Scotii, who had originated in the north of Ireland, though it was split into a numbers of clans. Fiachnae had had several small scale skirmishes with the Dál Fiatach branch, but matters were far from resolved. The situation wasn't helped by Congal Claen's continuing infatuation with the Dál Fiatach girl he'd abducted, or by the fact that she was now pregnant with his child.

Domnall asked Oswald if he would lead a small force to show his support for Fiachnae and try to negotiate a sensible settlement to the dispute. Oswald was anxious to return to Arran and his family but he felt that he could hardly refuse Domnall's request. The new High King had more or less promised him his support if he had a reasonable opportunity to regain the crown of Northumbria. Privately, Oswald thought that Domnall was promising a lot of support to a lot of people and, if he honoured them all, he'd be stretching Dal Riada's meagre force of warriors extremely thin.

In the end, Oswald set off for Larne with three birlinns and a hundred and fifty warriors. However, he sent Rònan back to Arran with those of his men who had been wounded during the fight for Dùn Add. The young man was loathe to leave Oswald, but he had suffered several minor wounds and they needed time to heal.

'Do we even know that Fiachnae still controls Larne?' Alaric asked him as they sailed southwards down the western side of Kintyre with the wind on their beam.

'No, but hopefully we'd have heard if the place had been taken.'

They were interrupted by the sound of Osguid being violently sick again. At twenty, he was the next oldest of Oswald's brothers. Once a monk on Iona, he had now been ordained as a priest and had been sent with the expedition to care for their spiritual welfare. At the moment it seemed that he was the one more in need of care. It hadn't helped that he had spewed first over the windward side of the ship and it had blown back into his face, much to the amusement of the crew.

Oswald beckoned to one of the ship's boys and told him to take care of Father Osguid and try to keep him alive until they landed. The boy smirked and nodded.

'It isn't even as if the sea is rough,' Alaric commented.

'No, but there is something of a swell and the birlinn is rolling a bit. It can make you queasy if you're not used to it.'

'Queasy? I'd say your brother is a damn sight more than queasy!'

Thankfully, the rolling motion eased as they sailed into the calmer waters in the lee of the Irish coast and Osguid started to feel a little better, even if his face was still pasty white and had a sheen of clammy sweat over it.

Fiachnae made no secret of his delight in seeing Oswald and his men. They had lost three more settlements to the Dál Fiatach in the past month and the old warrior was itching to take to the field to drive them back into southern Ulster. To make matters worse, the Uí Néill had settled their own internal differences and were preparing to take advantage of the internecine warfare amongst the Ulaidh to take over all of Ulster.

When they walked into the king's hall, Oswald and Osguid were surprised to be greeted as 'cousins' by a young man of about twenty. At that moment, Eochaid came striding over and he and Oswald threw their arms around each other with some enthusiasm, overjoyed at their reunion.

'I see you've met your cousin Oswin,' Eochaid stated with a grin. 'He's a grand fighter, too; must run in the family.' Osguid was feeling more than a little annoyed at being ignored.

'And how exactly is this renowned warrior our cousin?'

'Ah, Eochaid, you might not have recognised my brother Osguid. He is our priest for this expedition.'

Eochaid nodded at Osguid and gave him a brief half-smile before turning his attention back to his elder brother. The slight was not lost on Oswald and he frowned at his old friend.

'Just because he is a priest and not a warrior doesn't make my brother any less a man, Eochaid. When you disrespect him, you disrespect me.'

Oswin saw the colour rise in the Irish prince's cheeks and spoke before the debate got heated.

'Calm down, both of you. We came here to fight the Dál Fiatach and, if necessary, the Uí Néill, not each other. Now apologise to Osguid, Eochaid and watch your tongue, cousin – you are a guest here, as am I.'

'Oswin's right. I apologise for not being more hospitable, Osguid.'

'And I should not have spoken to you the way I did, Eochaid,' Oswald added.

'Good, now we're all friends again, let's sit down and drink to the success against the Dál Fiatach.'

'Pardon me for asking, but how exactly are we cousins, Oswin?' Oswald asked, reapeating his brother's query during a lull in the conversation.

'Your father and mine were brothers.'

'You're Ælfred's son?'

There had been four brothers: Æthelfrith, being the eldest, had succeeded as King of Northumbria; Theobald and Ecgulf had served him as commanders and had died in battle, both childless. The fourth, Ælfred, had left Northumbria and no-one had heard of him again, until now.

'Yes, my father came to Ulster when yours became king. He was a younger brother and had no wish to be seen as a hanger-on, begging for scraps from the king's table. I was born here and my mother was Eochaid's aunt, so he too is my cousin.'

Oswald ignored the implied criticism that Ælfred had been ill-used by Æthelfrith. He knew from what his father had told him that he had treated all three of his brothers the same. The truth was that Ælfred had been too proud to serve his elder brother and had, instead, ended up serving a petty Irish king. Although the Irish called their tribal leaders kings, many ruled a relatively small area and were lucky if they could field a hundred warriors. In reality, they were no more than chieftains. By contrast, Northumbria was four times the size of the whole of Ulster.

Despite the obvious resentment Oswin harboured towards his family, Oswald found himself warming to the young man. He was two years younger than him, but had fought in just as many battles and skirmishes. He was evidently held in high regard as a warrior and as a leader, but he didn't boast about his accomplishments, unlike most. Osguid also liked his cousin and as the ale wore away the young priest's inhibitions, he found himself laughing at Oswin's bawdy humour. Eochaid also relaxed and the slight awkwardness of their reunion was forgotten.

At one stage, Congal Claen came across and joined them and the mood immediately changed. It was evident that he and Oswin disliked each other and each kept making barbed comments at the other's expense. Oswald didn't like Congal either, but he tried to hide it. Oswin didn't.

Fiachnae was now an old man and it wouldn't be many more years before Congal became king in his place. Oswald didn't give much chance of either Oswin or Eochaid surviving for long after that; one would die to settle a grudge and the other to remove a rival to the throne. He determined then and there to try and persuade them both to return to Arran with him after this campaign.

~~~

Thankfully, Necton had liked the new Bishop of Pentir, but Aidan didn't leave the Land of the Picts immediately. He stayed for another year to found a new monastery on the east coast, at a place called Ceann Phàdraig. Then he and Ròidh took passage on a trader that was headed around the north of Caledonia to Ireland. The master had agreed to drop them at Iona for a fee. It was an exorbitant one, but as it would be months quicker than walking back the way they had come, he agreed to pay up.

Varar had originally intended to come with them, but faced with the opportunity of becoming a monk amongst his own people or travelling to a monastery hundreds of miles away where they spoke a different language, he chose to stay at Ceann Phàdraig. Ròidh had been with Aidan for two years by then and had long ago decided that his destiny was linked to that of the young monk. The boy had taken his vows at the new monastery, so he now dressed the same as Aidan and displayed the conspicuous tonsure.

The voyage was uneventful until they reached the Isle of Skye. The ship had put in to a deserted beach and the crew had set off with their empty barrels to search for fresh water. Aidan, Ròidh and three sailors had been left behind to guard the ship, though what help two unarmed monks, one a fifteen year old boy, would be wasn't clear.

The Picts appeared from nowhere. There were about twenty of them, poorly armed, but nevertheless they outnumbered the three sailors and two monks. The sailors prepared to sell their lives dearly, but Aidan told them to lay down their weapons and he and Ròidh strode forward to greet the Picts with smiles on their faces.

For their part, the Picts were surprised to be greeted in their own tongue and were even more astonished when one of the monks claimed to be the son of King Murchadh of Ardewr. The Picts hastily conferred amongst themselves before one of them stepped forward.

'I'm sorry to be the bearer of sad tidings, Prince Ròidh, but we heard six months ago that your father is no longer King of Ardewr. His brother, Sionn, is now king and he has married your mother, Queen Genofeva.'

'What! How? I mean, what happened? How did my father die?'

The Picts conferred once more before their leader continued.

'It may not be true, but the tale is that he caught Sionn in bed with Genofeva and challenged him to fight. Sionn won.'

153

Aidan thought back to when he was at the Crannog on Loch Ness and remembered how close Sionn and Genofeva seemed. The story had the ring of truth about it. He even wondered whether Ròidh might not be Sionn's son, rather than Murchadh's, though he would never voice such a doubt to the boy.

Ròidh didn't say anything and when Aidan put a comforting hand on his shoulder, he shrugged it off and walked away up the beach to be on his own. Aidan explained to the Picts that they just wanted to collect fresh water and they nodded assent. When they offered to sell them some dried meat and fresh bread, Aidan readily agreed, knowing that the ship's master would think it a small price to pay to avoid a fight.

When the ship was ready to sail, Ròidh still hadn't re-appeared and the master reluctantly gave Aidan a little time to go and find him. He knew that it was only because Ròidh had saved them from an attack by the Picts that he'd been given the time. Normally the ship would have sailed whether or not the boy was back on board.

He found him sitting on a rock a mile away.

'Ròidh, I know how upset you must be and I feel for you, but the ship is sailing. If we don't board now they will leave us here.'

'You go. I must return and avenge the death of my father.'

'How long have your mother and Sionn been close?'

'What do you mean?'

'Is their relationship new or of long standing?'

The boy shrugged. 'They have always been close, closer than my father was to her, I suppose.'

'Do you think that you might have been Sionn's son, rather than Murchadh's?'

'What? You think...?'

When Aidan nodded, the boy started to weep. Aidan pulled him to his feet and hugged him to comfort him and Ròidh clung to the monk as he sobbed his heart out.

'Take comfort in the love of God, Ròidh, for the love of man is flawed. Come, let's return to the ship and head for Iona and the protection of the Holy Church.'

When they got back to the ship, it was already afloat and they had to catch a rope and be hauled aboard. As the miles passed and they neared the Isle of Mull, Ròidh tried hard to shrug off his sombre mood. He and Aidan spent a long time in prayer each day and to some extent he found that it comforted him. Finally, as they rounded the Ross of Mull and the monastery on its small island came into view, Ròidh felt at peace, as if he was coming home.

~~~

Oswald sat on his horse beside his cousin and together they surveyed the enemy drawn up in the valley below them.

'There doesn't look to be too many of them,' Eochaid said cheerfully as he rode up to join them.

'No more than two hundred, I'd have said and half of those are not that well-armed,' Oswin agreed.

'I have an uneasy feeling about this,' Oswald replied. 'It seems almost too easy.'

'Our combined war band numbers one hundred and fifty seasoned warriors; King Fiachnae has another hundred, half of who are trained fighters and Congal Claen has another one hundred men, almost all seasoned warriors. How can we lose?' Oswin scoffed.

They had encountered the Dál Fiatach near a hamlet called Leithet Midind earlier that morning and the two sides had taken up battle positions facing each other. Fiachnae had divided his command in three, with himself leading the centre, Eochaid the right and Congal the left.

The priests, including Osguid, had blessed the men and gone amongst them with consecrated bread and wine. The same had happened amongst the enemy. At last the two sides seemed ready for the coming battle and the three men rode down and handed their horses to boys who took them to the rear. They took their places in the front rank and waited to see who would charge first.

Being October, the weather wasn't warm, but at least it wasn't raining. A cold wind swept in from the west and the sky overhead was overcast. Oswald was just thinking that they needed to get started or they'd be fighting in the dark, when the Dál Fiatach roared their war cry and started to run towards Fiachnae's clan – the Dál nAraidi. The enemy archers were in the rear and they sent their arrows high in the air to descend on the still static Dál nAraidi. Loosing an arrow on the run wasn't likely to do much damage and those which were on target merely thumped into shields. Of the two hundred loosed, only five hit someone and then they only inflicted flesh wounds.

The two volleys sent in response were fired by men standing still and hit men running holding their shields at their sides. More than two dozen of the Dál Fiatach fell. It seemed as if the battle was already half won, but

155

then, when their foes were still fifty yards away, something totally unexpected happened. Congal Claen suddenly wheeled his men around until they were facing his grandfather's flank and charged into them.

Fiachnae was caught completely off guard as he was hit from two sides and the Dál nAraidi centre collapsed. The old man still hadn't realised that Congal had betrayed him before his grandson chopped off his head and held it up with a yell of triumph.

Oswald, Eochaid and Oswin, on the right wing, were at first oblivious to what was happening in the centre. Their line overlapped that of the Dál Fiatach and so their foes found themselves in a similar predicament to the Dál nAraidi centre when Congal had treacherously attacked that flank. Oswald faced a giant of a man, wearing little but wielding a long axe. The man raised the axe and, had the blow landed, it would have cleaved Oswald in two, shield notwithstanding. As it was, when he raised his axe above his head, he exposed his bare belly and Oswald slashed his sword across it, splitting it open so that grey intestines spilled out along with a fair quantity of blood. The man collapsed in a moaning heap and provided Oswald with a barrier knee-high between him and the next attacker.

That gave him time to punch his shield into the face of the man facing Eochaid to Oswald's left. The man fell back and Oswald's sword snaked out to pierce the mouth of the man attacking Oswin. The three found themselves with a clear space in front of them and then they realised that the enemy were retreating and doing so rapidly.

Oswin glanced to his left and saw to his horror that the centre of their line had collapsed and that, having almost defeated the enemy to their front, they were about to be engulfed from the flank. Even more worrying was the fact that their foes were trying to cut off their line of retreat. Eochaid, who was now in command, had to act and act swiftly, if they were to save their own lives and those of their men.

~~~

Osguid admired his elder brother tremendously, but he had no illusions about his own abilities as a warrior. He felt in his heart that he was a coward, and that that had been his primary reason for staying on Iona and becoming a monk and then a priest, instead of returning to Dùn Add to train as a warrior. He was with the other priests, the servants and the boys, including his brother Oswiu, watching the battle. At first he couldn't believe his eyes when he saw the turncoat Congal join the enemy side.

'What's he doing? He's killing his own people!'

'It's that Dál Fiatach bitch he's infatuated with, I'd stake my life on it,' one of the older warriors who had been left to guard the baggage train told him. 'I'll bet you a gold arm ring that they've promised to let him marry her if he betrayed his grandfather.'

'But he's his heir!'

'Aye, so he is. He's no fool; with King Fiachnae out of the way he'll be scheming to unite both clans under his rule, you mark my words.'

'But surely the Dál nAraidi will never accept him as king now? Not after this.'

'They will if it unites the Ulaidh so that they can face the Uí Néill. I can see you don't know much about Irish politics, lad. Yesterday's enemy is today's ally all the time. We don't much care who we're fighting, just so long as we are.'

From their elevated position, Osguid could see that the Dál nAraidi centre had broken and they were fleeing from the field. Fortunately for the rest of the Dál nAraidi army, many of the Dál Fiatach and Congal's men set off in pursuit. However, enough remained so that Eochaid's wing were now forced to stage a fighting retreat. He could see that his brother and the rest were struggling and so he did something that he had thought up until then was entirely contrary to his nature. He picked up a sword and shield discarded by one of those who had been routed.

'You say the Irish love a fight? Well, come on then. Rally the others and arm the boys. Let's give those treacherous bastards a surprise.'

Oswiu clapped Osguid on the back and hastily organised the ships' boys and those who acted as servants to various groups of warriors, making sure that they all had a weapon of some sort. By this time Eochaid's wing were hard pressed and their line of retreat was almost closed off. Oswald wept when he saw his new-found cousin cut down, but there was nothing he could do to save Oswin. He was fending off three men as it was. Eochaid was standing shoulder to shoulder with him, but their retreat had almost ground to a halt and they were losing men all the time.

Oswald was tiring, but he managed to lift his shield to fend off one blow and block another's sword thrust at the same time. Then an axe came down on his helmet. The metal held, but it was badly dented and he fell to the ground unconscious. The last thing he heard was the strange sound of unbroken boys' voices mixed in with the deeper shouts of men, all yelling 'Whiteblade!' Then the blackness overcame him.

When he awoke, he was being gently rocked to and fro. He had a splitting headache and when he tried to open his eyes and sit up, he felt sick. He lay down again and groaned.

'He's awake!' he heard Osguid's voice yell in relief.

'He must have a skull as thick as a plank.' That voice he thought was Eochaid's, but he didn't understand what he was doing there. Then he remembered the battle.

'What happened?' he managed to croak out, as Oswiu knelt by his side and gave him a drink of water.

'You should have seen your brothers!' Eochaid told him whilst Osguid blushed and Oswiu beamed with pleasure. 'The two of them led the baggage train guards and the boys to our rescue. Oswiu and his boys were only armed with daggers and seaxes, but they got in amongst the surprised Dál Fiatach and hamstrung them or stuck their blades into their groins. Anyhow, they created enough of a diversion to allow us to fight our way clear and then we fled back to Larne.'

'Did we lose many?' Oswald croaked.

'Yes, a fair few warriors and a dozen of the boys were slain, too.'

He stopped speaking when he realised that Oswald had lapsed back into unconsciousness. Oswiu stayed with him, which saved his life. When he awoke again he was sick and would have choked on his own vomit if his brother hadn't had the presence of mind to turn him on his side and thump his back to clear his throat. When he was satisfied that his brother had stopped choking, Oswiu rolled him onto his back again. Oswald thanked him, then looked puzzled and asked where he was.

'We're aboard the Holy Saviour. Don't you remember?'

When Oswald shook his head and asked if Oswin was with them, Oswiu became concerned and sent one of the other boys to find Eochaid. However, when he arrived Oswald was mumbling incoherently and soon slipped back into a stupor.

A little later Oswald seemed lucid again and asked if the birlinn had enough men, given the losses that they had suffered. Eochaid nodded.

'Yes, we made up our numbers with those of the Dál nAraidi who refused to bend the knee to that treacherous cur, Congal. He's now been accepted as King of all the Ulaidh, after the King of the Dál Fiatach was also killed in the battle.'

'And Oswin; I thought I saw him fall?'

Eochaid nodded. 'They put his head on a spear as some sort of grisly trophy.'

Oswald groaned. 'One day I will kill your nephew.'

'Not if I get to him first,' Eochaid said grimly.

~~~

Gytha writhed in agony. The birth of Œthelwald had been relatively easy, but her second child was proving to be a very different matter. Acha knew what was wrong – it was a breech birth – but all her efforts to turn the baby had failed. Now Gytha was bleeding badly. Subconsciously, Acha felt that Gytha's death would be no bad thing for her son. She was the daughter of a minor Mercian noble and not a suitable consort for the King of Northumbria. Although it had been eleven years since her husband had been killed and they had fled into exile, she had never given up hope that one day Oswald would rule at Bebbanburg.

The struggles of the baby gradually grew weaker and Acha feared that the umbilical cord had become trapped, depriving the foetus of oxygen. It had been trying to come out bottom first and Gytha wasn't big enough to allow this to happen without severe tearing of the birth channel. She had already lost a great deal of blood and as Acha and the women helping her couldn't get the baby out so that they could try and repair the damage, Gytha's chances of survival were now extremely slim.

Finally they managed to deliver the baby girl, but as Acha had already concluded, she was dead. They did their best to stitch Gytha up, but she was now very weak and continued to bleed, despite the women's efforts. An hour later, she too died.

Although Acha tried to tell herself that it was God's will and it left her son free to marry a princess, she knew that he would be devastated and more than likely, he would hold her responsible. If he did, she couldn't blame him. She had made no secret of the fact that she had disapproved of the marriage and although she had tried her best to get on with Gytha, there was always a gulf between them. Now she would have to act as mother to four-year old Œthelwald, at least until Oswald returned.

At that moment, her eldest son was unconscious again and calling out in delirium as Eochaid changed his mind and the small fleet reversed course and headed for Iona instead of Dùn Add. Informing Domnall Brecc of the disaster in Ulster could wait.

~~~

Aidan and Ròidh were surprised to see three birlinns drawn up on the beach as their ship neared Iona. They could see a body being lowered from the side of one of the birlinns onto a stretcher and then four warriors carried it up to the monastery. Half an hour later the two monks disembarked, to be greeted by Ségéne mac Fiachnaíhe.

'Brother Aidan, we had given up hope of seeing you again, it's been so long since we had tidings of you. I am delighted to see you alive and well.'

He paused and looked at the young monk standing by Aidan's side.

'I see that you have a new acolyte.'

'Not new, Father Abbot.' Aidan smiled. 'This is Ròidh, a Pictish prince who has been my aide for the past two and a half years. He served his noviciate on the road and at the new monastery at Ceann Phàdraig, where he took his vows.'

'Welcome to Iona, Ròidh. Do you plan to stay with us now, or will you continue to accompany Aidan when he leaves us again?'

'I would like to stay here awhile, if I may, Father Abbot, to improve my knowledge of Holy Scripture and to learn new skills. But I wish to accompany Brother Aidan on his next journey, so I'm hoping he'll stay for some time, too.'

He and Aidan exchanged smiles and Ségéne realised that the two were close friends as well as colleagues.

'Ròidh has the making of a good healer as well, Father Abbot. I've taught him what little I know, but I'm hoping he can spend some time with Brother Brendan as well.'

'Well, why don't you go up to the infirmary now? You know Oswald, who they call Whiteblade, of course. He was badly concussed at a battle amongst the Ulaidh and has a nasty swelling on his head.'

'I've seen this before,' Ròidh told Brendan. 'It's not just a bad bruise. We had a wise woman when I was a boy who cut into the head to relieve pressure on the brain of one of our warriors. She kept the cut open until all the muck had drained out. When he recovered, the man was the same as before.'

'When you were a boy?' scoffed Brendan's assistant, a monk who was a year or two older than Ròidh. 'You still are a boy. What do you know?'

'An awful lot more than you do, I suspect.' Ròidh retorted angrily.

The two glared at one another and Aidan sighed. It was unlikely that Ròidh could work with Brendan, given the antipathy between him and the other youth.

'Brother Judoc, unless you have something useful to contribute, keep quiet,' Brendan told him with some asperity. The infirmarian also seemed to dislike his new assistant. Perhaps Ròidh's chances of working with him weren't hopeless, after all. Brendan bent over Oswald's head and gently pressed the swelling. It certainly seemed as if there was a lot of liquid under the skin.

'What were his symptoms when he was conscious? Was he sick? Headaches? Stiff neck?'

Eochaid nodded. 'Yes, all of those and he seemed confused at times. Oswiu was with him most of the time, so he may be able to answer more fully.'

The boy nodded. 'One moment he didn't seem to remember the battle, or even where he was, but the next time he awoke he was totally coherent again.'

'I think Ròidh may be right in his diagnosis,' Brendan said thoughtfully. 'It's not just a simple case of concussion. Judoc, fetch me that small knife and hold the blade in the flame of that candle to cleanse it, then hold the candle over here so I can see what I'm doing. Aidan, do you remember where the tubes are?'

'I think so; what do you want?'

'Any small length will do; a short section of artery from a cow would be ideal.'

Aidan nodded and sorted through a chest full of small square boxes before he found what he was looking for. He handed it to Brendan, who had made a small cut in the skin above the swelling. He pushed the tube in and watched as the pus, blood and muck ran out.

'Right, all we have to do now is wait until it's all out. When it heals up, he should be back to normal.'

'I'll sit with him,' Aidan volunteered and Brendan nodded.

'I want to stay, too,' Oswiu added.

'Your brother is in good hands now, Oswiu. Don't forget you are primarily one of my crew and can't decide to suddenly desert me.'

'I didn't mean that. It's just that I am concerned for him.'

'I understand that. He's probably my closest friend, as well as your brother, so I'll be staying for another day or so to make sure he is recovering before we leave. Alright?'

'I suppose so.' Then Oswiu realised he was just being petulant. 'I mean, thank you, Prince Eochaid.'

'What should I do?' Ròidh asked.

'Go and drown yourself,' Judoc muttered under his breath, but not quietly enough that Brendan didn't hear him.

'Brother Judoc, I'm afraid I've reached the inescapable conclusion that you are unsuited to the work of an infirmarian. I'll ask the abbot to find you something more suited to your talents.'

Judoc glared at him and then at Ròidh before storming out. Eochaid and Oswiu followed him, saying that they would be back later to check on Oswald.

'I wonder why Judoc became a monk,' Aidan mused. 'He doesn't exactly seem to have the temperament for it.'

'Perhaps you should take him with you when you leave. A year or two as a missionary might teach him to grow up and have some compassion for others,' Brendan suggested with a smile.

'I assume that you are in jest, brother. It's bad enough already, having to put up with this lad.' Ròidh looked at Aidan in astonishment and then smiled good-naturedly when the other two grinned at his reaction.

~~~

It took Oswald several weeks to recover and build up his strength again. During that time he went for long walks with Aidan and discussed what Christianity meant six hundred years after the death of Jesus. He came to admire Aidan's selfless dedication to spreading the Word of God to pagans and his austere disregard for the comforts of life.

Eochaid had sailed on with the rest of the fleet to Dùn Add, to let Domnall know what had happened in Ulster. Oswiu wasn't happy at leaving his brother behind and was concerned that it would be some time before he saw him again, but he had a job to do and he got on with it.

After a week at Dùn Add, they sailed back to Arran, where they learned about Gytha's tragic death. Eochaid didn't want to have to be the one to tell Oswald, but he knew that his friend would rather hear it from him than from anyone else, so he set out again in a small birlinn with a crew of just twenty, to go and collect Oswald. Oswiu had begged to go with him, but Acha had insisted that he stay with her.

'It's time you started your training as a warrior,' she told him, 'instead of following Oswald everywhere like a puppy. You'll stay here until you learn how to fight properly; then perhaps you might have a chance of surviving your first battle.'

'I've already done that!' he almost yelled at her in his frustration. 'If it wasn't for me and Osguid, Oswald would be dead, instead of just injured.'

Acha cuffed him about the head.

'Osguid's a priest, not a warrior; you don't know what you're talking about. I won't have my sons telling lies,' she stormed at him and refused to believe his account of what had happened.

After that, Oswiu refused to speak to her and nothing she tried, neither withholding food nor threatening to beat him, had any effect on him. Both were proud and stubborn people and neither would give in. Oswiu enjoyed the training with the other youths of his age, but he dreaded returning to his mother's hut every evening and in the end, he moved into the hut with the other trainees.

That had deeply hurt Acha, but instead of trying to heal the deepening rift, she now ignored her son completely. With Offa now a novice on Iona, she had grown closer to her daughter, Æbbe. However, when she started to mention possible suitors to the eleven year old girl, Æbbe astonished her by stating that she had decided to become a nun. It wasn't what Acha had in mind for her at all and their growing closeness all too quickly turned to confrontation. So instead, Acha focused her affection on Oswald's son, Œthelwald.

~~~

Oswald could tell that something was badly wrong as soon as he saw Eochaid disembark onto the beach below the monastery.

'What is it? Has Domnall accepted Congal as King of the Ulaidh?'

'He has, but that's not what I have to tell you.'

'Oh, I see. Is it my mother? I know she is getting on in years now…'

'Oswald, it's not Acha; she's fine. It's Gytha.'

'Gytha? Oh yes, the baby must have been born by now -' His voice trailed away as he saw the desolate look in Eochaid's eyes.

'She's dead, isn't she?' he said flatly.

He sat down in the sand and wept. Eochaid tried to comfort him, but Oswald said he wanted to be alone and wandered off to the other side of the small island with just his thoughts for company. He remembered all the happy times Gytha and he had enjoyed and the love that they had shared. He regretted not being together more, but he knew that he wouldn't have been happy just staying at home. He was a warrior, not a farmer or a fisherman. At one stage he cursed God for taking her from him and then realised that he was being foolish. Death in childbirth was not that uncommon. He did wonder, however, how hard his mother had tried to keep Gytha alive.

He spent the night sleeping in a small beehive-shaped hut built of stone that the monks used when they wanted to be alone to commune with God. He woke the next morning feeling hungry and if not reconciled to his wife's death, at least ready to face others again.

Eochaid told him what he knew about the stillbirth and said that Œthelwald was now being cared for by Acha. Oswald didn't reply, but Eochaid could tell that Acha's care of the little boy would cease as soon as Oswald returned to Arran. Rightly or wrongly, he would blame his mother for not preventing his wife's death.

'I need to go to Dùn Add first. I have to confront Domnall over his acceptance of Congal. I mean to lead an army to kill him.'

Eoachaid took him gently by the arm. 'I don't think that would be wise, Oswald. It would put Domnall in a difficult position and he could well exile you and your family from Dal Riada. Then what would you do? Don't forget, you will need his support if you ever have the opportunity to return to Northumbria and seize your father's throne.'

Oswald was silent for a long time, then his shoulders slumped dejectedly.

'I suppose you're right. But how do you feel? That traitor Congal killed your father and took the crown that should by rights be yours.'

'You know I never wanted the throne – too much responsibility and everyone expects too much of you – but I don't want my murderous nephew to have it, either. Like you, I'll have to play a waiting game for now.'

Oswald sighed. 'Reluctantly, I have to agree with you; but it's been eleven years already. How much longer can I wait? Edwin seems to get stronger all the time.'

'You are building a reputation as a warrior and a leader. Men will follow you, but you need to wait for the right opportunity. You're only twenty three, so time is on your side.'

'Sage advice, Eochaid, but sometimes it's hard to do the sensible thing. So, what now? I'll go back to Arran and visit my wife's grave, then make proper provision for my son's upbringing, but what do I do then? Ulster is no longer a possibility and Domnall will want to consolidate his position as High King before he does anything else.'

'I'm not so sure. He's talking of recovering the Dal Riadan territory lost in the past fifty years. He wants to conquer the Cowal Peninsula on the other side of Loch Fyne and retake the Isle of Skye from the Picts.'

'Strathclyde borders Northumbria to the south, so it wouldn't be sensible for me to antagonise Belin. Skye and the Picts are a different case, though.  My half-brother is a Pict and he has a better claim to Northumbria than I do, so they are unlikely to help me.  Perhaps I'll go and visit Fergus after I've been home.'

# Chapter Eleven – Arran

## Autumn 627 to Spring 628 AD

Oswiu was waiting eagerly at the dock in Duilleag Bán na Cille when Eochaid returned with Oswald. Acha had also wanted to be there to greet him, but she was wise enough to realise that her presence would lead to an awkward confrontation in public. She recognised now that her domineering attitude was gradually driving all her children away from her, but she didn't know what to do to rectify matters. In the end, it was Rònan who resolved an uncomfortable situation.

He had joined the crowd waiting to greet Oswald, but at first he hung back. Then Oswald spotted him. With one arm around Oswiu's shoulder he made his way towards him and flung his other arm around the shoulders of his former slave.

'It does my heart good to see my brother and one of my closest friends again. I've missed both of you. Tonight we three and Eochaid are going to get uproariously drunk to celebrate my homecoming.'

When he awoke the next morning, Oswald groaned at the pounding in his head and rushed outside to vomit. When he walked back into the hut he wondered where he was, until he saw Rònan asleep across the other side of the hut with a very pretty girl in his arms. A baby lay wrapped in furs near them and a woman, presumably their slave, slept close by with a small child. Evidently Rònan had somehow brought him home last night.

He went down to the river, dunked his head in the saline waters of the river estuary and rinsed the sour taste out of his mouth. Fresh water had to be brought down from the non-tidal part of the river each day and he resolved that one of the first things he would do was to dig a well in the settlement. There had to be underground springs of fresh water somewhere. It would be a good diea to see if there was a water supply under the fortress as well, instead of having to keep the storage tank full.

He started to make his way to his own hut, but then he remembered that Gytha was dead and a wave of sadness washed over him. Eochaid and the body servant he had brought with him from Larne now occupied it. His friend had rightly assumed that he wouldn't want to live there now; there were too many memories. Oswald was certain, however, that Eochaid had said something about building him a new hut, but he didn't know where it was.

Suddenly a small boy hurtled into him and gripped his legs so tightly that he nearly fell over. He was about to rebuke the boy and push him away when he realised that it was his son, Œthelwald. He picked the little boy up and threw him in the air, swinging him around when he caught him and making the child giggle with delight.

'You'll make him sick. He's just eaten,' a voice said quietly.

Oswald turned to see Acha standing a few feet away, looking nervous and uncertain.

'Good morning mother. I was coming to see you; we need to talk.'

His tone was neutral – neither warm nor cold – and Acha couldn't discern his mood. However, it certainly wasn't too encouraging, considering the time they'd been apart and his brush with near death. She turned to the slave woman standing behind her.

'Take Œthelwald back to the hut for now. You can spend time with your father later, child.'

The boy unwillingly took the hand of the woman and walked away with her, looking back over his shoulder at his father and his grandmother. Even at the young age of four, he could sense the tension between the two people he loved most and it worried him.

Oswald was just about to ask his mother what had happened when Gytha had died, when they were joined by a slightly out of breath Rònan. He took Oswald gently by the elbow and steered him away.

'I need to talk to you, or rather my wife does, before you talk to Acha.'

Oswald was somewhat taken aback. Although they were friends, Rònan had never forgotten that he was once Oswald's slave and had always treated him with a certain degree of diffidence. However, there was nothing diffident about his insistence that his friend postpone his discussion with his mother for now.

Oswald was tempted to put Rònan in his place, but his curiosity was piqued and so, telling Acha that he would come and find her later, he went back to Rònan's hut with him.

'I was there during the birth, Lord Oswald and I know exactly what happened,' Rònan's wife said softly.

'Go on.'

She proceeded to tell him in detail – some of which he could have done without – how they had discovered that the baby was in the breech position and how hard Acha had fought to save both the child and the mother.

'It was almost as if she was desperate to save Gytha. I mean, naturally, we did everything we could, but it was almost as if your mother was fighting to save her own life. When your wife died, Acha was beside herself with grief.'

Oswald took the young woman's hands in his own.

'Thank you. I can tell that it was difficult for you to go through that again. Any woman would want to put it out of her mind as quickly as possible, so I'm grateful to you for making me understand what really happened.'

He turned to Rònan, who was standing just outside the hut trying not to listen.

'You were quite correct to bring me here before I spoke to my mother. I was ready to accuse her of not really trying to save Gytha and I know now how unjust that would have been. It would have probably done irreparable damage to my relationship with her. It took courage to risk my anger and I know now what a true friend you are. I shan't forget.'

As Oswald strode away in search of Acha, Rònan was left wondering whether the blow on the head and its aftermath had changed Oswald. He seemed somewhat more level-headed and tolerant now, rather than the impulsive character he used to be.

'Mother, I know now how hard you tried to save Gytha and my daughter. I can never thank you enough.' Much to Acha's astonishment and delight, her son took her in his arms and kissed her forehead.

'Now, I suppose I'd better find a place to live. I'm far too old to be living with my mother.'

Acha laughed, feeling as if a great weight had been lifted from her shoulders.

'Eochaid had a new home built for you as soon as he moved into your old hut. It's inside the stronghold on the spit of land that sticks out into the loch. Go and find him; it's appropriate that he should be the one to show it to you. Oh! And come to eat with me and your sister tonight. Bring Oswiu with you. If you invite him, he might come.'

Not only had Eochaid built Oswald a large hut next to the hall where the single warriors lived, but he'd found two slaves to look after him. They were a brother and sister, who he had captured on a raid south of Ulster a month ago. The girl was fourteen and the boy, nine. Even in the gloom inside his new hut, Oswald could see what a stunning beauty the girl was. His first thought was how much he wanted to bed her; then he felt ashamed. Gytha was hardly cold in her grave and he was already lusting after another. Besides, she was a slave and he had never compelled anyone to have sex with him.

The siblings were named Keeva and Jarlath and they seemed pleased to be serving him. Willing servants were always better than coerced ones, but he could see nothing but problems. Living as they were in the fortress, there were only a dozen or so female slaves and a handful of boys. The girls who looked after the warriors manning it were used to being passed around for the sexual pleasure of their masters. Keeva was too pretty to be safe from his men's attention when he was away and he frowned, unsure how to voice his concerns to his friend whilst not seeming ungrateful. Eochaid must have sensed his quandary.

'If you're worried about preserving her virginity, don't be. I've made it clear to the oafs who live in the hall that she and her brother are off limits. One fool tried to mess with Keeva and Jarlath threatened him with a knife. Normally a slave would die for that, but I'd warned them and so, instead of punishing Jarlath, I had the man flogged and banished him from Arran.'

'Thank you, but couldn't you have found me an ugly couple of slaves? God knows, there are enough of them in Ireland!'

'I don't suppose you'll marry again in a hurry, after Gytha, but you're no celibate monk. I thought a pretty face might cheer you up.'

'Hmmmm,' Oswald replied noncommittally.

Many Celtic monks were far from celibate, though they were meant to be. Suddenly he realised that both of his new slaves had understood what they were saying and there was no mistaking the interest in Keeva's eyes. He blushed and the two siblings giggled, but they soon stopped when he looked at them sternly.

'Keeva, you are in charge of my home. I expect it to be kept spotless and for the meals you prepare to be tasty and nourishing. My clothes and my bedding are to be washed regularly and dried properly. You, Jarlath, will look after my armour and weapons. If I find a spot of rust anywhere, you'll regret it and my sword and seax must be sharp enough for me to use for shaving. Do you understand?'

The two nodded vigorously and looked fearful until Oswald smiled.

'If you look after me as I expect, you'll find me an easy master and I'll look after you; but don't let me down. Now go and find out where my chests are and bring them here.'

The two scuttled off and Oswald put his hand on Eochaid's shoulder.

'Thank you for the hut and for those two scamps. I have a feeling that we'll get on well together,' he said with a twinkle in his eye. 'Now I had better go and find Oswiu and see if I can persuade him to come and eat with our mother this evening.'

~~~

Two weeks later, the Holy Saviour rounded the Mull of Kintyre and headed north towards Dùn Add. Oswald had relieved Rònan at the steering oar an hour before they neared the rock-strewn top end of the Sound of Jura. His friend had resumed his job as steersman now that he'd recovered from his wounds and Alaric had set up a yard to repair ships and built new ones.

Oswald had sent Jarlath up the mast to keep an eye out for patches of white water, which would mark where the rocks were and the boy sat confidently astride the yard arm to which the sail was attached, with his bare brown legs hanging free and one arm loosely wrapped around the mast.

He had settled into his dual role of ship's boy and Oswald's body servant easily and seemed to love the sea. His happy disposition endeared him to the crew and they soon forgot that he was a pagan Irish slave. From Oswald's point of view, the only unfortunate thing was that he looked like his sister and was a constant reminder of her.

Keeva had made no secret of the fact that she was attracted to Oswald, even if he was nine years older than she was. She flirted with him and Oswald had to admit that he liked it. He had loved Gytha, but now it seemed as if he had to fight to keep her memory alive. He had resisted the temptation to bed Keeva so far, though none would have blamed him if he had. He felt guilty at even thinking of doing so; as if it would be betraying his late wife. It would have salved his conscience somewhat if he could have married her, but, unlike Gytha, she wasn't nobly born. It was unthinkable.

One night she had slipped naked under the covers with him and the urge to make love to her was almost overwhelming. However, he had gently kissed her forehead and told her quietly to return to the bed she shared with her brother. Instead of being angry at his rejection, she had nodded and kissed him back on his cheek.

'I understand. It is too soon after Lady Gytha,' she had whispered. 'But you know I'm ready whenever you are.' She slid out of bed and put her shift back on before re-joining her brother, who had been watching them with interest by the light of the dying fire.

He was jolted back to the present by a shout from Jarlath.

'Breaking water fine in the left bow.'

Oswald chided himself for not paying attention and moved the oar over to take them more into the middle of the channel.

'Well spotted, Jarlath.'

He had an uneasy feeling that the boy was well aware that Oswald hadn't been as alert as he should have been. This annoyed him and he glared up at Jarlath sitting cockily on his precarious perch. The confused look on the boy's face made him realise that he wasn't being fair. He knew that he had to make a hard decision when they returned to Duilleag Bán na Cille. Either he would make Keeva his lover, or he would have to get rid of her and her brother. Perhaps then she would stop distracting him when his mind should be concentrating on the job at hand.

Oswiu sat halfway down the bank of rowers, proud at being selected by his brother as a warrior for this journey. The evening meal with their mother on Oswald's second day back had started awkwardly, but the boy had relaxed a little after the first goblet of mead. Oswald had supported his sister's desire to become a nun and to everyone's surprise, Acha had agreed, provided she waited until she was fourteen. The rifts between mother and her offspring had been healed that evening and Acha understood at last that her task was nearly done. Now she had to let them go. Offa was due back from Iona in a year's time and she would support him, whether he decided to become a monk or a warrior, though from what Oswald had told her, the latter seemed highly unlikely.

Oswald hardly knew his youngest brother. The two had spent a little time together whilst he was recovering on Iona, but novices didn't get a lot of freedom and in any case, they had quickly found out they didn't have much in common. They were divided by a lot more than the ten years that separated them in age. Offa's goal in life seemed to be to live as a hermit, away from his fellow man, spending his time in prayer.

When they arrived at Dùn Add, Domnall asked Oswald what he thought of Congal Claen, but when he found out that Oswald shared Eochaid's view of him, he came to the reluctant conclusion that he would have to let Ulster seek its own destiny for now and concentrate on expanding Scottish Dal Riada. To do so, he needed to make it powerful enough to beat Strathclyde. He dismissed the Picts as backward and disunited and seemed unhappy about Oswald's proposal to aid Fergus in his conquest of Skye. He felt it was wasting the young warrior's talents.

Next, the High King turned to the question of Arran. Its Lord, a man called Barra, had been appointed by Connad to rule the whole island, but the man had contented himself with ruling the south of the island, leaving Oswald to look after the north. Barra had been a second cousin of Connad's and had refused to recognise Domnall Brecc as the new High King. He had lost his head in consequence and his family had fled to the Cowal Peninsula, though it seemed that sanctuary there might be short-lived.

'I need someone I can trust to rule Arran. Its strategic position will be crucial in the coming war with Strathclyde. Furthermore, I can't secure Cowal unless we invade the Isle of Bute, as that lies between Cowal and Arran.'

Oswald was quiet for a moment or two.

'My base on Arran would seem to be rather vulnerable, lying as it does less than ten miles to the south-west of Bute, once we go to war with Strathclyde.'

'Correct; which is why I want you to rule Arran for me and to conquer the Isle of Bute. Then you can be Lord of both islands; you can even call yourself *King of Arran and Bute* if you wish, but subject to me, of course.'

'The only kingdom I want to rule is Northumbria,' Oswald replied rather curtly. 'But I am grateful for the offer, my Lord King,' he added as an afterthought, when he saw Domnall's eyes darken in anger. 'Perhaps *Thegn of Arran* would be a more fitting title?'

Oswald wasn't interested in ruling Arran and Bute so much as the fact that it would give him a good source of warriors if there was ever an opportunity to try and recover Northumbria. Bute was much smaller than Arran, but it was a prosperous island with one main settlement at Rothesay. The rest of the island, which was much flatter than Arran, was covered in small hamlets, single farmsteads and a few small fishing settlements on the coast. If he could take Rothesay, the island would be his.

'I am delighted by the trust you place in me, King Domnall. I happily accept the Lordship of Arran and your instructions to capture Bute. How many men will I have for this?'

Domnall looked surprised. 'Whatever you can raise from Arran. I propose to invade Cowal next spring and you should aim to be ready by then.'

'I see. Very well, then. I'll let Fergus know of the change in my plans on the way home. I'll need to build or acquire more ships, but we'll be ready by the middle of April.'

172

~~~

On Oswald's first night back at Duilleag Bán na Cille, he sent Jarlath to spend the night with Oswiu and the other trainee warriors. He didn't fancy being watched whilst he made love to the boy's sister, though he knew that he would have to get used to that; he couldn't send the boy off every night.

At first they kissed tentatively and then with more passion. Their foreplay didn't last long before he took her virginity with more violence than he had intended, but she was even more inflamed than he was, if anything. They made love three times more that night. The first was over far too quickly, as they both sought release from their pent-up lust for each other, but after that, Oswald was gentler and made sure that Keeva enjoyed the act of love just as much as he did.

He was surprised to find deep, bloody scratches on his back the next day and Keeva was still tending to the wounds she had inflicted when Jarlath returned. The boy's eyes grew wide and he giggled, drawing annoyed looks from both of them.

'You can stay here at night from now on, boy, but you are to avert your eyes. If I find you watching us, I'll beat you until your back looks like mine.'

'Yes, master. I understand.' Privately the boy thought that, if they got that carried away when they made love, they wouldn't notice if all the boys in the settlement came to cheer them on.

The next six months were busy ones for Oswald. Alaric started to construct the extra birlinns he'd need and his warriors intensified their training. One pleasant surprise was the arrival of Oslac to serve as his senior priest. He had been away in Lorne when Oswald was on Iona and the two hadn't seen each other for years. He was four years younger than Oswald, but the two had always got on reasonably well together, allowing for the fights that brothers always have as children. Oslac was devout, but unlike Offa, he was also a man of the world and he joined his brothers and companions in getting drunk to celebrate his arrival.

In addition to Eochaid's Gift of God and the Seraphim, now captained by a man from Arran called Lorcan, he would need two more large birlinns so that he could ferry two hundred warriors to Bute; not that he was sure he could raise that number on Arran. His priority was, therefore, to tour the southern half of the island and assess the loyalty of the various

173

chieftains and settlement headmen, whilst Alaric and his apprentices continued to work on the two new boats.

The new Lord of Arran let it be known that he had adopted the title of thegn, one that was used throughout Anglo-Saxon England and parts of Scotland to signify a noble who held land from the king. After some deliberation, he decided that a show of strength was not the way to get the islanders to accept his rule. He therefore took only Eochaid, Oswiu, Lorcan, Oslac, Cormac – now a young warior of eighteen - and Jarlath with him. Both Acha and Keeva pleaded with him to take more men, but he was adamant. He found leaving Keeva a wrench, much more so than when he had left Gytha, but he couldn't take her with him all the time, especially when he invaded Bute, so he'd have to get used to it.

He decided to tackle Brodick first. It was the nearest major settlement to Duilleag Bán na Cille and it was the one where the previous Lord of Arran had based himself. When he approached the settlement, he found the gates shut against him. Signalling his companions to remain where they were, out of arrow shot, he rode forward and asked to speak to whoever was in charge.

'What do you want here, Whiteblade? Have you come to slaughter Lord Barra's wife and children, as Domnall Brecc did their father? If so, you'll be disappointed. They are not here.'

'I know that, old man. They have fled to Cowal, though I would never have harmed them unless they opposed my rule. I am now the Thegn of Arran and your Lord. Now open the gates and stop trying my patience.'

'You swear you mean us no harm, Whiteblade?'

'If I did, I'd have brought a damn sight more than four warriors, a priest and boy with me.'

Oswiu grinned delightedly at being termed a warrior.

The old man introduced himself as Turlough, the chief of the elders of the settlement, before calling a boy forth from the silent crowd to take them up to the Lord's Hall.

'You'll find the place deserted since Barra's demise,' he warned them. 'It's in a bit of a mess, too.'

Oswald grunted. No doubt the settlement's people had looted it after Barra's family had fled.

'Send up some servants to clean the place up then, and some food and mead or ale for us tonight. I'll address the settlement council tomorrow morning and then speak to everyone at the marketplace at noon. Please make sure you spread the word.'

A sullen, watchful group of boys appeared to sort out the hall and then some men arrived with a handcart carrying a little bread, cheese and a small barrel of ale.

'They don't intend to spoil us, then,' Eochaid muttered.

Oswald gave one of the men a sliver of silver – far more than the provisions were worth.

'Now go back into the settlement and bring us more bread, meat, fruit and a barrel of water.'

The man looked surprised, then smiled.

'Aye, Lord. I will, but there's good fresh water in the well outside the hall.'

Oswald's simple gesture in paying for their meal had paid dividends. The people were far less surly than they had been yesterday when the small group walked down to the church where the council usually met and the councilmen themselves seemed eager to hear what Oswald had to say.

One of the council was dressed as a priest, though his robe had seen better days and the crucifix attached to the rope around his waist was a crude thing made from two small sticks. Oslac made his way over to him and after a minute or so the two made their way to the altar.

The local priest intoned a prayer or two and then Oslac placed the Bible he always carried with him on the lectern and opened it at a marked passage. He then proceeded to recite the Ten Commandments, before concluding with a prayer for prosperity and a blessing on Brodick.

The simple religious service had been a useful way of preparing the ground. It calmed down the more excitable of the council and it reminded them all that they were Christians.

'Thank you all for coming this morning. I wanted to introduce myself to you properly, though many of you who were here when we drove the pagans from Strathclyde out will already know me. King Domnall Brecc has appointed me as your thegn and I will govern your settlement, with your advice, with a firm but fair hand. At first I proposed to remain at Duilleag Bán na Cille, but I can see that might not be sensible as Brodick is the largest settlement on the island, so I will be moving here shortly. My warriors will accompany me, but Prince Eochaid will remain at Duilleag Bán na Cille with his men to protect it. For the better defence of Brodick, I propose to build a fortress here, as I have at Duilleag Bán na Cille, to protect you during the coming war with Strathclyde.'

There was a stir at the mention of war and the councillors looked at each other in concern.

'I need to raise a force of two hundred warriors, so that we can fight and lay waste to the land of Strathclyde, rather than our homeland. They will need to be young, unmarried men who are good fighters. Married warriors will remain here to protect their families and yours, of course. So what I need to know first is how many trained young warriors you have.'

Silence greeted Oswald's little speech, whilst the council tried to take in what he had said.

'Lord Barra wasn't a warlike man,' Turlough said hesitantly, after a long pause. 'We have hunters and some elderly warriors, but most of us are farmers, merchants and fishermen who settled here after Belin's men were driven out. There has been no programme of training for our young men, such as we hear that you have introduced.'

This came as a body blow to Oswald. Brodick was twice the size of Duilleag Bán na Cille and he had counted on the settlement providing at least forty men to crew one of the new birlinns.

'How many boys and youths do you have? By that I mean between fourteen and twenty.'

'Perhaps fifty, maybe a few more.'

'And how many of those are hunters or fishermen?'

'Less than half, I would think.'

'I see. And how many married men are warriors who could defend you?'

'We have the settlement watch. They are volunteers who have had some military training, but not much. There are twenty of them and perhaps a dozen or so veterans.'

Oswald groaned inwardly. It would take a great deal of time and effort before Brodick could even defend itself, let alone provide him with men for the invasion of Bute. If this was the state that Barra had left his principal settlement in, he dreaded to think what the other smaller hamlets and the settlements in the south of the island were like.

That night he sat down with his companions and they discussed the situation. As Turlough had predicted, there were nearly fifty youths and unmarried men who came forward at the meeting to train as warriors, as well as a fair number of the married ones, who wanted to volunteer to defend their settlement. However, none had armour, helmets or weapons.

'There are quite a few of the Dál nAraidi who are less than happy to serve their king's betrayer,' Eochaid pointed out. 'I could sneak back to Ulster and see how many I can bring back with me.'

Oswald was unwilling at first, but in the end it was agreed that Eochaid would take the Gift of God and the Seraphim with skeleton crews and try to come back with as many warriors as they could carry. He left the next day, taking Lorcan with him.

Oswald waited until ten of his best warriors arrived to start training the men of Brodick and some carpenters to supervise the building of the new fortress, then he set off with Oswiu, Rònan, who had come across the island with the rest of the men, Cormac, Oslac and Jarlath to tour the rest of the island. The situation was just as bad as he had feared and he promised to send some men to help them train when he could do so. He just hoped that Strathclyde didn't invade in the meantime.

Rònan fitted into the small group well. He was now in his mid-twenties and seemed to have forgotten all about his time as a young Pictish prince and then as a slave. He was one of Oswald's best warriors and he thought about making Rònan master of one of the new birlinns. He knew how to steer but not how to trim the sail and navigate. However, it wasn't far across the sea to Bute.

He had been back at Duilleag Bán na Cille for about a week when Keeva told him that she was fairly certain she was pregnant. Oswald was all concern for her, remembering what had happened to Gytha, but his mother told him to stop fussing.

'You are meant to be helping Keeva, not panicking her. Everything will be fine. Gytha was just unlucky. Now, haven't you got a ship being built that you need to inspect, or some warriors to train?'

'Sorry, mother,' he said as he led her away out of earshot. 'I just can't bear the thought of losing her, too.'

'She'll be fine. I'll ask the wise woman to check her later on in the pregnancy, just to make sure that the baby is in the right position. Now stop worrying.'

Oswald stopped her as she turned to go back into his hut.

'There is something else. Now that I'm the thegn, I need to move to Brodick. Duilleag Bán na Cille is too remote from the southern end.'

'I see. Do you intend to invite the rest of the family to come with you?'

'Yes, of course. Why wouldn't I?'

'How long have we got until we have to move?'

Oswald could tell that she was upset by the news.

'You don't have to. I'm merely inviting you, not forcing you. I'm not going until Eochaid gets back in any case.'

'I see. If we come, where will we live?'

177

'I had thought of extending the present hall to include separate chambers for you and Æbbe, me and Œthelwald and for Oslac as my chaplain. Eochaid can become the Headman of Duilleag Bán na Cille.'

'Good. I was wondering when you'd remember that you had a son, but of course you've been too busy bedding your slaves.'

Oswald was about to utter an angry retort, but managed to stop himself just in time. He took a deep breath before replying.

'Do you really want to drive me away again? If so, you are succeeding,' he said calmly but firmly. 'You really do need to think before you speak, Mother. I'm not a child anymore and I won't let you speak to me like that. Perhaps you had better stay here, after all.'

Before she could reply, Oswald turned on his heel and walked away.

The two hadn't spoken since, but Oswald soon forgot the petty argument when Eochaid arrived back with his two birlinns overflowing with men and the odd woman and child.

'I could have brought more. It seems that few are keen on King Congal. They think he's mean spirited, vindictive, greedy and paranoid about being assassinated.'

'Is that all? I could think of a few other things to call him. How many have you brought?'

'Fifty four warriors, five of who are married and a few children.'

'Excellent. With our three crews and a few others under training, we will be able to man all five ships and have about a hundred and fifty men for the invasion.'

'You didn't have much luck finding any men elsewhere?'

'No, the other places are in much the same shape as Brodick. We are training more, but we'll need them to supplement what we have now for the defence of the island.'

He hesitated before continuing.

'I'm moving to Brodick, as that is best place for my hall and I'd be grateful if you'd be the new headman here.'

Eochaid nodded. 'But you must expect me to be a frequent visitor, with my wife.'

'Your wife?'

'Yes, this is Dervla. She's a cousin who was as anxious as anybody else to escape Congal's clutches. She's his cousin, too and he was about to marry her off to a dreadful old chieftain in Munster that Congal wants to ally himself with. We always got on well as children, so just before we left, we wed.'

178

Oswald thought initially that it was a marriage of convenience, as Dervla could have hardly joined a boatload of men on her own as an unmarried girl, but the more he saw them together, the more he believed that love had slowly developed between them and he was glad for his friend. He wished that his children by Keeva could have been legitimate, as those of Eochaid and Dervla would be, but he would do his best for them.

He was slowly getting to know Œthelwald and discovering that the little boy had an unattractive side to his character. He ordered Keeva and Jarlath around as if they were dirt beneath his feet and he seemed very self-centred. He wasn't quite five, so Oswald hoped he'd grow out of it, but he blamed his mother for spoiling the boy. He tried to make allowances for the fact that he'd lost his mother and probably resented Keeva taking her place in his father's bed, but it wasn't easy. Whenever he told the boy off, he felt that he was driving a wedge deeper between them. Perhaps when he was older and he could take him hunting or on voyages their relationship would improve. He certainly hoped so.

For her part, Keeva took over responsibility for looking after Œthelwald, but he knew it was difficult for her.

'I'm sorry my son is such a brat towards you and your brother,' he told her one night after they had made love. It hadn't been as satisfactory as usual and he blamed the fact that they now shared the hut with both Œthelwald and Jarlath.

'He's only a little boy and he must feel very disorientated,' she replied softly. 'First he lost his mother and then he was taken away from his grandmother to live with people he doesn't know; it can't be easy for him.'

'I'm not sure I could be so understanding if I were in your position. Perhaps that's why I love you so much.'

Oswald solved some of the problems with Œthelwald by bringing back an old woman from the settlement to look after him and Keeva. He also changed the design of the extended hall in Brodick. Œthelwald seemed much happier now that he had the old slave to look after him, and the fact that his father paid him a lot more attention helped as well. He even stopped pinching Jarlath whenever he thought no-one was looking.

Finally the day came in early December for the move to Brodick. The first snows had fallen on the mountain tops and the wind had the cold edge of ice in it; he daren't delay any longer. Oswald hugged Eochaid and bade farewell to all those who were remaining behind before stepping aboard the Holy Saviour, holding Œthelwald's hand. The little boy beamed with pride as his father picked him up so that he could see over the gunwale and wave at the crowd on the receding shoreline. The Seraphim followed them out of the sea loch; then they turned right to go around the north end of Arran.

Instead of turning south east as usual, as soon as they were clear of the point known as the Cock of Arran, Oswald kept heading east towards Garrock Head at the southern tip of the Isle of Bute. He wanted to see for himself how good a landing point the beach in Kilchattan Bay might be. From there, it was only five or six miles to Rothesay.

The fishing hamlet at Kilchattan was built in the lee of a hill to the left of the bay and the shore in front of it was rocky and strewn with boulders. However, there was a good sized sandy beach at the far end of the inlet where a few fishing boats were drawn above the high tide mark. Presumably the site had been chosen to gain shelter from the prevailing wind.

The Seraphim had continued along the coast of Arran, but now it came racing back towards him. What wind there was had died and the rowers were pulling for all they were worth. Because they were carrying families and possessions, both birlinns were only lightly crewed by warriors and as soon as he saw the three Strathclyde birlinns in pursuit, all crammed with warriors, he knew they were in trouble.

He suspected they had come from Ard Rossan on the Strathclyde mainland. He was surprised if King Belin was flexing his muscles. Tension had grown between Dal Riada and Strathclyde recently, but Oswald had assumed that Belin would be preoccupied by the current border dispute with the Kingdom of Rheged to the south.

He decided to try a bluff. Although there was no wind, he ordered the sail unfurled to display his symbol of a white sword with rays coming from its blade on a red background. At the same time he had the older boys and the women grab weapons and don helmets before lining the bows of the Holy Saviour. At a distance it might look as if his ship, too, was crammed with fighting men.

Taking his bold reaction as their lead, the Seraphim displayed its red sail with the white-bladed sword too and headed back towards their pursuers. The ploy worked. The Strathclyde birlinns might carry more men, but they obviously had no appetite for a fight at sea with the cursed Whiteblade and his tough warriors. Both ships erupted in cheers as the three enemy ships scuttled back towards Ard Rossan.

Œthelwald had been beside himself with excitement at the prospect of a fight and was bitterly disappointed when the enemy turned tail.

'Never mind, Œthelwald. If you like, I'll teach you how to fight with a seax when we get to Brodick,' Jarlath told him kindly.

'Would you?' the little boy's eyes lit up with excitement, then they narrowed in doubt. 'But you're too young to be training as a warrior and you're only a slave. You've no more idea of how to use a seax than I have!'

Oswiu, who had overheard the exchange, gripped his nephew's arm firmly.

'Now you listen to me, you little shit, Jarlath is one of the ship's boys and they are taught the rudiments of fighting with a seax so that they can help defend the ship.'

'Ow, let go of me. You're hurting!'

'I'd do more than bruise your arm if I were your father. Jarlath's offer to teach you was generously meant and you spat it back in his face. He's twice the man you'll ever be.'

He gave the little boy a look of disgust and released his arm. Oswald had overheard the conversation, but hadn't intervened. Oswiu was his favourite brother by some way and it pained him to see him clash with his son. He'd seen the venomous look that his son had given his brother as he walked away and he had a nasty feeling that the obvious antipathy between them would get worse as the boy grew older, but he was at a loss to know what to do about it. He just hoped that their relationship would improve with time. It would turn out to be a vain hope.

# Chapter Twelve – The Invasion of Bute

## Spring to Summer 628 AD

The Monday after the celebration of Easter was set as the time for the two invasions – Domnall Brecc's landings on the Cowal Peninsula and Oswald's on Bute. By that time Oswald had settled into his new home in Brodick and Keeva's belly had gradually grown larger. As his family each had their own rooms in the newly extended hall, he and Keeva now had much more privacy. Their slaves lived with the others in the main hall, but that didn't include Jarlath. Oswald had freed him and his sister as soon as they arrived at Brodick, but the boy continued to be his servant, sleeping outside the room he shared with Keeva.

He had hated leaving her with three months of her pregnancy still to run, but he hoped that this time he would be able to return in time for the birth. As usual, the sight of Jarlath as one of his crew reminded him of his lover. The two still looked remarkably alike, though the boy's jaw line was firming up, making him look a little more masculine now that he was nearly eleven.

It was a dozen sea miles from Brodick to Kilchattan Bay and, as they had left just as dawn was breaking, he expected to arrive no later than mid-morning. Allowing for securing the inhabitants of the settlement, he expected to be able to reach Ascog, another fishing hamlet, before dark and spend the night there. They would then be a mere two miles from Rothesay and well placed to make a dawn attack on the settlement.

It was vital that no-one escape to warn the inhabitants of his approach, therefore he sent the Seraphim in first so that their crew could set up an ambush astride the track that led north on the road between Kilchattan and Rothesay.

A few brave souls put up brief resistance, but it was all over in less than an hour. Leaving ten of his men behind as guards, they had just left the bay when they met the crew of the Seraphim, escorting two women and three children. The three men who had escaped with them were all dead.

'Take them back to the settlement. I've left ten men there with the ships' boys to look after our birlinns and the inhabitants. Once you've handed them over, follow us up to Ascog.'

Lorcan, the shipmaster of the Seraphim, nodded, but then asked how so few men would be able to bring the five birlinns up to Rothesay on the next day.

'I had thought to send enough men back here once we'd won the place, but it might make more sense to man one ship and that one can tow the rest.'

Oswald thought for a moment before making his mind up.

'I want to have as many men as possible with me for the assault on Rothesay as we don't know how many warriors they have. But the fleet is exposed where it is and, as it's only three miles from the Island of Cambrae to Kilchattan, it can be seen from there and so might be attacked. It'll take the enemy time to muster men and ships to do that, but I'd rather have the fleet secure at Rothesay by nightfall tomorrow. Take your crew and remain at Kilchattan until dawn tomorrow, then use them to man the Seraphim and one other birlinn. You can use one of them to tow the other three the seven or eight miles up to Rothesay. If we haven't captured the settlement by the time you arrive, we'll have failed anyway.'

'What about the fifth birlinn?'

'I want that in position by dawn, to cut off any escape from the settlement by sea.'

'Very well, Lord. What about the inhabitants of Kilchattan?'

'You can tell them before you leave that they're free, but are now subjects of Dal Riada, not Strathclyde. It won't make a huge difference to them, so I expect them to accept the change. Once we have Rothesay, we can send warriors to the other few settlements and make sure they know of the change in their masters, too. I don't anticipate any serious opposition from them. The main threat is of a counter-attack from the mainland, but as Belin's in the south conducting a war with Rheged and soon he'll know that Cowal had been invaded as well, he'll no doubt have other priorities.'

Rothesay lay on the south coast of a bay of the same name, at the end of a valley surrounded by two dominant hills. Oswald's plan was to send a ship's crew to secure each of the two hills above the settlement and then advance down the valley, with one crew on each bank of the river that ran from a small loch inland down to the sea. That way the inhabitants would be trapped in the settlement.

He was aware that there were likely to be fishing boats, and perhaps other craft, which people could use to escape to sea, and Rothesay Bay was quite extensive. Lorcan would just have to do his best to intercept them. If a few got away, it wasn't the end of the world.

It rained that night, which made for an unpleasant trudge into position above Rothesay. The rain stopped just before the eastern sky behind the dark clouds grew lighter. Oswald and thirty men moved down one side of the river whilst Oswiu led the same number down the opposite bank. Both stopped at the same moment when they saw the palisade that protected the settlement from the landward side in front of them. They retreated out of sight of the settlement and each sent a runner to tell Eochaid and Gwrtheyrn, the other shipmaster, to stop where they were for now.

Oswald crept forward to examine the palisade and the gates, which were to one side of the river that ran under the palisade through a grid made of stout cross timbers lashed together. He made his way parallel to the palisade until he reached the sea. The palisade ended in a stone wall four feet across and eight feet high that ran out into the sea, well beyond the depth where it would be possible to wade around it, even at the lowest tide. Someone had gone to a lot of trouble to protect the settlement from a landward assault.

The day was getting brighter as the sun rose behind the clouds and he still had no idea how he was going to capture the settlement without a significant loss of life. Then he had an idea.

The gates had been kept closed until farmers started arriving with their produce to sell in the settlement. There was no point in occupying the low hills above the settlement, as the only exit points for the inhabitants to flee were out of the gates or by boat, so he called in his men from the hills above Rothesay and they joined the others in the undergrowth on each side of the river. There were two tracks that led to the gates, one alongside the river and the other from the west. Oswald decided to lay his ambush on the latter, as his men had blocked the other route. A few carts laden with vegetables passed his hiding place, but it wasn't a cart he was looking for.

Meat had been scarce in the winter, but now that spring had arrived with its crop of new-born lambs, piglets and calves, drovers had started to bring their spare livestock into the local market. When he saw a man and three young boys herding about thirty sheep down the track, Oswald nudged Oswiu and signalled across the track to Rònan. It didn't take ten men to subdue the four, but he didn't want there to be any chance of one escaping. Three warriors surrounded the man whilst two more grabbed each boy. Another half a dozen prevented the sheep from panicking and escaping in the confusion.

Suddenly, one of the boys twisted out of the grip of the two men who each held a shoulder and he raced away dressed in just trousers, leaving his rough woollen tunic behind. Except, now that the child's torso was uncovered, Oswald could see that it wasn't a boy at all, but a young girl of perhaps twelve or thirteen.

One of the men went to put an arrow in her back, but Oswald knocked his bow aside and went racing after the girl. He didn't have to go very far, as she tripped and fell. She had been looking fearfully over her shoulder instead of looking where she was going and stumbled into a pothole in the track. Oswald pulled her up by the hair and marched her back to join the rest.

'Put this on, girl and don't be so stupid,' he told her, thrusting her tunic at her. 'We're not going to harm you, just borrow your sheep for a while.'

He turned to the man, presumably her father.

'Why do you dress your daughter as a boy?'

He shrugged. 'It's easier to herd sheep in boy's clothing and it's safer if strangers think she's a boy, now she's thirteen.'

Oswald laughed. 'Well, she had me fooled. Now you and your children are to stay near here with three of my men for a few hours. If you behave, then you'll come to no harm. Try to run and they'll kill, not just the one who runs, but all of you. Do they speak Gaelic or do you need to translate?'

The man looked puzzled. 'We all speak Gaelic. What did you think we spoke?'

'Brythonic, as you're from Strathclyde.'

'Not on Bute. We may be ruled by Belin, but we were Scotii from Ulster, originally.'

'So you wouldn't object if you were part of Dal Riada?'

'Makes little difference to me who rules us; they'll bleed us dry with taxes whoever they are, but yes, we'd rather be ruled by our own kind.'

'I'm Oswald, Thegn of Arran. Domnall Brecc wants to incorporate Bute into Dal Riada.'

'That's why you and your warriors are here? I see. Well, that's fine, but the Lord of Bute is one of King Belin's nobles and his warriors are from Strathclyde, too. They won't be so happy to see you,' and then added belatedly, 'Lord.'

'No, I had rather assumed that. How many warriors does he have?'

'About fifty in all, though some are scarcely more than boys.'

'Not experienced fighters, then?'

'No, Bute has been peaceful for awhile, so most of them are inexperienced.'

'Right. Oswiu here will go with you after he's made himself look more like a farmer. He'll take a seax, though; that shouldn't be too obvious. What I want you to do is to keep the sheep in the gateway for long enough so that the guards can't close it quickly. That'll give us a chance to rush the gates and capture them. Am I correct in assuming that the rest of the enemy will be in the fortress near the beach?'

The man nodded. 'Look, Lord Oswald, if there's going to be fighting, I'd rather my children stayed here and I took another man or two with me to help control the sheep.'

Oswald nodded and told two more of his men to take off their helmets and padded jerkins.

It was only then that Oswald noticed that his brother couldn't take his eyes off the girl. He hadn't looked at her before, but he could see that, under the dirt, she had an attractive face. Her hair was filthy, too, but washed and allowed to grow a bit longer, she might be reasonably presentable. He was well aware that the girl he slept with wasn't his wife, so he couldn't object if his brother wanted a lover too. However, this girl was the farmer's daughter, not his slave, and he might not be too happy at turning his barely pubescent child over to Oswiu.

Frowning at his brother and shaking his head disapprovingly made the young man blush and Oswiu set off with the sheep and the others without a backward glance.

There were only two men on guard at the gate and to save themselves effort, they only opened one gate of the two, to let the sheep in. Oswiu didn't bother to use the sheep to block the gateway; he and the other two warriors killed the sentries and threw open the other gate. They then drove the sheep off to one side outside the palisade so they didn't get in the way.

Before anyone inside the settlement realised it, Oswald and seventy of his warriors were running through the streets making for the fortress. The rest stayed with Oswiu to guard the gates.

'I don't suppose there is any chance of a market today, so I might just as well take my sheep back home for now,' the farmer said to Oswiu as the last of Oswald's men disappeared from sight.

186

The young man grinned. 'No, don't do that. We'll buy quite a few of them for a feast tonight to celebrate the liberation of Bute.'

'Oh, I see.' Then he narrowed his eyes suspiciously. 'No, I don't think so.'

'Why not?' Oswiu asked, surprised.

'Well, Lord Oswald is hardly likely to give me a fair price, is he?'

'Yes, he has every reason to. In any case, he's an honourable man and a fair one. If we were raiding, we'd kill you, take your sheep and also your children as slaves. But we're not. Oswald is to be your thegn and will deal with you justly.'

'Oh, very well. We'll stay, then. I'll need to get the beasts corralled, though.' He turned to his children. 'You three start cutting saplings to make a few hurdles so we can pen them against the outside of the palisade.'

Leaving six men guarding the gates, Oswiu and the rest helped make the hurdles and soon had the sheep confined. By then the farmer had noticed the calves' eyes that his daughter kept making at Oswiu, before casting them down demurely to the ground. It was obvious that her interest in him was reciprocated.

'Fianna,' he yelled at her angrily. 'Go and sit over there with your brothers, away from these men.'

Turning to Oswiu, he upbraided him quietly.

'You may be able to kill me, God knows I'm no warrior, but my daughter is not a whore for you to use for your pleasure. I've eyes in my head and I've seen you flirting with her, so don't deny it!'

To his surprise, Oswiu smiled at him instead of getting irate.

'I confess that she interests me and I think I interest her. I'm sixteen, not much older than Fianna and like her. I'm a virgin and, even if I wasn't, I'm not the sort of person who would take a girl to bed, deflower her and abandon her, and I resent the implication that I am. I don't know your daughter, but I'd like to see if our attraction for one another is more than a passing interest. If it is, I can't promise her marriage – my mother would have a fit – but I can offer her a home and treat her as if she was my wife. My brother is not married to the girl he shares his hall with, either, but Keeva is loved by him and well cared for.'

The farmer looked doubtful and said nothing for a while.

'You say you want to see if yours is just a fleeting physical attraction or whether there can be more to it. How do you propose to find out? You don't expect me to leave her here with you?'

Oswiu shook his head. 'No, of course not. Tell me where you live and as soon as my brother can spare me, I'll come and pay you a visit. Is that acceptable?'

The farmer nodded. 'I'm Bedwyr and my farm is three miles along this track on the left. The house is on top of a small hill. You can't miss it.'

As soon as Bedwyr had left Oswiu's side, Fianna came running up to him.

'What did he say? Were you talking about me?'

'Why would he be interested in you, girl? God knows, your brothers look better than you do, dressed like that.'

'Stop teasing me; you know they're as ugly as sin because they look like you. You always told me I have my mother's good looks.'

'Well, he says he might come and visit us in a few days. Perhaps he would like you better if you put on a kirtle and tried to make your hair look less like a bird's nest.'

'So he is interested! How old is he? I know he's called Oswiu and he's the Thegn of Arran's brother.'

'Sixteen, so he says, though he looks a little older. He doesn't know if he likes you or not, child, so don't start imagining you're in love or anything silly like that. He'll only break your heart.'

He knew as he said it that he was wasting his breath.

~~~

As he ran towards the fortress near the sea, Oswald felt elated. He hadn't expected to gain the settlement so easily and without a drop of blood spilt, apart from the sentries at the gate. Now he was praying that he could surprise the garrison in the fortress. It was a vain hope.

The gates to the compound around the hall were shut and archers in the watchtower sent a few arrows towards the attackers before they managed to seek shelter behind nearby houses. Oswald noted that the palisade around the hall was much lower than that which defended the settlement on the landward side. It was no more than five feet high and presumably designed to give the hall privacy rather than be a serious defensive wall. Now some defenders had found something to stand on so that they could see over the wall, but what bothered Oswald more was the sight of several men, including one dressed in a long blue tunic and a red cloak embroidered in gold – presumably the hitherto Lord of Bute – making their way down the beach towards a currach. Two women and three children followed the group, struggling to keep up. If, as he assumed from the fine clothing of one of the women, she was the Lord's wife, her husband was more intent on saving his own skin than he was on protecting his family. Oswald's lips curled in distain. Such a man had no honour and deserved to die.

He called across to his best archer and pointed at the fleeing Lord of Bute. The man looked sceptical, but he nocked an arrow to his bowstring. He took careful aim and allowed for the breeze blowing from the south. He and Oswald watched as the arrow sped on its way, but it missed its target, lodging in the back of the man trudging through the sand next to him. The Lord looked back in alarm and increased his pace.

'I'm sorry, Lord Oswald, he's out of range now.'

Oswald nodded and thanked the archer, resigned now that the man would escape. Then, as the small group clambered into the currach, the two women lifting the children in before being pulled aboard themselves, the Seraphim sailed into view around the headland. The men started rowing frantically, leaving stranded the two who had pushed the currach off the beach. It did them no good, though. It took the Seraphim no more than ten minutes to reach the currach. The Strathclyde warriors obviously had more pride than their Lord, as they sent a few arrows towards the birlinn before a much greater answering volley ended their resistance.

Less than half an hour later, the birlinn and the currach slid their prows onto the beach and Lorcan strode towards Oswald. There had been no more showers of arrows from the hall's palisade after the brief encounter at sea. Oswald greeted him and congratulated him for arriving at the opportune moment. Just then, another birlinn hove into view, towing the rest of the fleet. Apologising to Oswald, Lorcan sent his birlinn back into the bay so that the crew could sail the unmanned birlinns onto the beach.

'I'm sorry, Oswald,' Lorcan said when he returned, 'I fear that the Lord of Bute was killed, along with five of his men; two more were wounded, but they'll live.' He looked at the ground for a moment. 'The lady was killed, too.'

'I see. It can't be helped. I'd have only sent them to Domnall as hostages.'

'The other girl is a slave, who looks after the three children: two boys who look to be about five and three and a girl of four. What do you want done with them?'

Oswald thought for a moment and then called his brother over.

'Oswiu, once we have secured the hall, I want you to take the previous Lord's children and their nursemaid out to that farm you're so keen to visit. Ask the farmer and his wife if they'll look after the children until I decide what to do with them. Oh! And just make sure you're back by nightfall. I don't want to have to send men looking for you.'

Oswiu gave him a broad grin. 'Nightfall today or tomorrow?'

Oswald sighed. 'Tomorrow, if her father hasn't cut off your balls by then.'

'Thank you. I suspect that either I'll be back long before then, or I won't be alone.'

~~~

'Your Lord is dead and you're surrounded. Come out unarmed and your lives will be spared.'

Oswald now had over a hundred and twenty men with Lorcan's crew, so they outnumbered the Strathclyde men three to one.

'Get stuffed, you Irish bastard,' someone inside the palisade called out defiantly.

'I'm a Northumbrian Angle and my mother would cut off your manhood for implying that she wasn't married to my father. Now if you're quite finished trading insults, are you going to do the sensible thing and surrender, or do you want us to jump over this poor excuse for a palisade and slaughter you all?'

There was a fair amount of heated discussion before the voice called out again.

'What'll happen to us if we surrender?'

'You'll be allowed to live and be sent as slaves to Arran to work on the land.'

'We have no master now. If we surrender, we'll become your men and serve you loyally. We'd rather die than become slaves.'

'Are you Christians?'

'Some of us are. Why?'

'If you all agree to become Christians and swear on the Bible to serve me, I'll re-settle you on Arran as my warriors.'

There was another pause for discussion before the gates swung open and a large man in a byrnie and a helmet with a nose guard appeared and threw his sword, seax and shield onto the ground in front of him.

'We accept, Whiteblade. We'll serve you on Arran.'

# Chapter Thirteen – The Death of Kings

## 633 to 634 AD

In the five years that had passed since he became Thegn of Bute as well as Arran, Oswald had been kept busy ruling his two islands, settling disputes and administering justice. He'd made Oswiu his deputy on Bute and he and Fianna now had a girl of three and a boy of one. Domnall Brecc had used the three children of the Lord of Bute as negotiating tools for the treaty which he'd finally signed with the embattled King Belin of Strathclyde. Domnall had retained Bute and the Cowal Peninsula and in exchange, the children, who turned out to be Belin's cousins, were returned. Domnall also promised him help if there were any incursions into his territory by his neighbours.

Belin had used his new alliance to force Rheged to make peace with him. That was something of a relief to Oswald, as the prospect of war with Rheged had dismayed him. When his father ruled Northumbria, Rheged had been a client kingdom and the last thing Oswald wanted was to make himself unpopular with a potential ally.

Keeva had given birth to two girls and Oswald did his best to hide his disappointment that they hadn't yet managed to have a son. Œthelwald was now nine and although Oswald loved his son, he knew that he wasn't a particularly likeable child. He berated himself for looking forward to the day that he could send Œthelwald off to Iona to be educated and leave him there until he was fourteen, when he'd be old enough to start training as a warrior. It wasn't the way a father was supposed to feel about his son and he wondered what he could do to bring them closer.

Fergus had managed to conquer Skye with little difficulty, so Dal Riada was now more powerful than it had ever been. The one thing Domnall hadn't managed to do was to be reconciled with the Ulaidh and their king, Congal Claen. The struggle between him and the Uí Néill for control of Ulster had continued sporadically, with Congal initially getting the upper hand. He had gathered allies from the other provinces of Ireland, mainly in Leinster and Meath and in 629 he made a bid to be crowned as High King of Ireland. However, he was thwarted by the southern Uí Néill.

Eochaid and Dervla had also had children, a boy called Lethlobar and a girl named Megan. They remained at Duilleag Bán na Cille and Oswald saw them when he visited there, which wasn't often. Gradually he and Eochaid grew apart.

'I don't really understand how you can continue to accept Congal Claen as King of the Ulaidh when he killed your father. I know there is nothing I want more than to rule Northumbria.'

'That's you; it's not me. I've never wanted to be a king and, although I would like to see my father's killing avenged, I'd rather Congal ruled the Ulaidh than I was forced to do so.'

They didn't argue about it, but Oswald's failure to understand his friend's indifference lay between them and gradually their relationship cooled.

Since his successful conquest of Bute, Oswald had continued to build up his force of trained warriors. He couldn't afford to keep most of them permanently employed, but many of his farmers and fishermen had undergone training as warriors when they were younger, and those who were primarily warriors were kept gainfully employed raiding Ireland and the Isle of Man, which was part of the Kingdom of Mercia.

Then Oswald's brother Osguid arrived with the news that he'd been waiting for. His mother's brother, Edwin, King of Northumbria, had fallen out with Penda of Mercia. Cadwallon, King of Gwynedd, who Edwin had defeated a few years previously, had quickly allied himself with Mercia against Northumbria. It was the first serious setback Edwin had faced since usurping the throne sixteen years previously.

'What's the latest you've heard, brother?'

'Cadwallon and the Penda have invaded Elmet and Edwin has decided to take action against them before they move into Deira.'

Elmet was a small kingdom to the south of Northumbria that Edwin and Mercia had both tried to take over in 616. Edwin had finally managed to incorporate it into his kingdom in 627, when the previous Mercian king died. Obviously, that had rankled with the Mercians for some time and Penda had seized this opportunity to invade.

~~~

Penda sat on his horse and examined the low wetlands in front of him. A mile and a half away lay the confluence of the Rivers Trent, Ouse and Idle. To the north-west lay the course of the River Thorne, into which several other small rivers ran. There was an area of peat bog to the left of the Thorne and another, larger, one on the left bank of the River Idle. Penda wondered how best to use this area, known as Heathfield Chase, to defeat Edwin. Although the King of Northumbria had the reputation of being the most powerful ruler in England, Penda despised him. Edwin held the throne because he was an Ætheling and was only king because he was born to the right father. So was Cadwallon, although *Ætheling* was a purely Anglo-Saxon term that roughly equated to *prince*. Penda didn't have much respect for his ally as a military commander, either.

Penda had been the son of a noble who had risen to become the leader of Mercia through his abilities. At first he was content with the title of hereræswa – or war leader – but when the last king of the direct royal line died, he had been elected by the Witan as the best man to rule them.

Beside him sat his two sons, Paeda and Wulfhere. Turning to them, he asked for their ideas on how to lay out his army.

'Well,' Paeda, the eldest, began hesitantly. 'We could draw it up in the triangle formed by the Ouse, the Idle and Thorne Moor. They would defend our flanks and provide an obstacle to our front.'

He smiled at his father, pleased with his solution, but his pleasure faded into dejection when he saw the contemptuous look on the king's face.

'We'd be trapped, you fool. He'd use his archers to weaken us and then drive us back into the Ouse to drown! Wulfhere, have you got any more sensible ideas?'

His younger brother, who had been relishing Paeda's discomfort, stopped grinning and swallowed anxiously several times, so that his prominent Adam's apple bounced up and down.

'Well, if we don't want to be trapped there, I suppose we want to try and lure King Edwin there.'

'Humph! That's blindingly obvious from what I just said to Paeda. Any brilliant ideas how we do that?'

Wulfhere's nervousness vied with his irritation as Paeda smirked at him behind their father's back.

'Well, I suppose we could um, er, drive him northwards between Hatfield Moor and the Trent.'

'Have you forgotten that he outnumbers us? How exactly do we force him to retreat?'

Both brothers examined the grass being cropped by their horses, not daring to look their father in the eye. Penda snorted noisily to convey his exasperation with his sons. Then he muttered an oath under his breath as Cadwallon and three of his chieftains trotted up to join them.

'Any ideas, Penda?' the black-haired Briton asked with a smile.

'Yes,' Penda replied shortly. 'We'll set up our tents there, between Thorne Moor and the confluence of the three rivers, tonight and wait for Edwin to attack the camp at dawn tomorrow. I'll need some of your men who can swim to keep the campfires going tonight.'

'But, father, you've just said it would be suicide to get trapped there!' Paeda objected.

'We won't be there, you little fool. We just need Edwin to think that we are.'

'Where will we be, then?' asked the puzzled Wulfhere.

'Camped miles away. We'll move into position here, in these woods to the east of Hatfield Moor, once Edwin attacks our supposed camp. Your men, Cadwallon, will need to move into position between Thorne Moor and the Ouse to cut off their escape. Then they'll have a choice. Fight and be slaughtered, drown trying to cross the rivers, or surrender.'

~~~

Edwin was moving down the far bank of the River Trent when his scouts came in to report that the enemy were putting up their camp just south of the Ouse, where it joined the Trent and the Idle.

'We have them!' Edwin told his two eldest sons, Osfrith and Edafrith, when the scout had departed. 'No-one in his right mind would camp there and Penda's no fool. It must be Cadwallon's army. We'll deal with them first and then go looking for the Mercians.'

'Wouldn't it be better to locate Penda first?' Edafrith asked.

'Yes, but I don't want Cadwallon to escape.'

'When do we attack, father?' Osfrith's eyes were alight with excitement. At seventeen, he was two years older than his brother and like his father, he was impatient to teach the Welsh invaders a lesson.

Eadfrith felt that they were being reckless to plan an attack without knowing exactly where their enemies were, but he held his counsel. He could see that he would be wasting his breath trying to dissuade them. This was the first time his father had taken him to war with him and he wasn't going to risk making him regret it.

Edwin's army was mainly composed of his own trained warriors, drawn from all over Northumbria, and the fyrd – the muster of armed freemen – from Elmet and Deira. The fyrd of Bernicia hadn't been called out, as the battle wouldn't be fought near their territory and Edwin felt that he had more than enough men. In all, his army numbered nearly a thousand, whereas Cadwallon was reputed to have about three hundred and Penda another five hundred.

Although Edwin had converted to Christianity, mainly to please his wife and father-in-law, he didn't encourage his subjects to do likewise. No priests accompanied his army, something that Eadfrith deplored. Unlike his brother, who was still a pagan, he was an ardent believer in the new faith and regularly attended mass with his mother. Bishop Paulinus could have accompanied them but he had remained at Bebbanburg on Edwin's instructions.

As dawn broke, Edwin advanced on foot with his two sons, surrounded by his professional warriors. The fyrd followed on, commanded by the nobles of Elmet and Deira. It was obvious almost immediately that the set-up was a trap; the tents were unoccupied and those few men that there were in the camp fled immediately. Edwin looked around him, wondering where the enemy were, when a roar and the clash of weapons gave him the answer. He was being attacked in the rear.

Edwin and Osfrith immediately started to force their way back through their men to see what was happening, leaving Eadfrith in charge of the experienced warriors in what had been the vanguard. Eadfrith stood there, uncertain what to do, until fighting erupted on his left flank. He immediately wheeled the front ranks to face this new threat, yelling for the nearby men of the fyrd, who by now were completely confused, to form up behind the leading warriors. It was the right thing to do and soon Eadfrith was forcing Cadwallon and his Welshmen back.

Meanwhile, Edwin and his other son had reached the fighting between Hatfield Moor and the River Trent. The rear half of the fyrd had been taken by surprise and several of their leaders had been killed before they could turn to face the Mercians. Consequently, they were on the point of rout when King Edwin reached them. Although many rallied to him and Eadfrith when they arrived, they had already sustained a large number of casualties. When Osfrith led his men off to fight Cadwallon, the fyrd finally had the space in which to retreat, rather than face the better armed and experienced Mercians.

Edwin thrust his sword into the belly of a large, rotund Mercian and the man sunk to his knees. Then out of the corner of his eye Edwin saw his favourite son being attacked by two men, both in byrnies and helmets and armed with swords and shields. He went to help him, but was confronted by a Mercian wielding a battle axe. Edwin swung his shield up to defend himself from the axe blow and his arm was jarred by the impact. Unfortunately the shield started to split with the axe embedded in it. Whilst the axe man struggled to pull his weapon free, Edwin shoved his sword up between the man's neck and chin. The point entered his brain and he slumped to the ground. Edwin tried to free his sword, but it was trapped; he released his grip on it, drew his seax and cut the leather strap which attached his sword to his wrist. His shield was also useless, so he let go of it. When he turned to go to Osfrith's aid, he saw that he was too late. His son was dead and his slayers were heading towards him.

Edwin looked around him for his men, but they had been driven back and he found himself on his own. In addition to the two men who had killed his son, there were several Mercians between him and the rest of his army. He prepared himself for death, but it wasn't to the Christian God that he prayed; rather it was to the old gods of his ancestors. He had no illusions that his conversion was anything other than political and now there was no reason to pretend anymore. He tore the crucifix from around his neck and picked up a discarded shield.

The Mercians closed around him, but didn't come within range.

'You see, King Edwin, my men are well trained. They know that I want the pleasure of killing you myself.'

There was a slight sneer when the man said the word 'king'. Edwin turned to regard the bear of a man standing behind him. Penda of Mercia stood a few inches taller than most men of his time, had broader shoulders and was stocky of build, but not fat. His biceps bulged out of the short sleeves of the leather tunic he wore under his byrnie and his striking ice blue eyes stared out of the holes in his helmet. Like many rich Anglo-Saxons, his steel helmet had a ridge of gold running fore and aft over the crown and a gold circlet around the bottom of it. His eyes and nose were protected by a curved piece of steel with eye holes, riveted to the brim of the helmet and a chain mail aventail protected his neck.

Penda hefted his sword in his hand and pulled his shield, bearing the golden horse of Mercia on a blue field, closer to his body. He circled Edwin and the latter nervously held his borrowed shield in front of his chest. He was well aware that, unlike his own shield, which was made of lime wood covered in leather and banded in bronze with a large metal boss, his borrowed shield was made of several lengths of oak nailed onto cross slats. He doubted if it would withstand more than one blow from Penda' sword.

196

~~~

Eadfrith watched elatedly as the beaten Welsh continued to fall back under the onslaught from his warriors. Cadwallon's men had little armour and few helmets. Their half-naked bodies were painted in blue whorls and other designs and some had spiked their hair with lime. Their circular shields were half the size of those carried by the Northumbrians and they carried more spears and axes than swords.

However, their line was becoming shorter, because they were now hemmed in by a bend in the River Ouse on the left and the peat bogs of Thorne Moor on their right. This not only protected their flanks, but it meant that the superior numbers opposing them meant little. Cadwallon knew that if he retreated much further, he would be trapped at the junction of the Ouse and the River Aire.

It was at this point that a messenger arrived to tell Eadfrith that his brother was dead and the other half of the army was on the point of defeat. Cursing, Eadfrith left the senior noble in command with instructions to give the Welsh no mercy and raced back towards the south, where he could see the routed fyrd running towards him.

He tried to halt them and managed to gather a few to his side, but most kept on running – though there was nowhere for them to go except the battle with the Welsh. They could wade across the River Idle, as he'd just done, but not across the Ouse or the Trent. He pushed on south and forced his way through the press of men still confronting the Mercians. When he got to the front rank, he saw his father engaged in single combat with a man who was plainly playing with him.

Penda brought his sword down and Edwin deflected the blow with his shield. The blow had loosened one of the planks from which it was made and this now hung at an angle, making it near on useless. However, Edwin had crouched down and took advantage of his position to stab his seax into Penda's massive thigh. It must have been painful, but if it was, Penda gave no indication.

The wound wasn't serious, but the Mercian king was losing blood and he wasn't as quick on his feet now. He had also lost some of his confidence, which had been replaced by rage. He swung his sword in a sweeping blow aimed at decapitating Edwin, who ducked just in time. The sword struck the golden crouching lion ornament riveted on top of Edwin's helmet, slicing it in half and knocking the helmet back with some force. It was anchored in place by a leather strap under Edwin's chin and this now tightened, nearly throttling him, before it broke and the helmet went flying behind him.

Edwin gasped for breath whilst Penda stumbled. He had expected the blow to meet the resistance of Edwin's neck, so striking the ornament hadn't checked the blow as he'd anticipated. He halted his momentum by going down on one knee before springing up and round. He wasn't quick enough. Edwin was gasping for breath, but he forced himself into action and brought his seax down towards Penda's back.

One of the Mercian archers, believing that his king's life was in danger, had an arrow already nocked to his bowstring. As Edwin's blade darted forward, the arrow was released. The archer hadn't had time to draw back his bow fully, so the arrow lacked power; had it struck Edwin's byrnie, the chain mail would have been enough to stop it. It didn't, though; it drove into the king's unprotected neck, severing an artery on the way.

Seeing his father fall with blood spurting out of the wound, Eadfrith ran forward and threw himself onto his knees, cradling his father's dying body in his arms.

'How touching,' Penda jeered. 'I presume that you're Edwin's surviving son, Eadfrith? You had better tell your men to throw down their weapons before I order my men to kill every last one of them.'

Dumbly the boy nodded, stood dejectedly and gave the necessary order. Had he known what fate had in store for him, he would have died there and then trying to kill Penda.

~~~

Oswald had just returned to Brodick from Rothesay when he heard the news from an over-excited Oswiu.

'Aidan's here. Edwin's been slain in battle by Penda of Mercia!'

'Aidan? Here? Edwin, dead? Who's now King of Northumbria?'

Oswald's mind was in a turmoil. He had got used to his life as an exile, but he was still a young man and he had far from given up the idea that one day, he might be able to return to Northumbria as its ruler. It was evident that Aidan hadn't told Oswiu, or anyone else, any more than the fact that Edwin and one of his sons had been killed in a battle somewhere in Elmet or Deira, Oswiu wasn't sure.

Oswald embraced Keeva and his two daughters, who were waiting on the beach with the rest of his family, before greeting his mother and sister and then grasping the nine year old Œthelwald by the shoulders and smiling at him. Oswald had taken every opportunity over the past few months to take him hunting and had promised him that next year he could come with him as a ship's boy. Once the idea of being at everyone's beck and call would have horrified him, but Œthelwald had mellowed. He still didn't get on well with Oswiu, though.

'Aidan, I'm delighted to see you, old friend. How are you?'

Then he noticed the young monk by Aidan's side. At first he didn't recognise him, but then he hadn't seen him for years. He quickly calculated that he must be in his early twenties by now.

'Rònan, I wouldn't have recognised you if you hadn't been standing by Brother Aidan's side.'

The two smiled at one another.

'It's good to see you again too, Prince Oswald.'

'You're being very formal.'

'It's appropriate, now that you're the brother of a king.'

Oswald looked bewildered and Aidan suggested that they all sit down and he would tell them what he knew.

The three took a seat and Oswiu came in and joined them, signalling to a boy to go and fetch wine and refreshments.

'Water and a little bread and a bite of cheese, if you have it, will suffice for us. Thank you, Lord Oswiu.'

Oswald smiled. It seemed that Aidan had grown more frugal and ascetic as he grew older. Both he and his acolyte looked as if they would get blown away by a strong gust of wind.

'Now, I only know what I gathered from the Picts, but they were all full of Edwin's death and the election of your brother Eanfrith to the throne of Bernicia by the Witan. Sadly, although Eanfrith had become a Christian and I had baptised him during his time in the land of the Picts, I am told he has now reverted to paganism.'

'Do you know why?'

'I suspect because, although Edwin converted on marriage, most Northumbrians are pagans still and Penda of Mercia, who Eanfrith seeks to appease, is a pagan.'

'What of Edwin's wife and children?'

'I heard that Osfrith was slain with him and Eadfrith was captured. His wife and the younger children have fled to her father in Kent, or so the story goes.'

'I wonder why he left Eadfrith alive.' Oswiu pondered.

'Perhaps Penda thought to make him a puppet king. Might he try to put him on the throne of Deira and Elmet?'

'If so, he's too late. The Witan in York has chosen your cousin Osric as its new king.'

Oswald sat lost in thought for a while. It seemed that he had missed an opportunity to take advantage of Edwin's death, but of more concern was the fact that the kingdom was divided again after his father had managed to unite it, and that made it even more vulnerable to the depredations of Penda and Cadwallon. He was as certain as he could be that they would take advantage of their victory and plunder the land. Not only would it make both men and their armies rich, but it would destroy the power of Northumbria and allow Mercia to become the dominant kingdom in England.

'Where will you go?' he asked Aidan.

'Back to Iona, for now. Like Eanfrith, Osric has renounced Christianity and reverted to paganism. I need to discuss with the abbot how we can persuade them – and their people, this time – to follow Christ. What will you do?'

'Go and see Domnall Brecc and get him to release me and my men from our oaths to follow him. From what little I know of my half-brother and my cousin, I don't believe that either will survive long, as neither Penda nor Cadwallon have agreed to their enthronement. I need to be ready for the next move in this dangerous game.'

~~~

Osric – the son of Ælfric, the King of Deira who had been killed when Oswald's father had united the two halves of Northumbria – had struggled to raise another army after the disaster at Heathfield Chase. He was the obvious choice to succeed Edwin, his cousin, when the latter was killed, but instead of being accepted by the whole of Northumbria, Bernicia had opted to crown the eldest son of the man who had slain Osric's father. It was hardly a move calculated to unite opposition against the invaders.

Had Northumbria remained a single entity, it might have been able to withstand the advance of Penda and Cadwallon, but Osric couldn't bring himself to form an alliance with Eanfrith. Instead, he took advantage of the fact that Penda had returned to Mercia to deal with a problem there and promptly besieged Cadwallon and his Welshmen in Eoforwīc as soon as he had gathered enough men.

The King of Gwynedd had lost almost a hundred men at Heathfield Chase, so was believed to have no more than two hundred with him in the city and some of those would be wounded. Osric, therefore, believed that the three hundred he had managed to raise would suffice.  What he had ignored was the fact that his army included old men and boys as young as thirteen, and that many of them hadn't been trained to fight.

Much of the old Roman city of Eboracum had been flooded after the Romans left and had been abandoned for a time.  The Angles had rebuilt the city on higher ground to the north of the River Ouse, renaming it Eoforwīc.  It was protected by a palisade twelve feet high with three gates, to the north-west, north-east and south-east.

'He evidently doesn't know much about sieges,' Cadwallon sneered to his chieftains as they watched the Deiran army divide into three roughly equal parts and camp two hundred yards back from each of the gates.

His eleven year old son, Cadwaladr, looked up at his father before asking, 'What should he have done, father?'

'Kept his army together and erected a fortified camp to protect it.  He should have only put a small force in front of each gate to give warning of a sortie by us and to prevent supplies reaching us.'

'Oh, I see.  So, because he's split his army, you can defeat them one section at a time?'

Cadwallon looked at his son with approval.

'Precisely.  At dawn tomorrow we'll sally out and wipe out one of the detachments, then carry on and attack the rest, by which time our numbers will be more even.'

He examined the men setting up their camps for a while and grunted in satisfaction.

'Do you notice anything else about this so-called army of Osric's, Cadwaladr?'

The boy peered at them for a while before a grin spread over his face.

'Quite a few of them appear to be no more than a few years older than me and there are a lot of old men, too.'

'Yes, I estimate a third of them or more are not normally members of the fyrd.  They'll be unused to war and will panic easily.  They'll be more use to me than to that fool Osric.'

Cadwaladr was disappointed to be left behind with a small force to protect the city when his father led his army out of the north-east gate, but he watched from the top of the gatehouse as the Welsh swept into the Angles' camp.  Most of them were still asleep and the alarmed cries of the few sentries didn't give them enough warning.  Before the sun had fully risen into the sky, flooding the area around the city with light, Cadwallon had killed nearly one third of Osric's army and the survivors had fled, throwing away their weapons.

Cadwallon left a few of his men behind to go around the camp killing those of the enemy who were badly wounded. Just to make sure that none were playing at being dead, they stabbed everyone in the throat, dead or not.

Osric had hastily roused his men when he heard the sounds of fighting coming from the north, but no enemy appeared. He sent out scouts to find out what was going on and they returned a little later to tell him of the slaughter at the middle of the three besiegers' camps.

'What about the one to the north-west?'

The scouts looked at each other uncomfortably.

'Cadwallon is attacking that now, Lord King. Our men are fighting bravely, but the cursed Welsh are forcing them back towards the river.'

'Come on,' Osric yelled, 'there is no point sitting here waiting for Cadwallon to attack us. We must go to the rescue of our countrymen.'

Osric set off, followed by most of his men, but about thirty of them took the opportunity to desert. When they reached the middle camp they saw a hundred corpses or so strewn about the place and his men became fearful. Carrion birds were already picking out the eyes of the dead and tearing at their flesh. Even Osric felt his courage seeping away. A few more men started to run away and the trickle soon became a flood. By the time Cadwallon had finished obliterating the north-west camp, Osric had joined the rest of his men in flight.

The short-lived King of Deira had left too late. By the time that he'd decided it was time to retreat and wait for another opportunity to tackle Cadwallon, his mounted scouts had fled and someone had taken the king's own horse to aid his flight. Osric and his bodyguard ran away from the debacle at Eoforwīc, but they had gone less than three miles when a group of mounted Welshmen caught up with them.

Osric glanced behind him and saw a group of nearly naked men mounted on small Welsh ponies with bodies covered in blue patterns closing on him fast. He and his ten warriors turned to face their pursuers. They were outnumbered by two to one, but the Welsh decided not to risk their own lives. Three of them carried bows and they dismounted to send arrow after arrow into the tightly packed warriors. Most did little more than lodge in the Angles' shields, but a few got through to pierce legs, arms and, in one case, a neck.

Osric didn't know what to do. He was conscious of the fact that the main body of Welshmen on foot would be getting nearer all the time. Eventually he decided to attack. After whispering his orders he yelled and led his men towards the group of horsemen. They caught the archers by surprise and killed them before they could mount. The rest rode off, then turned and charged back. Two of Osric's men were in the process of lifting the king onto one of the dead archer's ponies when a spear took Osric in the middle of the back, breaking apart the links of his chain mail byrnie and shattering his spine. He fell to the ground, as his two bodyguards died of other spear thrusts. Then one of the Welshmen dismounted and proceeded to hack at Osric's neck with his blunt sword until it parted company from his body and he stuck it onto his spear.

Lifting the grisly trophy on high like a banner, the scouts chased after the rest of their routed enemy.

~~~

Oswald knelt nervously in front of Domnall Brecc in the latter's hall at Dùn Add. For just a moment, he was taken back in time seventeen years to when he had stood by his mother's side in front of King Connad. That seemed a long time ago, now.

'Why should I release you from your vows and those of my men living on Arran and Bute who want to go with you? I would be losing one of my best leaders and many of my trained warriors. Of what advantage is that to me?'

Oswald got to his feet and looked Domnall in the eye.

'I have served you loyally, Domnall Brecc. I was instrumental in putting you on the throne on which you now sit and I won you the Isle of Bute. Prior to that, I brought Arran back to Dal Riada. I was hoping that you might do as I asked to acknowledge the debt you owe me!'

Had Oswald not been so angry at Domnall's attitude, he might have thought before he spoke to the king so intemperately. As it was, his anger was matched by that of Domnall.

'You are being impudent and unwise, Oswald. Watch your tongue or I'll have it cut out.'

'I'm sorry, Cyning. I apologise.' Oswald took a deep breath to control his fury at being denied his heart's desire. 'You ask what's in it for you. I'll tell you. The border of Northumbria runs with that of Strathclyde from halfway along the Roman Wall in the south to where the river flows into the Firth of Forth, near Stirling in the north. In my foolishness, I imagined that you might welcome an ally threatening your ancient enemy.'

Domnall opened his mouth to yell at Oswald again for being sarcastic, but then the import of what the man had said sunk in. If he forbade him to leave, he might just go anyway, with or without his blessing. In the unlikely event that he succeeded in winning back Northumbria, he didn't want him as a friend to Strathclyde. Under the right king, Northumbria had the potential to be far more powerful than either Dal Riada or Strathclyde.

'If I agree, and I'm far from convinced that I should do so, how many warriors would you expect to take with you?'

'If the reports are correct, Cadwallon has over two hundred men with him. However, they are a long way from home and some will slip away back to Gwynedd with their ill-gotten plunder. The number of desertions will increase as winter approaches. Penda's whereabouts are uncertain. There are some stories that Mercians attacked Bebbanburg and were repulsed, but it's not clear whether Penda was with them. Others say he is still in Mercia. So my priority is to defeat Cadwallon first and then move against Penda if I have to.'

'All very interesting and it shows that you have both good information and a plan, but I asked you about the numbers you are hoping to take with you.'

'Yes, I was coming to that, but I thought it important that you appreciate why I need the numbers I do. To move overland would advertise my strategy and might give the two kings time to unite their forces to oppose me. I therefore propose to take ship to Caer Luel in Rheged and then move along the Roman Wall into Bernicia.'

'But I thought that Cadwallon was in Eoforwīc?'

'He is, or was. But from the Roman Wall I can strike either north or south and the ruined fortifications along it will protect us as we advance.'

'So the numbers you take will be limited by the number of birlinns you have?'

'Yes, Lord King. At the moment Eochaid and I have four, so enough to carry some one hundred and fifty warriors, plus helmsmen, ships boys and so on.'

'Do you have a hundred and fifty men who are willing to risk their lives on this mad venture?'

'Yes, Lord. Over two hundred, so I can pick who I want.'

'I see.'

Domnall looked at Oswald thoughtfully for a moment, before the silence was interrupted by Fergus of Islay, who was visiting and who had sat quietly by Domnall's side up to that point.

'You'll need more than a hundred and fifty, laddie. If Domnall doesn't object, I'll pledge a hundred warriors and two birlinns until you wear the crown – or are dead. In either event, they are then to return home.'

Domnall gave him an annoyed look for forcing his hand.

'What about your elder brother and Oswin?'

'Half-brother. They are hardly friends, so Northumbria will remain divided whilst they rule. I don't expect either of them to be able to defeat Penda and Cadwallon on their own. If they are still alive by the time I arrive, I will deal with them after ridding my kingdom of the wretched Welsh and the Mercians.'

'Very well, you may go in the spring. But if there is little prospect of your succeeding, you are to return here. Understood?'

~~~

Oswald was beginning to think that things might be going his way. He hadn't been back on Arran for more than a month when Aidan and Ròidh arrived. They had travelled down Loch Fyne from Fibach in the Land of the Picts and had managed to get a fisherman to take them from Cowal to Brodick. They were making their way back to Iona, so Oswald took them the rest of the way himself.

He was still there visiting his brothers when tidings came of Osric's death. Furthermore, it now seemed certain that reports of Penda's return to Northumbria were false. It appeared that he was still in Mercia, though some of his men had apparently joined Cadwallon in order to plunder the country. It was much later that he heard about the fate of Eanfrith.

Both Osguid and Oslac were keen to go with him and the three went to see Abbot Ségéne mac Fiachnaíhe.

'So you believe that you can become the King of Northumbria, do you, Oswald?'

'With God's help, Father Abbot, yes.'

'Then I believe that the community of Iona must support you against the apostate Eanfrith.'

'Apostate?'

'Yes. Having been converted by Brother Aidan years ago, he has now renounced his Christian faith and become a pagan once more, perhaps to curry favour with Penda. If so, it hasn't done him much good. The pagan Penda is back in Mercia and Cadwallon is a Christian, though he doesn't seem to act like one half the time. He's gone into winter quarters at Corbridge, I understand, presumably waiting until spring before continuing his rampage across the kingdom. The last I heard, your half-brother, Eanfrith, was seeking ways of avoiding war.'

Oswald sniffed to indicate what he thought of that. Eanfrith didn't have the strong character that he and Oswiu had. When he was elected by the Witan of Bernicia, it was far from a unanimous decision. Many nobles and thegns had been in favour of Oswald, but when Eanfrith arrived and no-one had yet been in contact with Oswald, the vote swung in his favour. Now it appeared he was seeking to make peace with Cadwallon. Oswald was certain that the only peace that Cadwallon would agree to was complete submission. He could then get Eanfrith to pay him a hefty tribute annually at no cost to himself. Oswald struggled to stop thinking about his half-brother and concentrate on what the abbot was saying.

'We have a few islanders who are trained as warriors who would like to go with you. Of course, I'm happy for Osguid and Oslac to accompany you, to look after your spiritual welfare.'

Oswald smiled. He had known that Offa wouldn't want to leave Iona, where he lived as a hermit in a beehive cell on the far side of the small island. His other brother, Oslaph, had died of a fever the previous year.

Oslaph's death had hit Acha hard. She hadn't seen him for years and now she never would. She became deeply depressed when she heard the news. Soon four of her sons would set out on an extremely hazardous venture and she was concerned about their survival; perhaps she'd never see them again, either. The fact that Æbbe, now seventeen, had recently left her to become a novice nun had increased her loneliness and depression.

It was Keeva and Fianna who had lifted her out of her black mood. They started to bring their children round to see their grandmother almost every day and Eochaid's wife, Dervla, also became a frequent visitor with her two children. Of course, Acha knew why she was getting this sudden attention and she was touched. She had never approved of Oswald's relationship with Keeva and she had been just as angry when Oswiu, scarcely more than a boy at the time, had brought the elfin Fianna back with him from Bute. Dervla was different. Firstly she was an Irish princess and therefore a member of the same class, and secondly she was married to Eochaid, not a concubine. From the start, the two women had got on well.

However, Acha soon regretted her former antipathy to her sons' lovers and looked forward to their visits. She had just turned fifty and was beginning to feel her age. Her hair, once a bright auburn, was now almost entirely grey and the wrinkles on her face were getting deeper. Her joints ached, too. However, she still held herself proudly and was determined not to die before she saw her son crowned as King of Northumbria.

~~~

Unlike Oswald, Eanfrith had spent his period in exile quietly. He had married the daughter of one of the Pictish kings and they had a son, Talorgan, who didn't follow his father when he returned to Northumbria. He was his grandfather's heir and the boy viewed the pagan Northumbrians as barbarians. His family, along with most of the kingdom, had been converted to Christianity by Aidan. Eanfrith had also become a Christian to conform, more than through any deeply held beliefs in the teachings of Aidan.

Once back amongst his own people, he immediately abandoned Christianity and reverted to paganism. This didn't endear him to Cadwallon, who was a Christian. In fact, the King of Gwynedd held Eanfrith in deep contempt. Not only was the man an apostate, but he was no warrior. Instead of training to fight, he had spent his time among the Picts in idleness. His passions in life were hunting, fishing and feasting; consequently his rotund body stood out amongst his lean fellow countrymen and was another reason for Cadwallon's dislike of the man.

'Twysog, there is a messenger from Eanfrith for you.'

The sentry had poked his head inside the door of the small room that had been constructed to give the king some privacy within the hall that had been built by the Welsh inside the ruins of the old Roman fort at Corbridge. Cadwallon regarded the man with annoyance. *Twysog* meant prince or chieftain and he would have preferred to be called *Brenin*, meaning king, but if he stood on his dignity he feared that he would look foolish. Twysog was what those who had followed him into exile had called him and they had continued to do so when he'd returned from exile and seized the throne of Gwynedd eleven years ago.

Cadwallon divested himself of the furs on his bed and shivered as he stood up in just his under-tunic. The small room might give him privacy, but it had no fire and the snow falling outside swirled in through the gaps in the poorly made shutter that covered the small window. At least there would be a fire blazing in the central hearth of the main hall. The girl who shared his bed pulled the furs back around her naked body and snuggled down into them. He envied her.

The king pulled on a long woollen robe and stuffed his feet into a pair of leather shoes. Pulling a fur-lined cloak around him, he followed the sentry back into the hall. He was surprised to see that Eanfrith's messenger was little more than a boy – sixteen years old, at most.

'Well, what does the King of Bernicia want with me?' he asked in the Anglo-Saxon tongue.

'Brenin, my lord Eanfrith wishes you good fortune and great health.'

Cadwallon was pleased to be addressed in his own tongue as king, but the flowery language didn't impress him.

'Stop the drivel, boy and come to the point.'

'Yes, Brenin, of course,' the youth said nervously. He took a deep breath before continuing. 'King Eanfrith believes that an alliance between your two great nations would be of much greater benefit to both of you than a war.'

'Does he, now? Is that because he is a coward, do you think?'

The messenger blushed. That was exactly what he and many other Bernicians, thought.

'Bernicia is strong and has many allies -' the lad began, but Cadwallon cut him off.

'Who are these allies? The Picts in the North? They haven't forgiven him for his apostasy. The Deirans? They are weak and leaderless; they can't even agree on a king to replace Osric. Rheged? Rhun acknowledged Æthelfrith as his overlord, but Edwin ignored his obligations to support him when he was at war with Strathclyde. I don't suppose that Rhun's son, the present king, will be disposed to help Bernicia, do you?'

The young messenger was silent after that. Cadwallon regarded him for a while and the youth looked him in the eye, determined not be cowed. Suddenly Cadwallon made up his mind.

'You have more spirit than your king, boy. Tell him I'll meet him here. He is to come with no more than a dozen men as escort. He has until two weeks hence to accept my offer.'

The messenger gasped. It had taken him over a week to get to Corbridge through the December snow and it would take him just as long, if not longer, to return to Bebbanburg. There was no way that his king could reach Corbridge in less than a week.

'Thank you, Brenin. However, two weeks is not long enough for me to return and for King Eanfrith to journey here. I would ask you for three weeks.'

Cadwallon smiled. He'd known that the deadline was impossible.

'Very well, boy. Three weeks it is – that's the middle of January. We are just about to celebrate Christ's Mass. I suppose there is no point in inviting you to stay?'

'No, Brenin, but thank you. If I could have a fresh horse in exchange for mine, I'll be on my way.'

'Very well. Have a meal before you go, though.'

The youth nodded his thanks.

'And boy, I like you. Don't come back with your king. Use exhaustion as an excuse; I doubt if it'll be far from the truth.'

~~~

Eadfrith, the captured son of the unfortunate Edwin, lay bound in the small hut where he had been dumped when Cadwallon's army arrived at Corbridge. Like the king's bedchamber, it was freezing cold but, unlike Cadwallon, he didn't have a bed of furs to keep him warm. His teeth chattered and his belly kept cramping for lack of food.

Cadwallon had kept him alive in the hope that he could install him as his vassal in Deira, but Eadfrith had refused time and time again to do what Cadwallon wanted. Each time he refused, the conditions he was kept in got worse. Now he was only fed a few scraps every other day or so and given very little water. Eadfrith knew that he couldn't live much longer like this and started to pray for death to escape the cold, the hunger and his raging thirst.

He was barely surviving when he was taken out of his hut in the middle of January and half carried, half dragged into the presence of Cadwallon in his hall. At first he was grateful for the heat of the fire, but then he began to wonder why he was there.

Gradually he became more conscious of his surroundings and saw that a dozen men dressed like Northumbrians sat around the hearth in front of Cadwallon's throne. A Welshman sat beside each of them, as they feasted on meat and a mess of grain and root vegetables mixed together in a bowl. They had been laughing and quaffing ale when he had been brought in, but gradually the hall fell silent.

Propped up between his two guards, he heard Cadwallon speaking, but at first he couldn't make out the words, although they were Anglo-Saxon English. Then he realised that the king was speaking about him.

'- but he was too pig-headed to pay me homage and agree to become my vassal. Had he done so, he could be living comfortably in Eoforwīc now, instead of enjoying my poor hospitality.'

Eadfrith worked his mouth to try and generate some saliva so that he could speak.

'Cadwallon,' he croaked. 'You would have made my people slaves.'

The words were hardly audible, even though the hall was quiet as the men listened to Cadwallon.

'You spoke, worm? Come on, speak up so we can hear you.'

'Water,' croaked the wretched Deiran prince.

He was given a bowl and he eagerly slurped it down before clearing his throat and repeating what he'd said before.

'That's true, but you would have been free. Instead of that, you will shortly die in agony, whilst I will raid Deira again after I've finished with Bernicia.'

At that, King Eanfrith tried to get to his feet to protest, but the two Welshmen sitting either side of him pulled him down.

'King Cadwallon, what's the meaning of this? You invited me here to discuss peace between us and now you talk of raiding my country?'

'No, you assumed I'd invited you here to discuss peace. In fact, I invited you so that I could offer the same terms to you as I offered to poor Eadfrith.'

'Never. An honourable peace, yes. I was even prepared to offer you a gift to take back to Gwynedd with you, but I'll not subjugate my people to you. I'd rather die!' he exclaimed dramatically.

'Is that's your final word?'

'It is.'

'Very well. Your wish is granted.'

With that Cadwallon signalled to the men sitting beside the Bernicians and they each produced a dagger and proceeded to cut the throats of their dinner companions. The blood spurted out of the severed carotid arteries and some reached the edge of the fire, where it sizzled and gave off the odour of molten copper.

Eadfrith was horrified and started to speak, but Cadwallon cut him off.

'Kill him, too. He's of no further use to me. Then throw all the bodies onto the midden heap. No doubt the dogs and carrion birds will be glad of the meat at this time of year.'

~~~

Tidings of the treacherous way that both Eadfrith and Eanfrith had been killed reached Oswald on Arran at the beginning of April, just as he was preparing to set out. It had taken some time for word of the killings to reach Bebbanburg and then it was a month or more before a messenger could reach Arran with an invitation from the some of the nobles of Bernicia for Oswald to take the throne, if he could defeat Cadwallon.

He sailed three days later after a tearful farewell from his mother, Keeva and their two children. He had long since freed both Keeva and her brother, Jarlath, now sixteen. Jarlath was now part of his war band and one of his closest companions. Oswiu bade an equally poignant farewell to his family and even Osguid and Oslac embraced their mother emotionally before boarding the Holy Saviour.

A fair wind from the north-west carried them out of Brodick Bay and the four ships headed for the Mull of Kintyre, where they would meet up with the two birlinns from the Isles of Islay and Jura. It wasn't until the next day that the latter arrived and the fleet could set sail once more. The fresh westerly wind took them around the end of Galloway and into the Solway Firth.

They soon discovered that the wide expanse of water wasn't all that it seemed to be when one of the birlinns from the Isles stuck fast on a sandbank. As the sun was close to setting, Oswald took the decision to anchor where they were for the night. At some stage, the tide started to come in again and just before dawn the stranded birlinn floated off the mud.

Without a pilot Oswald came to the conclusion that they had better stay where they were until low tide revealed where the deep channel was. There had to be one because he knew that trading vessels and fishing boats sailed all the way into the River Eden. Halfway through the morning the course of the navigable channel became obvious and the small fleet set off again. However, the incoming tide slowly swallowed the seemingly endless sands until Oswald was about to call a halt again. It was Œthelwald, who was serving on the Holy Saviour as one of its ship's boys, who spotted the line of posts from his roost up on the yardarm.

'Father, there's what looks like a line of saplings or maybe posts running inland from about half a mile ahead of us. Might they be channel markers?'

They proved to be thin posts buried deeply into the mud, which marked the way through the estuary of the River Eden. Once past them, the river ran between pastureland and rough moorland all the way to Caer Luel, the capital of Rheged. It was late afternoon before they reached the old Roman town and Oswald told the rest of the fleet to moor beside the bank half a mile short of the town walls whilst he went ahead and spoke to Royth, the current King of Rheged.

Oswald was greeted by closed gates set into high stone walls, manned by spearmen and archers. He tied up alongside the wharf and disembarked, taking just Osguid and Œthelwald with him. His son carried the banner of Northumbria – alternating vertical bars of gold and red – which Acha had made for him - and Osguid carried a cross on a long pole.

'That's far enough, Whiteblade. What do you want here? Have you come to invade us, as your father did in my grandfather's time?'

'I come in peace, as you can see. I bring with me only my young son and my brother, who is a monk from Iona.'

'So you say, but you have an army moored downriver.'

'They mean you no harm, unless you were party to the treacherous murder of my brother Eanfrith by Cadwallon.'

'No, I swear not. We live in fear of an invasion from him as he overwintered not far from our border with Bernicia. He is not there any longer, however. I'm told that he has moved east.'

'Then we have an enemy in common. Let me in and we can discuss it like civilised men, instead of bawling our business for everyone to hear.'

'Very well. But make sure your men remain on board.'

'They know. I have already told them.'

A few minutes later, Oswald and Royth were sitting in his hall – a grand house which had been that of an important Roman until they had left Britannia for good more than two hundred years ago. The Britons, who were the race inhabiting Rheged, had done their best to repair it, but the roof was thatched instead of tiled and gaps in the stone walls were filled with wattle and daub. The hypocaust heating system didn't work either; instead, there was a fire blazing in the middle of what had once been a rather beautiful mosaic floor.

'Rheged was once part of my father's kingdom, although ruled by its own king. I believe that the arrangement was beneficial to both of us then. It's a pity that Edwin let the arrangement die, but I would like to restore it,' Oswald began.

'You would like me to become your sub-king, your vassal?'

'It's not the way I'd have put it. You benefit because you'd have a powerful ally in your constant struggle with Strathclyde and currently against the Mercians and men of Gwynedd. I benefit because a united North can become powerful enough to keep out our enemies.'

'Edwin never came to our aid and Eanfrith -'

'Was a fool. I'm not him, nor am I Edwin or my father. If we become allies now and you support me against Cadwallon and Penda of Mercia, I'll treat your enemies as my enemies from now on.'

'No tribute?'

'No tribute, but we meet our own war expenses, whoever is aiding who.'

Royth still looked doubtful.

'I'll even swear an oath on Holy Relics.'

'No, I believe you, but I will agree to become a part of Northumbria if you marry my daughter, Rhieinmelth. She is the last of our royal line, so, in time, you will become king when I die.'

'How old is she?'

'Fourteen.'

'I'm thirty and I'm sure she won't want an old man like me to bed her. However, my brother Oswiu is only eight years older than Rhieinmelth. Would marriage to him suit you?'

Oswald had no intention of marrying Rhieinmelth, even if it meant he became the heir of Rheged. He had married once for love and now he was determined that, when he married again, it would bring with it an alliance with a great power. Rheged was scarcely that.

'Bring your brother to dine with us tonight. The two young people can meet and see whether they are suited.'

Oswald nodded. He realised that he had just betrothed his favourite brother without discussing it with him. He just hoped that the Princess Rhieinmelth was pretty.

~~~

Cadwallon sat before Bebbanburg and cursed. His sixteen year old son, Cadwaladr, sat on his horse beside him and shared his father's frustration. The latter had arrived in April with reinforcements for their attack on Bernicia. They had raped and pillaged their way across the country, but now that they had reached the mighty fortress on its basalt rock by the coast their progress had ground to a halt.

Bernicia might be without a king, but it was still a powerful nation. Cadwallon had heard rumours that the Goddodin in the north and those nobles who lived south of Bebbanburg were mustering an army and, although he now had over four hundred men, he was worried about the size of the force he might be facing. However, Bebbanburg housed the treasury and he was a greedy man.

'There's no way in, father. The palisade to the east and west runs along the top of the rock and the gates to the north and south are too strong.'

It was a conversation they'd had before. They had stormed both sets of gates over the past two weeks and both times they had succeeded in taking the outer gates, admittedly at the cost of a lot of men, but they had then been trapped between the outer and inner gates, where they had been slaughtered. In all, sixty men had died and even if his men were willing to try again, the Mercians with him had flatly refused.

The two rode back to their camp in silence. Cadwallon knew that his son was right and that he ought to abandon the siege, but to do so would weaken him in the eyes of his men. So far they regarded him as invincible and he shared their opinion. To just cut and run would diminish him in his own eyes, as well.

The next morning was wet and dismal, so was the news that one of his scouts brought. He had sent out small groups of men on ponies to scour the country and find out the truth about rumours that the Bernicians were raising an army. The scouts had returned from Corbridge, which Cadwallon had retained as his base, mainly as a place where his wounded could recover.

'Twysog, we bring news of Oswald, the one they call Whiteblade.'

'I thought he was in exile in Dal Riada. Where is he now?'

He knew of Oswald, but he had disregarded him as a threat. He was well aware that Oswald had established something of a reputation as a warrior serving the kings of Dal Riada, but he couldn't see how such a man could raise an army that could be any sort of threat to him. Even after his losses at Bebbanburg, he still had nearly four hundred experienced warriors.

'He's in Rheged with a small army, or so rumour has it.'

'How small?'

'A couple of hundred, or so those who come in to sell supplies have told us.'

Cadwallon smiled. He now had the excuse he needed to abandon his attempt to take Bebbanburg without losing face. Furthermore, his defeat of this Whiteblade would restore his reputation once more.

'Thank you; you've done well. Cadwaladr, tell our chieftains and the Mercian thegns that we leave tomorrow to march west to confront this Oswald and his pathetic army.'

~~~

Oswiu wasn't best pleased when his brother told him about Rhieinmelth. He loved Fianna and had no intention of betraying her by

214

marrying some girl he'd never even met, however royal. Besides, she had just presented him with a son – Aldfrith. He had planned on marrying Fianna to make the boy legitimate.

'If you want to gain an ally, why don't you marry her yourself?' he spat at Oswald.

'Because I may have to marry later to create an alliance with one of the major kingdoms of England. For me it will be for duty rather than love as well. If you refuse, we'll lose Rheged as an ally and we might as well go back to Arran now.'

He paused and looked at his brother's angry face.

'Look, you know I wouldn't ask this if it wasn't vitally important. At least meet the girl tonight at the feast. That can't do any harm, can it?'

When Rhieinmelth came in and sat between her father and Oswiu, Oswald, who was sitting on King Royth's right, gasped and wondered if he'd made the right decision in turning her down himself. He didn't think that he'd ever seen anyone so beautiful. He thought Keeva was stunningly attractive, but he had to admit that she wasn't as lovely as this girl. Rhieinmelth had kept her eyes down demurely when she took her place, but when she was introduced to the brothers she gave each a radiant smile. If Oswald was captivated, Oswiu was overcome with desire for her. All thoughts of betraying Fianna were suppressed and he concentrated on winning the heart of the princess.

After Oswald's initial feeling of regret at passing up the opportunity to marry Rhieinmelth, he consoled himself with the thought that the alliance with Rheged was now assured.

~~~

In early June, Oswald reached Hexham, or at least the blackened ruins of what had been the settlement. The people had returned after the sacking by Cadwallon, but lived in makeshift shelters. Many had been killed by Cadwallon, but even more had died during the harsh winter. They greeted Oswald as their saviour and he assured them that he would help them to rebuild their settlement once he was king. That night he camped beside the River Tyne on the west side of Hexham.

His army had been swelled by another forty warriors from Rheged. He had hoped for more, but, not unreasonably, Royth hadn't wanted to weaken his own forces too much in case Oswald lost and Rheged had to face an invasion by Cadwallon. He had also given Oswald horses, supplies and several guides.

Two of these returned the next morning to inform him that Cadwallon was camped at Corbridge, a mere two and a quarter miles away on the other bank of the Tyne. Oswald's first problem was crossing the river, but the local people told him of a ford that was passable in the summer months near Riding Mill. The mill was the nearest one to Corbridge; Cadwallon had spared it so that he could use it to produce flour for his army.

That evening Oswald's advance guard killed the dozen Welshmen who guarded the mill and crossed to the north bank without a problem. The next morning they advanced on the old fort at Corbridge, but the scouts returned to report that it was deserted.

'Do you think that they were ever there, after all?' Rònan asked.

He and Jarlath were two of a dozen warriors selected as Oswald's personal guards, his gesith, and like the other ten, were his friends as well as his bodyguards.

'All the signs are that a large army has only just left the place, including a few of their own men who were too badly wounded to take with them, who they killed. The corpses were less than a day old,' the chief scout pointed out.

'Right. Well, we need to find out where they've gone. We'll get rid of the corpses and camp in the old fort tonight. Tomorrow we'll send out the scouts to locate Cadwallon's army. Their trail should be easy to follow. Just pray that it doesn't rain hard tonight.'

Oswald and Oswiu, followed discretely by Rònan and Jarlath, toured the old fort and both became angry when they saw the remains of bodies in the midden heap.

'One of those is probably our half-brother. Whatever we thought of Eanfrith, he deserves a Christian burial.'

He asked for volunteers to carry out the unsavoury task of recovering what was left of the bodies and burying them together in a patch of ground consecrated for the purpose by Osguid and Oslac. Halfway through the following morning the scouts returned to report that Cadwallon had drawn up an army of between three and four hundred men on a low ridge some six or seven miles to the north-west.

Oswald decided to move to within two miles of the place and camp there for the night. At dawn the next morning he advanced to below the ridge and called Osguid and Oslac forward, together with several men with wooden shovels and metal picks. They proceeded to dig a hole in full sight of the Welsh and Mercian army into which the two monks placed a large wooden cross before the hole was filled in again and the earth packed tight.  Oswald drew his army up either side of the cross and the two monks led prayers for their success against the enemy.

Cadwallon was also a Christian, as were many of his men, but he had brought no priests or monks with him.  Seeing their foes being blessed, whilst they were not, unsettled them and the men started to murmur amongst themselves.  It was not a good sign, but there was little that Cadwallon could do about it.

'God be with you on this day, brother,' Oswald said to Oswiu, who smiled and nodded before taking his place in command of the right flank.  Eochaid took charge of the left whilst Oswald led the centre.

'What will you call this place, Oswald?'

He turned and smiled at Osguid.

'I'll call it the Field of Heaven if we win; if we lose it doesn't matter what I call it.'

'Heavenfield?  Yes, that's apt.  Christ guide your strong right arm and protect you.  Oslac and I will join the warriors of Iona.  We may not shed blood, but mayhap our cudgels will crush a few skulls this day.'

Oswald took a deep breath and ordered his archers forward.  The battle that would decide the fate of Northumbria was about to begin.

**TO BE CONTINUED IN**

# WARRIORS OF THE NORTH

# Other Novels by H A Culley

## (Published on Kindle)

**The Normans Series**

The Bastard's Crown

Death in the Forest

England in Anarchy

Caging the Lyon

Seeking Jerusalem

**Babylon Series**

Babylon – The Concubine's Son

Babylon – Dawn of Empire

**Individual Novels**

Magna Carta

The Sins of the Fathers

**Robert the Bruce Trilogy**

The Path to the Throne

The Winter King

After Bannockburn

## Constantine Trilogy

Constantine – The Battle for Rome

Crispus Ascending

Death of the Innocent


## Macedon Trilogy

The Strategos

The Sacred War

Alexander


## Kings of Northumbria Series

Whiteblade

Warriors of the North

41143199R00132

Made in the USA
Middletown, DE
04 March 2017